Cranberry Red

Books by Jerry Apps

Fiction:

The Travels of Increase Joseph

In a Pickle

Blue Shadows Farm

Cranberry Red

Nonfiction:

The Land Still Lives

Cabin in the Country

Barns of Wisconsin

Mills of Wisconsin and the Midwest

Breweries of Wisconsin

One-Room Country Schools

Wisconsin Traveler's Companion

Country Wisdom

Cheese: The Making of a Wisconsin Tradition

When Chores Were Done

Country Ways and Country Days

Humor from the Country

The People Came First: A History of Cooperative Extension

Ringlingville USA

Every Farm Tells a Story

Living a Country Year

Old Farm: A History

Horse Drawn Days

Audio Books:

The Back Porch and Other Stories

In a Pickle

Children's Books:

Eat Rutabagas

Stormy

Tents, Tigers, and the Ringling Brothers

Casper Jaggi: Master Swiss Cheese Maker

Cranberry Red

A Novel

Jerry Apps

Terrace Books
A trade imprint of the University of Wisconsin Press

Terrace Books, a trade imprint of the University of Wisconsin Press,
takes its name from the Memorial Union Terrace, located at
the University of Wisconsin–Madison. Since its inception in 1907,
the Wisconsin Union has provided a venue for students, faculty, staff,
and alumni to debate art, music, politics, and the issues of the day.
It is a place where theater, music, drama, literature, dance, outdoor activities,
and major speakers are made available to the campus and the community.
To learn more about the Union, visit www.union.wisc.edu.

Terrace Books
A trade imprint of the University of Wisconsin Press
1930 Monroe Street, 3rd Floor
Madison, Wisconsin 53711-2059
uwpress.wisc.edu

3 Henrietta Street
London WC2E 8LU, England
eurospanbookstore.com

1   3   5   4   2

Printed in the United States of America

Library of Congress Cataloging-in-Publication Data
Apps, Jerold W., 1934–
Cranberry red: a novel / Jerry Apps.
p.   cm.
ISBN 978-0-299-24770-6 (cloth: alk. paper)
ISBN 978-0-299-24773-7 (e-book)
1. Cranberries—Wisconsin—Marketing—Fiction.
2. Cranberries—Research—Wisconsin—Fiction.
3. County agricultural agents—Wisconsin—Fiction.
4. For-profit universities and colleges—Corrupt practices—Wisconsin—Fiction.
I. Title.
PS3601.P67C73   2010
813'.6—dc22
2010011523

To
Ruth, Sue, Natasha, and Kate

*C*ontents

Contents

Part 5

Part 6

Part 7

Contents

Acknowledgments

In September 2007 my son Steve and I were canoe-camping in the Boundary Waters Wilderness of northern Minnesota. It is here where this book began, as Steve and I sat on rocks overlooking John Lake. I had shared stories of my days as a county extension agent for the University of Wisconsin, and of my work raking cranberries in a cranberry marsh near Wisconsin Rapids. Steve suggested it might make a novel. When we weren't paddling or fishing, we worked on characters and plot.

Brent McCown, a horticulture professor and former colleague at the University of Wisconsin–Madison, steered me toward Chinese research on increasing antioxidant levels of fruits. Brent has also done landmark research on cranberry varietal development and cranberry culture.

Much of the information on cranberry history and present-day cranberry culture I gleaned from the Wisconsin State Cranberry Growers Association's collection of materials.

Several people read the manuscript and offered suggestions—many suggestions—for improvement. Special thanks to my wife, Ruth; my daughter, Sue; my son Steve's partner, Natasha; and Kate Thompson, freelance editor extraordinaire. I also appreciate the comments and suggestions from manuscript reviewers Dick Cates, Spring Green; Maryo Gard Ewell, Gunnison, Colorado; and Dennis Boyer, Dodgeville.

A special thanks to editors Amy Johnson and Sheila Moermond, who helped fine-tune the manuscript. Lastly, I want to thank Raphael Kadushin at the UW Press for his support of my work.

Many others helped with this book. I thank them all.

Part 1

Fred and Oscar

"Oscar . . . Oscar . . . I've hooked a big one . . . hooked a big one. Oscar, you hearin' me? I need help," Fred Russo yelled.

Fred, Oscar Anderson's lifelong friend and constant fishing companion since both of them quit farming twenty-five years ago, was on the front side of eighty-five. Oscar was a few years older. They both fished the Tamarack River from shore, as they had done once or twice a week every summer since they retired.

"Dammit, Oscar, I need help. Where the hell are ya?" Both men had spent too many years around loud farm machinery such as silo fillers and threshing machines and tractors that needed new mufflers. On a good day they could hear one another if they stood a couple of feet apart. Most of the time they talked outside this range, so conversations resulted in exchanges such as: "You thirsty, Fred?" "Nah, today's Wednesday; tomorrow is Thursday."

Fred yelled again, this time louder. "Oscar, dammit, where the hell you at?" Fred's fiberglass spinning rod bent in an arch as he cranked on the reel. The fifteen-pound test line kept tearing off the reel—even with the drag on near full, Fred couldn't turn around whatever had taken his bait.

Wearing an old Filson hat his kids had given him for his eightieth birthday, Oscar Anderson slowly appeared from around a bend in the river. He carried a spinning rod in one hand and a wooden walking stick in the other. Temperatures on that sunny May afternoon had climbed into the eighties with not a hint of a breeze.

"Hold your damn horses, will ya, Fred? I'm a comin' as fast as I can."

"'Bout time you showed up," Fred said. "I've hooked a big one. Helluva big one. He's a real pole bender."

"You sure you ain't snagged a stump or maybe an old tire somebody threw in the river?" Oscar said. He was near out of breath as he approached his friend, who was tugging on his spinning rod and twisting on the reel handle. Fred wore bib overalls and a straw hat, the same clothing he'd worn for years on the farm. He was tall and thin and sweat streamed down his tanned, deeply wrinkled face.

"He ain't broke water yet; figure he's one of them big old northerns," Fred said.

"You sure you got a fish on?"

"Dammit, Oscar. I got me a fish on this line and he's a lunker."

*T*he Big Tamarack River flowed lazily along the western boundary of Ames County before it dumped into the Wisconsin River to the west. It flowed through marshland, past several cranberry bogs, and through a nature preserve where sandhill cranes found a summer home along with beaver and muskrats and ducks and Canada geese too lazy to fly to their namesake country to nest and raise their goslings. The river twisted and turned and sometimes nearly came back on itself. Because of these characteristics it was a good fishing river, especially for those fishermen who baited their hooks for small and large mouth bass, and for northern pike.

On this day Fred Russo used a big bucktail spinner with number two treble hooks, the kind that fluttered and caught the light and was supposed to attract fish from some distance away. He'd caught other northerns with this spinner, so he knew it worked.

"I need a little help," Fred said as he continued cranking on the reel.

"So, what you want me to do?"

"Let's both grab hold my fish line and we'll haul that big bastard in hand over hand, like we do when we're ice fishin'."

"But this ain't ice fishin'."

"I know it ain't ice fishin', . . . but I think it'll work."

Oscar shoved his walking stick into the dirt so it stood up straight and grabbed the shaking fishing line.

"Okay, I got the line. Damn, it's a big something you got yourself hooked onto."

The two old men, not as strong as they once were, but both in good shape for their ages, slowly pulled on Fred's line. The fish tugged so hard the line vibrated as the two men pulled on it hand over hand, the heavy line nearly cutting their calloused hands. A pile of monofilament gathered in front of them.

"Shouldn't be long now and we'll see what we got."

"Probably a big old carp," Oscar said.

"Ain't no carp. No carp fights like this."

Just then Oscar glimpsed the fish in the water, coming toward them with its mouth wide open and the bucktail spinner hanging from a lower lip.

"Damn," Oscar said. "Damn. You got yourself a real fish."

"You just keep on pullin', Oscar. We let up and he's gonna shake that spinner loose and he's gone."

"I'm pullin'," Oscar replied. "I'm pullin'."

When the fish came within ten or so feet of shore, Oscar, still holding onto the line, waded into the water. He wore rubber knee boots, a pair he always wore fishing.

In the water no more than a few seconds, Oscar came splashing out. He dropped the fishing line, which Fred continued to hold.

"What're you doin'?" Fred asked.

"Son-of-a-bitch took after me."

"Whattya you mean, took after you?"

"Fish went right after me, its big jaws clompin' up and down. Tried to bite me on the leg."

"To hell, you say. Fish tried to bite you?"

"Sure as hell that fish tried to bite me."

"If you say so, Oscar. Grab hold this line again and we'll pull him in."

Fred had lost a little ground since Oscar had let go of the line and the fish swam farther out in the river. The two men continued pulling and this time they yanked the giant northern pike on shore, just out of the water.

The big fish lay in front of the two perspiring men, appearing to eye them.

"Big bastard, ain't he?" Oscar commented.

"Biggest fish I ever caught," Fred replied, pulling off his straw hat and rubbing a red handkerchief across his face. While Fred was still holding his straw hat, the big fish made a giant leap toward him, just missing his leg with its giant tooth-studded mouth.

"See, what'd I tell you. Fish went after you, too."

Fred jumped back, put on his straw hat, and stuffed his handkerchief into his back pocket.

"Mean son-of-a bitch," Fred said.

The fish leaped again, this time toward Oscar, who stood holding his walking stick. The giant fish missed Oscar's leg by inches and grabbed the walking stick, biting it in two with little effort.

"Good God, you see that?" Oscar exclaimed. "Damn fish bit my walking stick in two. It's made out of hickory."

With the tension off the fishing line, the big fish shook loose the spinner and continued flopping on the shore. With a giant leap, it flipped back in the water, where it hesitated for a moment or two before swimming off into the deep.

Oscar looked at Fred, then at his severed walking stick. "I don't think we should tell anybody about this," Oscar said quietly.

"I think we'd better go home," Fred said. "I've had enough fishing for one day." He balled up the tangled fishing line and stuffed it in his pocket.

2

Lost Job

Ben Wesley hadn't seen it coming; he should have, but he didn't. When the news came, it felt like somebody kicked him in the stomach. The University of Wisconsin was laying him off. Firing him. Putting him on the trash heap. Ben was forty-five years old and had worked as a county agricultural agent for twenty years. The best years of his life, at least to Ben's way of thinking. And now his career was finished. Kaput. Gone forever.

And he was mad as hell. Who was to blame? Had he done something wrong? Ticked somebody off—did something so bad that they complained enough to get him fired? Who could that be, who would have done it? After you're twenty years in a job you're bound to have some enemies, no questions about that. He thought about the people who probably didn't like him, didn't like the advice he gave, or perhaps even in a few cases were unhappy when he had given the wrong advice. There were a few times like that. He remembered the farmer who came into the office with his wife one day; both of them were about in tears. They said they were about to lose their farm, and would he put in a good word for them at the bank so they could get their loan renewed. He did that. He shouldn't have. They still lost their farm. Getting their loan renewed wasn't the problem, doing a decent job as a farmer was. These folks, as sincere as they seemed, just couldn't cut it. Ben hadn't taken time to look into their situation well enough; he'd let emotion affect his decision. The couple was mad at him and the bank loan officer never forgot the situation either.

Of course Ben wasn't the only county agent in Wisconsin to lose his job. They were all fired, every last one, because all the county offices were to shut down on July1. Hints and rumors about closing down the county agent offices in Wisconsin had been floating around for several years. It seemed every year the state budget was in worse shape than the year before, and lawmakers seemed stunned about what to do. Two themes emerge each time a budget crisis comes into focus: Cut programs. Raise taxes. This time the program cutters had apparently won the day. Ben didn't have much confidence in the state's lawmakers. Long ago he'd concluded that most of the lawmakers in the state capitol in Madison didn't know a blame thing about farming and didn't seem to care either. They spent most of their time worrying about where to build another prison, who shouldn't be eligible for welfare payments, and which highway bridge had to be fixed before it fell in the river.

Ben got the news of his dismissal in a terse e-mail message from Madison:

From: Joseph Higgins, Assistant Dean, UWAAP
To: Ben Wesley
Date: June 4
Subject: Job Elimination

I regret to inform you that the legislature has voted to eliminate the University of Wisconsin Agricultural Agent Program (UWAAP). Unfortunately, this means all UWAAP employees will be dismissed and all county offices will be closed on July 1 of this year. Our administrators have been fighting the possibility of this decision for many months, but ultimately the legislature has spoken. A letter will follow, including the status of vacation time and retirement benefits.

Ben couldn't believe it. Surely they didn't mean him. But they did. A stroke of a politician's pen and he and his colleagues in every county in Wisconsin would disappear. Like water spilled on a hot stove that evaporates in a little cloud of steam.

Lost Job

Ben Wesley's office was in the Ames County courthouse, a big, early-twentieth-century brick building with a statue of a civil war veteran on the front lawn standing straight with a musket at his side. Nothing fancy about his office. At one time four people worked there: Madeline Draper, who was family living agent; Floyd Evenson, 4-H agent; Delores Curry, the office secretary; and Ben Wesley. Now it was just Delores and Ben. Floyd and Madeline's jobs were eliminated three years ago in a round of budget cuts.

Ben should have paid more attention when their jobs disappeared— the handwriting was on the wall and he didn't see it. Ben's supervisor had said, "As soon as the budget is restored, we'll put those two positions back in your office." But that never happened. Three years ago, Ben had taken on the administration of the county 4-H program, which he added to his other duties. The family living program had lapsed into oblivion.

Ben leaned back in his chair and brushed his hand through his thinning hair. He figured his wooden desk arrived the same day the first agricultural agent came into the county—that was 1915. The desk was dirty brown and scarred here and there from smokers whose cigarettes fell out of the ashtray. Wooden bookshelves covered one wall of the institutional-gray room and likely arrived that same year. Some of the reference books and bulletins that he'd never tossed out came about that time, too: "How to Shoe a Horse." "Why Concrete Silos Make Sense." "Controlling Flies in Your Dairy Barn." "Best Methods for Growing Cranberries." "How to Prune Apple Trees."

Ben walked to the window and looked out on the courthouse lawn and the petunia bed that had just come into its own. "What am I gonna do now? Beth will have a fit," he said aloud.

He pounded his fist on the old desk. He could feel a tension headache building in the back of his neck.

Beth Wesley

*B*en Wesley quickly decided the worst part of losing his job was telling his wife. He and Beth had been married for twenty-one years. They had two kids: Liz, a junior at the University of Wisconsin–Madison; and Josh, in his first year at Mid-State Technical College in Wisconsin Rapids. It was no time to lose his job. With two kids in college, plus the mortgage on his house, his expenses had never been higher.

"I'm home," Ben said when he entered their modest house on Cedar Drive in Willow River, the county seat for central Wisconsin's Ames County. The lawn needed cutting and weeds had overgrown the flowerbed next to the sidewalk. The house could use a coat of paint. Josh was spending the summer at his grandparents' farm in Clark County, so he was not around to help. Liz had a summer job in Wisconsin Dells, at one of those water parks. Ben had hardly seen either of the kids so far this summer.

How should I break the news to Beth? he thought. He'd never been fired before—he hadn't been fired this time either—except come July 1, he wouldn't have a job. Comes out the same way. Laid off or fired. He'd still have no income.

"How's Mr. Agricultural Agent today?" Beth said by way of greeting. Ben couldn't tell by the tone of her voice if she'd had a good day or not. Beth never quite appreciated what being an agricultural agent meant, as she was a city girl, having grown up in Chicago. She, from the very beginning of Ben's career in Ames County, thought he worked too hard and put in too many hours for the pay he received. Just yesterday she'd said, "Ben, when are you going to start saying no? You're always working. Every evening. Almost every Saturday and Sunday. We never have any weekends together."

Ben knew she had a point. Over the years, Beth had by herself attended the kids' school events, taken them to the doctor and dentist, and listened to their problems because he was at some meeting or was out on a farm call dealing with some problem that couldn't wait.

"I'm beat," Ben said. "Bitch of a day."

"Well, you don't have to swear about it."

"'Bitch' isn't swearing."

"Sounds like swearing to me—thought we had a rule. No swearing in this house."

"Any beer in the fridge?" Ben was trying to think of a way of telling Beth his job was gone. He had a fierce headache, the kind that started just above his left eye and ended up in his neck. A stress headache, that doctor had once told him when he described the symptoms.

"How am I supposed to know if we've got any beer? I don't drink the stuff."

"Sounds like your day wasn't too great, either," Ben said, still wondering how he was going to say what he knew he must.

"What do you care about my job?"

"Well, I care. More than you think."

"I doubt that. What do you know about what I do? Next to nothing. I'm on my feet all day, running up and down hospital halls answering patient calls, listening to whining doctors. We're always shorthanded. Never enough aides. Every shift at the hospital someone doesn't show up. At least once a week I have to do a double shift. Bet you didn't know that." Beth's green eyes opened wide as she spoke.

"I've got some news," Ben said quietly as he opened the refrigerator, found a bottle of Leinie's Red, and popped off the cap. He took a long drink from the bottle.

"I hope you're gonna tell me you got a raise."

"No. I did not get a raise."

"So, what's the news?"

"I . . . I got laid off. The office is closing July 1. No more agricultural agent in Ames County."

"You've been fired." Beth raised her voice a bit. "The bastards in Madison fired you."

"Yup, I'm all through in two weeks."

"Why'd they fire you?"

"Fired all the county agricultural agents."

"All of them?"

"Yeah."

For a time they both just stood there in the kitchen, Ben looking at his beer, Beth looking out the window.

Then Ben started to explain. "The tax-cutting Republicans and a few weak-kneed Democrats got a majority on their side and cast the vote to cut our budget. Not just cut it. Eliminate it. Do away with it."

"So you don't have a job."

"Yup."

"No more income!" Beth had her hands on her hips, her green eyes flashing.

"That's about the size of it."

"How the hell we gonna live on my salary?"

"I don't know," Ben said quietly.

"Well, your getting fired really takes the cake. After all the time you spent, all the work you've done. Any way you can appeal? Tell those folks they made a mistake?"

"No."

"Why not?"

"It's done."

"Ben, decisions are never 'done.'"

"This one is!" Ben exclaimed.

"So you're not going to do anything?" There was exasperation in her voice.

"So, what am I supposed to do?" Ben slammed his beer down on the end table and some spilled on the shiny surface.

"Now look what you've done!" Beth shouted.

"I'll take care of it." Ben walked to the kitchen, tore off a length of paper toweling, returned, and wiped up the spilled beer.

"Ben, we've got to talk, boy, have we got to talk."

"I thought we were talking."

"This isn't talking. This is yelling at each other."

Local Agent Out

*T*he following article appeared in the *Ames County Argus*, the local newspaper, on June 11:

The Ames County agricultural agent's office will close July 1. In a surprise move, the Wisconsin Legislature voted this week to eliminate the budget for the University of Wisconsin Agricultural Agent Program (UWAAP). The governor is expected to immediately sign the legislation. The decision effectively eliminates an organization that began in the early 1900s and recently had employees in every county in the state.

"With an extremely tight state budget something had to go," said a legislative spokesperson who chose not to be named. "We simply can't pour any more money into Wisconsin's higher-education institutions."

Contacted at his office in the Ames County courthouse, Ben Wesley, current agricultural agent, said, "I was very surprised at the decision. Those of us who work as agricultural agents believe we have made a difference in improving Wisconsin's farming community and the related businesses that support agriculture."

When asked about his plans, Wesley replied, "I don't know. I just don't know. I didn't expect this to happen."

In addition to his work with farmers, gardeners, and cranberry growers in the county, Ben Wesley also administers the county 4-H program. With the UWAAP office closing, 4-H will be eliminated in

Local Agent Out

Ames County. The county fair, supported by the agricultural agent's office, will also be dramatically affected, as the fair depended heavily on 4-H member entries for its existence. Additionally, Wesley's weekly newspaper column and popular weekly radio program will end.

A week later, letters to the editor began appearing in the *Ames County Argus*:

Dear Editor:

It isn't often I have anything good to say about Wisconsin's legislature, but I want to applaud their recent decision to eliminate the University of Wisconsin Agricultural Agent Program (UWAAP). UWAAP lost its way about 25 years ago, when county agricultural agents began doing social-welfare work. The state already has too many welfare programs. The original idea of UWAAP was laudatory—helping to advance Wisconsin's agriculture. But when UWAAP began working with low-income food programs, assisting subsistence farmers, and doing other than transferring research results from the Madison researchers to those who could best apply the results—progressive farmers—UWAAP essentially became irrelevant.

Our lawmakers must continue to find ways to lower the state's taxes. The decision to eliminate UWAAP is an excellent beginning. Perhaps cutting the outrageous salaries offered to University of Wisconsin professors would be another avenue for them to pursue. Cutting about a third of the University of Wisconsin's professorial positions would be another effective approach to cost saving.

Dennis Culpepper
Link Lake

Dear Editor:

I milk 750 cows three times a day. I grow 500 acres of crops. I haven't worked with a county agricultural agent in ten years. When I want information, I get on the Internet and look for a specialist. It might cost me a little, but the information is up to date and accurate. Finally

the legislature is beginning to cut some of those obsolete state agencies.
I applaud them.

Clarence Higgins
Willow River

Shotgun Slogum

When the word got around that the legislature was closing all agricultural agent offices in the state, the phone calls began pouring into Ben Wesley's office. One of them was from Shotgun Slogum. Slogum operated a small cranberry bog and grew ten acres of vegetables and strawberries. He sold most of what he grew from a neat little stand that sat out by the road. "Slogum's Farm Fresh Vegetables," the faded, hand-painted, and slightly tilted sign read. Slogum sat in the stand for a few hours or so each day; during the summer season, he sold asparagus, radishes, leaf lettuce, sweet corn, tomatoes, beets, carrots, green beans, cucumbers, fresh cranberries, onions, dill. He also ran a pick-yourself strawberry patch where folks from all around came and picked berries.

Ben first heard about Amos "Shotgun" Slogum from Lars Olson, the county agricultural agent who had preceded him. Ben hadn't been on the job more than a day or so when Olson said, "You've gotta drive out and talk to Shotgun Slogum. He lives on the Tamarack River on the western edge of the county and is quite a character."

"Shotgun?" Ben remembered saying, wondering about the origin of the name.

"Yeah, everybody calls the guy by that handle. I'll bet you wonder why," Olson had said. "Well, Slogum runs this vegetable and fruit farm that his dad, old Felix, did before him. Slogum always had a big patch of watermelons way out on the back end of his farm, some distance from the house. They were good melons, too. Big juicy ones. In the 1960s, it was rather common for the local boys on cool autumn evenings to borrow a few melons, as they called it. Meaning they'd steal a sack full or so and then go off someplace and eat them, have themselves a little watermelon party."

"So," Ben said, waiting for the nub of the story.

"Well, one October evening, when the moon was full, four or five guys from Willow River drove out in Walter Houseback's pickup to Slogum's farm. Johnny Houseback, Walt's eighteen-year-old son, was driving and thus considered himself the leader of the little band of thieves. Everything went according to plan, if there can be a detailed plan for stealing watermelons on a warm fall evening when the moon is up and the night is as quiet as a cemetery in a January snowstorm.

"They'd sacked up about three gunny bags of melons when it happened. The blast of a 12-gauge shotgun shattered the quiet night air. Somehow Slogum had gotten wind of what these fellows were up to," Olson recalled. "This had been the third time that Slogum had lost melons. For Slogum losing melons once was a prank. Twice became a nuisance. Three times, well that pushed Slogum beyond the limit of his tolerance. These guys were stealing his melons, and he intended to teach them a lesson.

"As it turned out, Johnny Houseback was bending over picking up a melon and Slogum shot him in the ass with a fine shot. Slogum's idea had been an educational one—he didn't intend to hurt anyone. In fact, he didn't find out until the sheriff stopped out the next day and told him he'd shot a little too low and hit someone.

"The sheriff, it was old man Noble at the time, says to Slogum with a straight face, 'You know you shot a kid last night.'

"Slogum answered that he'd fired his shotgun but didn't intend to hit anyone. Then the sheriff says, 'You shot Johnny Houseback in the ass, about a dozen pellets got him. Doc told me about it. Doc also said that he didn't freeze his behind when he plucked out the pellets, that he wanted the young man to remember what he had done and the consequences of his action.'

"Then the sheriff began to laugh so hard his big belly that wanted to crawl over his wide belt jumped up and down. Sheriff said, 'I don't think you'll have anymore problems with that young man.' He could hardly talk he was laughing so hard. Then the sheriff got serious. 'But be careful. Next time you shoot, you might want to shoot over the heads of the watermelon stealers, probably scare them just as much.'

"That's how Shotgun Slogum got his name, and it stuck. That's what folks from around here call him to this day," Olson said.

Ben Wesley had spent considerable time with Shotgun Slogum over the past twenty years. Ben helped him select varieties for the fresh vegetable market; they talked about minimum use of fertilizer and pesticides to protect the soil and the groundwater. Amos worried about polluting the Tamarack River that ran by his place. He depended on water from the river to operate his cranberry bog. When he returned the water to the river, he hoped it was in as good condition as when he got it. He once told Ben he was not sure his neighbors who grew cranberries felt as strongly about this as he did.

Shotgun, some fifteen years ago, had been instrumental in helping Ben organize the Ames County Fruit and Vegetable Growers Cooperative, an organization of farmers dedicated to helping each other market their products. Additionally, with Ben's assistance, the cooperative sponsored annual meetings to keep growers up to date on everything from new varieties of fruits and vegetables to ecologically friendly pest control. Perhaps most importantly, the cooperative provided marketing strategies that allowed the members to compete as a group with much larger growers who had, before the cooperative was organized, essentially controlled the fruit and vegetable market in the area.

The cooperative established the Ames County Farmers' Market, one of its most successful endeavors. The market was held around the courthouse square in Willow River. Every Saturday from April to early November, members of the cooperative and others, too, had an opportunity to sell their products directly to consumers.

Letters about the closing of UWAAP were still being published in the *Ames County Argus*:

Dear Editor:

As a member of the Ames County Board, I have long been critical of our county agricultural agent's office. Ben Wesley has been a hardworking and loyal employee. Unfortunately, that has been the problem. He tries to do too much, spending more time than necessary working with low-income farmers who have refused or simply have not figured out how to enlarge their operations and become profitable. Of course, the large farm operators seek expertise elsewhere, as their special needs usually are beyond the capabilities of the local agricultural agent office. Wesley has also worked with the 4-H clubs in the county. It is high time that these clubs, although useful and well thought of, become self-supporting. After all, the Boy and Girl Scouts have always been on their own. It is time 4-H weaned itself from any tax-dollar support.

I am proud to say that I have been one of those who contacted legislators and urged that they cut the funding for the University of Wisconsin Agricultural Agent Program. It clearly is an outdated organization and should have been eliminated several years ago.

Cindy Jennings,
member of Ames County Board

Visiting Shotgun

Shotgun, now in his late seventies, invited Ben out to his place for a talk; he didn't say what about. Not everyone got along with Shotgun Slogum; as he got older, he had become even more ornery. Those who knew him, especially his close neighbors, put up with him. However, Ben liked Shotgun and considered him both a friend and someone who just might have an approach to farming that might one day become popular again. Shotgun wanted to keep things small and manageable. He listened critically to those advocating new technology whether it was a new machine to harvest cranberries or a new insecticide to control pests on his vegetables. Repeatedly, he'd say "no" to something new. His neighbors, who managed much larger cranberry marshes, saw Shotgun as someone hopelessly lost in history.

After Ben made a few routine phone calls, he hopped in his car and headed out to Shotgun's place; it was about a twenty-minute drive from Willow River. Mid–June was a beautiful time in Ames County. Although the western part of the county, where Shotgun lived, was sandy, in June everything was green and growing. The potatoes were up and Ben saw the green corn rows poking through the yellowish brown sandy soil. He drove through one of the richest vegetable-growing areas in Wisconsin. Vegetable growers here planted hundreds of acres of these crops. When the rains quit coming, and that was usually the case by July, these farmers turned on their irrigation systems, and the crops remained lush.

Ben heard the noise before he saw the small yellow airplane fly over the road in front of him, quickly drop down, and then, with its wheels but a few feet from the potato tops, turn on its sprayer. It flew to the end of the field and then with a loud roar of its engine quickly climbed to avoid a row of trees and power lines, banked sharply, descended, and began a return pass. It was surely an efficient, if somewhat costly, way to control insects and various diseases.

Ben's thoughts turned to his friend Shotgun Slogum. He remembered when he drove out to see him for the first time, now twenty years ago, along this same road. He had tried to follow Lars Olson's directions, but still drove past the overgrown driveway where a rusty mailbox sat on a crooked wooden post with one faded black word, "Slogum," painted on its side. Shotgun did not yet have the roadside stand. Ben remembered stopping, backing up, and driving along the snaky track that led to an unpainted house and other outbuildings planted in a little clearing.

He remembered climbing out of his car, expecting any minute to see a big, growling farm dog racing toward him, ready to tear off his pants. But no dog appeared. No movement. No sounds at all.

He had walked toward the house and around the side, because any country person knows you never approach the front door of a farm home. Farm people use their kitchen door; the front door was for show.

He remembered that on that first visit, he'd heard, "Hello."

"Hello," Ben replied. It was a rather high-pitched voice he'd heard.

"Hello," he heard again. "Screw you."

"What?" Ben said, surprised.

"Your mother wears bloomers."

"Slogum? Amos Slogum?" Ben called out.

"Hands up," commanded the voice. Then a man appeared. He had long black hair and a black beard. "Whattya you want?" he said gruffly.

"I'm . . . I'm Ben Wesley," he blurted out, "your new agricultural agent."

"Why in hell didn't you say so?" responded the heavyset man with deep blue eyes. "I'm Amos Slogum; everybody calls me Shotgun."

The man thrust out his big, rough hand to shake Ben's. "See you got acquainted with Joe."

"Joe?"

"Yeah, he's my pet crow. Talks pretty fair, wouldn't you say?" The big black crow flew down from its perch in an oak tree just beyond the kitchen, and landed on Shotgun's arm. The bird looked at his master and then he looked at Ben.

Ben remembered that day well. For some reason he and Shotgun Slogum had hit it off right away; over the years they developed a great respect for each other. Shotgun didn't always agree with Ben and the recommendations from the university. Ben didn't always appreciate Shotgun's stubbornness and resistance to change. But they had become good friends nonetheless.

This time Ben drove down past the sign that read "Pick Your Own Strawberries—follow the trail" and past the vegetable stand, where some kid Shotgun had hired was selling fresh-picked strawberries. The kid pointed to the trail Ben should follow, assuming he was there to pick berries.

Soon Ben was out in Shotgun's berry patch, about three acres of the finest strawberries found anywhere in central Wisconsin. Probably two dozen pickers were scattered along the rows.

When Shotgun spotted Ben, he waved. "Over here, Ben," he called.

Ben shook his friend's hand, calloused from years of physical work. Shotgun's hair and beard had long since turned white, and he walked with a little stoop. His deeply tanned face had become as wrinkled as an old washboard. However, the striking blue eyes remained the same. Bright and penetrating.

"Sure as hell sorry about what happened to you, Ben," Shotgun began. "Some of them ag agents deserved to be fired, but not you. Them god-damn politicians. All they got on their minds these days is cuttin' taxes. Got everybody thinkin' it's a good idea. But they ain't smart enough to pick out what deserves cuttin' and what don't. Bunch of dumb bastards."

"Shotgun, you're gonna raise your blood pressure," Ben said, smiling. He saw a big black crow sitting on the edge of the little table where strawberry pickers came to check out and pay for what they had picked. The big, black bird looked at Ben then back at its master.

"Well, it's too damn bad the ag agent office is closing. Too damn bad." Shotgun shook his head. His long white hair tied in back flopped back and forth like a horse's tail. "Weren't for you Ben, we wouldn't have the growers cooperative. Don't know what we smaller growers would do without it. Probably be out of business, that's what."

"Oh, I doubt that," Ben said, smiling. "Guys like you would make it."

"I'm busy as hell today, Ben. Ain't got much time to talk. But I wanted you to know my feelings. I put together some stuff for you." From under the table where the crow sat Shotgun pulled out a box, which contained six quarts of fresh-picked, red and lush strawberries, a big bunch of asparagus, and the reddest radishes Ben had ever seen, their tops held together with a rubber band. "Strawberries," the crow said, in its high-pitched voice. The bird flew up and sat on Shotgun's shoulder.

"What do I owe you?" Ben asked.

"Owe me? You don't owe me nothin'. All that you've done for me. All that you've done for the little guys in this county." The big man grabbed Ben's hand with both of his. Ben saw tears in his eyes.

*L*etters continued to pour in to the *Argus* about the end of the agricultural agent program:

Dear Editor:

I've just read the story about the legislature closing down all the agricultural agent offices in Wisconsin, including the one we have here in Ames County.

Do the people of Ames County realize that they will lose one of the most dedicated public servants we have ever known? Ben Wesley, our agricultural agent, works night and day to make this county a better place to live. He not only works with farmers, small and large, but he works with the youth of our county as well. Without his able assistance we would not have one of the most active 4-H programs in central Wisconsin.

Wesley also devotes many hours to the small vegetable gardeners in Ames County, those who live in the villages and cities, as well as those who live in the country. Sure, he works with the large vegetable growers, but if someone has a problem with a backyard vegetable garden, some insect is chewing up the potatoes, the sweet corn isn't doing well, a fruit tree has a problem, he is there to help with no questions asked.

It's about time we begin standing up to these legislators who have run amuck. We elected them. It's time to vote the rascals out.

Peter Swendryzinski
Willow River

Dear Editor:

I read with interest the story about closing the agricultural agent offices in Wisconsin. About time we began cutting the handouts to farmers. The rest of us have to get along without free help. I have to pay my attorney when he helps me. Same for my accountant and dentist. They don't come to me at taxpayers' expense. Look at these farmers today. They're all making big money. Dairy farmers get good money for their milk. Vegetable growers seem to be doing well—at least they drive big new John Deere tractors and hire airplanes to spray their crops.

It all started when old Franklin Roosevelt began handing taxpayer money to down-and-out farmers back in the 1930s. It's got to stop. Getting rid of these agricultural agent offices is a beginning.

Name Withheld on Request

Part 2

Fred and Oscar

This ain't much of a boat," said Fred Russo. He and Oscar Anderson were fishing in Round Lake, south of Willow River.

"What'd you say?" Oscar replied.

Louder this time, Fred repeated, "This ain't much of a boat."

"Don't 'peer to be leakin'," said Oscar.

"At least this one ain't leakin'," said Fred.

"That's what I just said. I said it weren't leakin', ain't you listenin'?"

"Ain't I what?" asked Fred.

"Ain't you listenin'?" Oscar said more loudly.

"Thought that's what you said. You don't have to shout."

"How deep you got your bobber set?" asked Oscar, changing the subject. They were fishing with sixteen-foot-long cane poles, having left their fancy mechanical fishing rods at home.

"My what?"

"Your damn bobber, Fred. How deep you got it?"

"Hell, I don't know. Maybe four feet. Little better than that maybe. You gettin' any bites, Oscar? Any nibbles?"

"Any what?" asked Oscar, turning his good ear toward his old friend.

"Nibbles, Oscar. Nibbles. You gettin' any nibbles?"

"Nah. Nothin'. Probably too nice a day. Sun shinin'. No wind. Nice and warm. Too nice a day," said Fred, who lifted his heavy green line with the red and white bobber and worm-baited hook out of the water and tossed it back in again. The bobber made a "plop" sound when it hit the water.

Fred and Oscar fished for bluegills, hoping to snag some the size of your hand and some bigger. Enough for a meal for both of them. Early summer was the time to catch them when the water was still cold and the fish's flesh was firm. Round Lake was one of several relatively small lakes in central Ames County. The lake was only about fifty acres but according to some maps was up to forty-feet deep in places. A good fishing lake.

The two old men sat quietly for a time, staring at their bobbers and enjoying each other's company. They saw a mother mallard near shore, six little ducklings strung out in the water behind her, paddling furiously to keep up. They heard a red wing blackbird singing from its perch on a cattail.

"You read about what happened to the ag agent?" Fred broke the silence.

"Who?"

"The ag agent? Think his name was Ben Wesley."

"Oh, him. Yeah, I did. Don't know what to make of it. Seems like a farming county like this one needs an agricultural agent."

"Farmin' ain't like it was," Fred said. "There just ain't many of us anymore, and the ones still workin' . . . well, they seem to have gotten so damn big it's just hard to know how they can make a go of it."

"Yup. Ain't like when we was farmin'."

"Sure not," said Fred. "Don't know where it's all headed. This business of farming. Can't tell what's goin' on. Too bad about the ag agent gettin' canned. Figured he was a pretty good guy. A straight shooter."

"A what?" Oscar asked.

"Straight shooter."

"He a hunter?" asked Oscar.

"I don't know if he hunts or not. What's that got to do with anything?"

"Just giving you the business," said Oscar. "I know what you mean."

Once more the two old men watched their big bobbers, which sat motionless on the smooth surface of the lake.

Fred and Oscar

"Whattya say we wrap up our poles and git outta here. Fish just ain't bitin' today," said Fred.

"Ain't that the truth," replied Oscar. "Sure a nice day though."

8

Phone Call

Good morning, Ames County Agent's Office, this is Delores. How can I help you?"

From his office, Ben heard the phone ring and his secretary answer. Delores was putting up a good front; both of them would be out of work on July 1. She'd been secretary in this office for thirty years, ten years longer than he had been here. It was the only job she'd ever known; she started the summer she graduated from Willow River High School.

After a brief pause, she said, "Just a moment, I'll connect you." The phone on Wesley's desk rang.

"This is Ben." These were the same words he'd used for twenty years whenever he answered the office phone.

"Mr. Wesley, this is Dr. Sara Phillips with Osborne University. How are you this morning?"

"I'm fine," Ben lied. "How can I help you?"

He took off his wire-rimmed glasses, placed them on his desk, and rubbed his free hand over his balding head.

"Are you familiar with Osborne University?" Phillips asked. The voice was coldly professional.

"Of course, you're only fifty miles from Willow River," Ben said.

"You'd be surprised how little people know about us," Phillips went on. "Some folks think we're another state university. We are not, of course. Few people realize that we don't cost the taxpayers a nickel of their hard-earned money. We're entirely self-supporting," Phillips said proudly.

Phone Call

By now Ben was wondering why she had called. He knew quite a bit about Osborne University. How could he not? The press had run feature stories about them nearly once a month since they opened a little over four years ago. They had a first-rate public relations office, no matter what else you might say about them. As a for-profit university, they offered bachelor's, master's and PhD degrees entirely online. Everything on the Internet. They had no campus; merely a building in downtown Oshkosh that at one time housed a furniture store.

As he listened to the woman, Ben became even more curious about what she wanted from him. Frankly, he'd been more than a little skeptical about what Osborne University was doing. *Guess I'm old fashioned*, he thought, *but I can't see how you can earn a degree by sitting in front of a computer.* Sure, the Internet can provide lots of help, give a person a pile of information, but earn a degree that way? Ben never said so to anyone, but he just couldn't see how earning a degree without looking your instructors in the eye was possible.

A year or so ago Ben had talked with one of the horticulture researchers in Madison. He told Ben that Osborne University was developing a research station in Ames County. Osborne University had bought an old abandoned farm on the Tamarack River and had constructed several green houses where they were doing research on vegetables and small fruits—strawberries and raspberries especially. The Madison researcher also mentioned that Osborne had restored a small abandoned cranberry bog where they'd begun working on cranberries. That was the first time he'd heard about their research program. Since then Ben had driven by the facility a few times; the gate was always locked and a big orange sign declared, "Private Property: Keep Out." Ben wondered why an online university had a research station; somehow that didn't make sense to him. If all the students were working online, who was helping with the research projects? At research universities, graduate students assisted with the ongoing research activity.

"I was wondering if you had some time to meet with me next week. You name the day and place," Phillips said.

"Sure," Ben said. Now he was really curious. She must have heard that he had been laid off and his office was closing. "I've got time next Tuesday."

I've also got time on Monday, Wednesday, Thursday, and Friday, he thought. "Is there anything I can help you with over the phone?"

"No, I've got a question I'd like to discuss with you in person. Could we meet for lunch? You name the place."

"Okay," Ben said. "How about the Lone Pine restaurant just outside Willow River on Highway 21?"

"I know the place. See you there at noon. Nice talking with you."

Ben put on his glasses and leaned back in his chair. "What does Osborne University want with me?" he said aloud. So far the for-profit university had completely ignored him and his office. In fact they always seemed quite aloof to anything and everyone connected to the University of Wisconsin. At least that's the impression he got from reading their news releases. He turned back to cleaning out file cabinets and packing boxes in preparation for the office closing. He found a stack of bulletins, "Growing Cranberries in Central Wisconsin." He had written the twenty-page booklet ten years ago, and it was still being used. He thumbed through the pages. "How to Establish a Cranberry Bed," "Water Requirements," "Controlling Pests," "Weed Control," "Harvesting Shortcuts," and more. He'd even included a few paragraphs about the health benefits of cranberries—how they contained substances that helped prevent urinary problems.

As he continued packing, the memories keep getting in the way of his work. Every object he picked up had a story to tell. He packed a picture taken at the county fair, where he stood in front of the horticulture building. He found the scrapbook where Delores had saved all his weekly newspaper columns, twenty years of writing. He remembered in the early days how he had trouble thinking what to write, and how, in recent years, he had more ideas than there was space in the newspaper.

Ben looked up to see Delores standing in the open doorway to his office.

"Ben, it's after five. Time to quit for the day."

"Yes, yes, it is," Ben said. He had scarcely begun packing away twenty years of memories.

Dr. Sara Phillips

*T*he *Ames County Argus* kept publishing additional letters as they came in:

Dear Editor:

    Our county agricultural agent is leaving. My goodness, what'll be next? Close the schools? Shut down the firehouses? Privatize the police departments? What's the country coming to? Just remember: Good things often aren't missed until they're gone.

Lizzy Hatliff

Link Lake

The following Tuesday, Ben arrived at the Lone Pine restaurant about ten of twelve, wondering what Dr. Sara Phillips from Osborne University had on her mind. Sitting on a little pine knoll, the Lone Pine, sided with cedar half-logs, once stood on the outskirts of Willow River. In the last twenty years, the city had come out to meet the restaurant and now an Ace Hardware, an antique store, an Amish furniture outlet, and a small-engine repair shop surrounded the little restaurant. The Lone Pine tried to promote itself as a Northwoods eating place. It had a mounted northern pike on the south wall, a ten-point deer head on the north wall, and a collection of shotguns and deer rifles displayed on the long wall above the counter. Willow River was actually a hundred miles south of where most people thought Wisconsin's real Northwoods began. Some said you had to travel at least north of Highway 29 for the Northwoods. The purists claimed you had to drive beyond Highway 8 to find the true north in the state. Willow River natives knew this, and although they did not agree on where Wisconsin's north began, they all knew it wasn't Willow River.

"Mornin', Ben," said Mazy, longtime Lone Pine waitress, when Ben came through the door. Mazy worked here when Beth and Ben first moved to Willow River the year after they married. Mazy had aged well. She maintained a positive attitude, even in the early morning when she came to work. She'd also developed a reputation for taking no guff from anybody, especially early morning truck drivers passing through town and stopping for breakfast.

"Woman here to see you, Ben," Mazy said. She talked out of the side of her mouth. "Over there in that side booth." She pointed with her pencil.

Ben walked over to the table. "Hi, I'm Ben Wesley," he said. A woman in her mid-thirties with short brown hair and wearing a cream-colored blouse and a hunter-green blazer with "Osborne University" stitched on one pocket held out her hand.

"Hello," she said. "I'm Doctor Sara Phillips from Osborne University. Have a seat. I haven't ordered yet." Ben noticed her fingers were long and thin. Her grip was firm. Her hand was warm.

He slipped into the booth, opposite the woman.

"Thanks for coming on such short notice."

"No problem, not much going on these days with my office closing down. You've no doubt heard that all the agricultural agent offices in the state are closing on July 1."

"Yes, I've heard that," she responded. Ben couldn't read the expression on her face, nor could he tell from the tone of her voice what she thought about the matter.

"How do you like living in Willow River?" she asked. Her voice was professional. Her face was without expression.

"I like it," he said, wondering why she would ask such a question. "My wife and I have lived here for twenty years. Didn't think I'd like it when we first moved here. But the place kind of grew on me. Good place to raise kids."

"Let's see," Phillips said, opening a folder. "You have a daughter, Elizabeth, who will be a junior at the University of Wisconsin in Madison next fall. And a son, Josh, who just finished his first year at Mid-State Technical College."

"That's . . . that's right. But how did you know?"

"Oh, I did a little homework," Phillips said. She smiled smugly.

"What else did your homework turn up?" Ben asked. His voice sounded more surprised than he intended.

"Let's see." She glanced at the papers in front of her. "You've been married twenty-one years. Your wife, Beth, is a registered nurse at Ames Memorial Hospital."

"How'd you find that out?" Ben stammered.

"Oh, we have ways," she said. "Not too complicated, just ask a few questions. Oh, and by the way, you have a bachelor's degree in agricultural education and a master's degree in horticulture from the College of Agricultural and Life Sciences in Madison." Her manner was business-like, cool and calculated, yet friendly.

"I . . . I do," Ben said. Now he was really curious what this nosey woman wanted. She went on reciting Ben's resume.

"You've won three awards for outstanding work as an agricultural agent. The people you've worked with speak highly of both your knowledge and your people skills. And your supervisor ranks you in the top 5 percent of all county agricultural agents in Wisconsin."

"How . . . how did you learn all that?" Ben muttered.

"I told you, I do my homework. I'll bet you're wondering why I wanted to meet with you," she said.

"That I am," Ben said. He had a perplexed look on his face.

The lunch menus sat in front of them unopened. Mazy appeared at the side of the booth, her pencil and order pad at the ready. "You two ready to order?" she said. She tapped the pencil on the order pad. "Special this noon is a half sandwich of your choice and a cup of either chicken noodle or vegetable beef soup."

"I'd like the special," Phillips said. "Turkey on whole wheat with a cup of chicken noodle."

Mazy wrote the order on her pad. "This all on one check?"

"It is," Phillips said. "I'm buying."

"Ben, what's for you today?" Mazy asked. She had a quizzical look on her face. It wasn't often she saw Ben having lunch with a well-dressed, good-looking woman from out of town.

"I'll have the same, except you can bring me the vegetable beef soup," Ben said.

Mazy scratched a few notes on her pad and left.

"As I was saying, you're probably wondering why I'm here," Phillips said.

"As a matter of fact, yes, and by the way, thanks for buying lunch."

"You're welcome. Let me start at the beginning." She stacked the papers in front of her into a neat pile and folded her hands on top of them.

"Osborne University is adding another dimension to its portfolio—we'd planned to do that even before the legislature voted to eliminate the University of Wisconsin Agricultural Agent Program. You know about our experimental work at the Osborne Research Station, I'm sure."

"Well, not entirely," Ben said.

"To summarize quickly, we've hired the top horticultural researchers in the world to staff our facility. We give them free rein—they work on everything from traditional plant breeding and variety development to genetic modification of plants to make them less susceptible to insect and weed pests. A special team of our scientists is working on a new product to enhance the health-producing qualities of cranberries," she said, emphasizing the words "health-producing."

"Is that right?" Ben said. "Sounds interesting."

"Yes, and besides this new material, our scientists are on the edge of several new discoveries, well ahead of public-supported universities, I might say, even the University of Wisconsin."

"Really?" said Ben. He wanted to challenge this woman who was beginning to get on his nerves. He wanted to tell her that she had no idea about the research going on in the College of Agricultural and Life Sciences in Madison. But he didn't. Maybe it was because he was curious. Maybe it was because she was so darn good looking. It's hard to tell a good-looking woman that she's full of it, at least for Ben it was. Or maybe it was because she was filled with enthusiasm. Ben's agricultural agent friends were all in a deep funk these days, wondering how they'd pay their mortgages and feed their kids after the first of July. This woman, this Dr. Sara Phillips, was filled with excitement to the point of bubbling over.

"Would you be interested in working for Osborne University?" she asked. She looked straight at Ben, with just a hint of a smile on her lips.

"What?" Ben was astounded.

"Would you like to work for Osborne University?" She continued smiling, her eyebrows raised as she repeated the question.

"To do what?" he blurted out. "I'm not a researcher."

"We don't need any more researchers right now."

"Then what?" He was sure she was enjoying the surprised look on his face. Her smile seemed to indicate that.

"We would like you to be our first Ames County research application specialist."

"Your what?"

She laughed. "We'd like you to be our county agricultural agent, except we call them research application specialists.

Mazy came by with the food, slid it in front of both them without comment, and breezed off.

Ben couldn't believe what he was hearing. Dr. Phillips was offering him a job, and it sounded like the same one he was about to leave—except he'd be working for a different university.

"Wait, let me get this straight. You're offering me a job after talking to me for fifteen minutes?"

"I am. It's not like I don't know you. I know a lot about you. More than you think."

"So, what does the job involve?"

"About the same duties as you do now. Except people will pay you for your work."

"Pay me?"

"Yes, it's a new day. People expect to pay for services these days, whether it's helping fill out an income tax form or landscaping your yard. Nothing is free anymore."

"Oh," Ben said. "And how much will I charge?"

"We have it all worked out—a payment schedule, if you will. Different payment rates for different services. When you consult with farmers about crops, we have one schedule. When you consult with cranberry growers, we have a different payment listing. When you teach a workshop, we have a workshop payment plan."

Working for both the University of Wisconsin and Ames County, Ben couldn't charge for his services. His work was supported by a combination of funds that came from the United States Department of Agriculture, the state of Wisconsin, and Ames County. The county agent system, called Cooperative Extension, was established by federal legislation passed in 1914. Cooperative Extension, with its county-based agents, was a response to the immense value the country placed on agriculture and the family farm. Ben was glad his services were free because he worked with many low-income farmers who couldn't have paid him a nickel.

"What about those people who can't afford me?"

"No problem. We have payment plans for those with limited income. Besides, they can pay you with a credit card. But we don't have to talk about these details now. Here's a folder that describes the position. We offer a special in-service training program that will tell you all you need to know about your job."

"Oh." It was all Ben could think to say. All this had taken him completely by surprise. He was extremely flattered that this university wanted him to work for them. So far, the only job he had looked at was head of the garden department for the big new Wal-Mart Superstore. It paid half of what UWAAP paid, and with limited benefits.

"One more thing," Phillips said. "We are prepared to offer you twice the salary you now receive."

"Twice my salary?" Ben sputtered.

"Yes, plus a percentage of your billed hours, a portion of the money earned from book and bulletin sales, and half of what you take in from workshop fees."

"I . . . I don't know what to say."

"Don't say anything." She reached over and touched Ben on the arm.

"Take this packet of materials home with you. Discuss the details with your wife and then let me know your decision within a week."

Dr. Phillips stood up, reached over, and shook Ben's hand. "Sorry, I have to run. I have another meeting in Stevens Point this afternoon. I know I'll enjoy working with you, Ben." She looked him in the eye when she said it. The soup stood untouched; she had taken one bite of her sandwich.

10

New Job?

*H*ow'd your lunch meeting go?" Beth Wesley asked when Ben returned home that afternoon.

"Okay," Ben said. He tossed his cap on the chair by the door.

"So, what'd the woman from Osborne University want? She knew you'd been fired, didn't she?"

"Yup, she knew that," Ben said.

"Well, what'd she want?"

"Wanted to talk about a position they have open at Osborne University."

"What kind of position?" Beth had that irritated tone to her voice that she sometimes got when Ben seemed to be avoiding giving her a straight answer.

"It's called a research application specialist."

"Well, what about it? She offer you a job?" Beth said it half joking, as she was quite confident that it would take weeks for Ben to find new work, maybe months. There just weren't many jobs available for people with Ben's qualifications.

"She did offer me a job. Osborne wants me to be one of their research application specialists."

"Really?" Beth began to smile.

"Yes."

"What kind of salary—more than the Wal-Mart job?"

"Yup, quite a bit more than the Wal-Mart job."

"So, how much?"

"Twice what I'm making as an agricultural agent."

"Twice!" Beth exclaimed. "Twice as much as you make now?"

"Yeah, that's what Dr. Phillips said. I haven't seen the offer in writing yet."

"You sure you heard right?"

"I heard right. She said I'd earn twice my salary, plus I'd also get a percentage of my consulting fees, part of what I make for giving speeches, and a portion of the money I take in for selling Osborne bulletins.

"Well, I hope you said 'yes.'"

"She said I had a week to think about it."

"You didn't say 'yes' right on the spot? Why not?"

"Beth, you don't say 'yes' to a job offer without thinking about it."

"Ben, Ben, Ben. In less than two weeks, you are a man without a job, and you're playing hard to get."

"I gotta talk to Lars about this, see what he thinks. Should talk to Shotgun Slogum, too. Then I'll do some thinking."

"For heaven's sake, Ben, what's to think about? Osborne University is offering you a plum position, and you have to think about it? That's been your problem all along. You just don't move fast enough."

"I've got to think about this, Beth. I never charged fees for my work before," Ben said. "Osborne wants me to charge people for my advice."

"Geez, Ben, isn't it about time you started charging people? People come to the hospital; we don't treat them for free."

"It's not the same, Beth. The hospital is not like a farm or a cranberry bog."

"Same principle applies. You want something, a new idea, a new way of doing something, you plunk down your money for it. What's the difference between a farmer with a sick corn plant and a mother with a sick child? The mom has to pay; why shouldn't the farmer?"

"I just don't know," Ben said. "Don't know about this new job."

"What are you afraid of? For heaven's sake, call this Dr. what's-her-name and tell her you'll take the job."

"It's just not that easy, Beth. I can't jump into this willy-nilly. Wouldn't be right."

"Good God, Ben. Here we are, soon out of money and you're worried about making the right decision. If somebody offered me twice the money I was making, I sure wouldn't waste any time saying 'yes.'"

"I expect you wouldn't," Ben said under his breath. He picked up the newspaper and settled into his chair.

Beth and Osborne University

*B*eth Wesley simply could not understand her husband, even after twenty-one years of marriage. Just when she thought she knew what interested him, he'd change and do something else. Or maybe *not* change; perhaps that was the better way of putting it. About five years ago the local farmers' co-op in Willow River had offered Ben a job as a field representative. It was a good job, too, with a chance to advance to the head office in Minneapolis. They wanted him to visit farmers, help them figure out their seed and fertilizer needs each year, and then sell them the products the analysis suggested was appropriate for the coming year. Ben had sat around and thought about it for a week or more, and then turned them down. Beth was furious at the time. She told him he was never going anywhere with his career if he kept passing by opportunities when they came knocking on the door.

At the time Ben had quietly explained that he enjoyed being a county agricultural agent and was quite satisfied with the work. They had a big fight over that job offer; Beth threatened to leave him, and she probably would have if both kids hadn't still been in school and living at home.

Beth couldn't figure out why Ben seemed to have no gumption, no sense of wanting to get ahead. Of course, she hoped upon hope that he'd find a new job that paid more than what a county agricultural agent got. She'd long recognized that you just don't make much money when the taxpayers foot the bill.

And now what was Ben going to do? Beth wondered. He was going to talk to Lars Olson, who hadn't been a county agent for twenty years, and, even worse, he wanted to talk with Shotgun Slogum, that old vegetable farmer who hadn't done anything different or new for more years than a person could count. *What kind of advice will he get from those guys?* Beth thought. He should be talking with somebody who thinks about the future—where agriculture is headed in the next twenty years, not where it's been the past twenty. He ought to be talking with people who know about new research and how agriculture is likely to be structured in the future, that sort of thing. Beth thought it was time she did some research of her own. She turned on her computer and typed "Osborne University" into the search engine. Soon she was looking at Osborne University's website. She first clicked on "history" and learned that Osborne University, officially known as Ira Osborne University, had been organized only five years ago. It was named after the former board chairman of the International Farm-Med Company. The Farm-Med Company had put up the money to start the for-profit institution, which was to be entirely online.

Beth then clicked on "philosophy of Osborne" and read:

> As a totally online university we pride ourselves in making our curriculum available to young and old alike. Some of our students are recent high school graduates, others are in their sixties and even older.
>
> Because all our offerings are online, students can study whenever, wherever, and for as long as they like. They can take three years to earn a degree, or they can take ten years; it is entirely up to the student, who knows his or her circumstances better than anyone.
>
> Students enrolled in Osborne University only need a computer with an Internet connection. If for some reason a student does not have a computer, we will include one at the time of enrollment, at a modest price.

Beth then looked at the programs the institution offered and was amazed at the array of degrees available. Everything from a bachelor's degree in liberal studies to a PhD in educational administration. She found a degree program for nurse-practitioner, a career-advancement position she had long sought. The more she read about Osborne University the more excited she got. Finally, she clicked on "employment opportunities":

Beth and Osborne University

Osborne University has an open position in its community outreach department, titled Research Application Specialist. Salary is competitive. Full description of the position is available by contacting Osborne University. Fringe benefits are generous, including free tuition for family members wishing to enroll in one of Osborne's many programs.

Beth sat back in her chair. This was the position Ben had been recruited for. How could he possibly turn down this opportunity? Osborne University was looking to the future, and her husband, Ben Wesley, could be a part of it. She wondered how she could convince him to take the job.

12

Shotgun's Advice

*B*en Wesley valued Shotgun Slogum's advice; he always did. Shotgun was one of those fellows who gave you his opinion whether you wanted it or not. That of course turned off some people. They didn't want to be reminded of a wrong-headed idea or something they did that Shotgun thought was off base and cockeyed.

True, Ben didn't always agree with Shotgun's critiques, but Ben always listened. As time passed, he listened more carefully, as Shotgun Slogum, different from a good many people, didn't open his mouth unless he'd thought through what he had to say. One of Shotgun's favorite sayings was "It's better to keep your mouth shut and be thought a fool than open it and remove all doubt."

Ben was especially curious what Shotgun would say when he told him about his job offer. Though no longer president of the Ames County Fruit and Vegetable Growers Cooperative, Shotgun still represented the main thread of the cooperative's thinking—providing a marketing opportunity for the small- and mid-sized fruit and vegetable growers in the area. Ben didn't want to do anything to undermine this group, which he'd helped create and still supported.

He chose to drive out to the Slogum place in the early evening, when he knew that the pick-your-own strawberry people had gone home and Shotgun might have a little time to talk.

A haze hung over the marshland as Ben approached Shotgun's farm. The sun was low in the western sky and he heard a sandhill crane call as he stepped from his car and walked the short distance to Shotgun's house. In the distance he could see the Tamarack River that bordered Shotgun's place. Lazy threads of thin horse-tail clouds rose from the river as the cool air of evening met the warmer river water.

"Ben, come in," Shotgun said when Ben knocked on the door. "Just finishing up my supper. Want a cup of coffee?"

"Don't mind if I do," Ben said as he sat down at the big wooden kitchen table. Shotgun poured a cup of coffee and handed it to Ben. It was strong, the kind of coffee Ben liked. Though he had long lived alone, Shotgun's place was neat and tidy, not at all like the places of some bachelor farmers that Ben knew.

"Good to see you again," Shotgun said. "Got any leads on a job?"

"Matter of fact I do," replied Ben.

"Well, that didn't take long. I knew it wouldn't. I don't wanna swell your head, but there ain't many Ben Wesleys around."

"Thank you," Ben said.

"Say, you want a chocolate chip cookie to go with your coffee? I stopped at that little bakery in Link Lake the other day and bought a couple dozen. Best darn bakery in all of Ames County, that one. Make cookies like my mother used to make."

"Sure," Ben said. Shotgun pulled a sack of cookies from a shelf behind him, took one out, and handed the bag to Ben. He broke the cookie in half, walked over to the door, opened it, whistled softly, and called, "Henry."

Ben saw a raccoon amble from around the corner of the house, crawl up on the porch, and gently take the broken cookie from Shotgun's hand. The raccoon turned and waddled off.

"Friendly little fellow," Ben said.

"Yup, raised Henry on a bottle. Car ran over his mother. Little guy would've died if I hadn't taken him in. He's found a home in my old corn crib. So, what's the job offer?" Shotgun asked, looking Ben straight in the eye.

"It's what I want to talk with you about. Don't know if I want to say yes or no to it."

"So, what is it? President of the bank?" Shotgun laughed when he said it.

"Not quite. It's working for this new Osborne University. You know about them?"

"Only what I've read in the paper. What do they want you to do?"

"They want me to be a research application specialist."

"A what?"

"Research application specialist."

"What in hell is a research application specialist?" Shotgun asked, smiling.

"Fancy name for a county ag agent. They want me to work with farmers, pretty much as I do now."

"That don't sound too bad. Different office. Different university. Same job."

"It's not quite that simple, Shotgun. I'll have to charge a fee for my work."

For a time it was quiet in the Slogum kitchen, the two men sitting across from each other drinking coffee and eating chocolate chip cookies.

Shotgun ran a big hand through his white hair. "Guess that's how it is these days. You want something done, you have to pay for it." He reached for the cookie sack and took out another cookie.

"What do you think I should do, Shotgun? Take this job or not? Beth is all for it. Can't blame her too much. I'll have no paycheck on July 1."

"Hell, Ben, quit frettin'. Take the damn job. If it don't work out, quit and find something else. You're still a young man."

"I'm forty-five, Shotgun."

"Forty-five. Hell, Ben, forty-five is like being a kid these days. You've got at least twenty, twenty-five good years left in you. If Osborne doesn't work out, you'll find something else."

13

Conversation with Lars

*W*hen Ben got home that night he called his old friend Lars Olson. "Lars, you got time for coffee tomorrow morning? I need to talk with you."

"Sure," Lars said. "Always ready to talk."

"Thanks," Ben said. "See you at the Lone Pine at seven tomorrow morning."

Ben arrived at the Lone Pine about five of seven. "You alone, Ben?" asked Mazy when he came through the door.

"No, I'm meeting with Lars Olson when he gets here."

"Take a booth, take a table, your choice," Mazy said as she carried coffee to the morning coffee klatch of old timers gathering around the long table in the back of the restaurant. Mazy had a breezy, confident way about her that customers appreciated.

Promptly at seven, Lars slid into the seat opposite Ben. Ben had selected a booth as far from the old-timer table as he could. He didn't want them overhearing his and Lars's conversation and starting a bunch of rumors about "that fired agricultural agent," as he was commonly referred to these days.

"What's up?" Lars asked. He had a way of knowing when to make small talk and when to get to the core of a conversation. Pushing seventy-five, Lars Olson continued to be the picture of health. He was tall and trim and could easily pass for someone ten years younger.

"I've got a job offer," Ben said.

"Well, good for you, Ben. That didn't take long."

"It's with Osborne University. They want me to be what they call a re-search application specialist." Ben went on to explain what he knew about the position, including the fact that he would have to charge for his services and that one of his major jobs would be to promote the university's new research findings. "Well, what do you think?" Ben asked. An uncomfortable silence settled between the two men. Lars was sipping on his coffee, which Mazy had brought while they were talking.

"You talk this over with Beth?" Lars finally asked.

"Yeah, most of it. She's all for it. Says it sounds like a great opportunity for me. She especially likes the idea of me getting a bigger paycheck."

"She have any problem with you charging people for your help?"

"No, not at all. She says they don't pass around much free advice at Ames Memorial Hospital, nor anyplace else she knows about."

Once more, silence.

Lars finally said, "Why'd you become a county agricultural agent?"

"Let's see. I heard about the job when you retired and I applied. I needed a job at the time; Beth and I had just gotten married."

"That all there was to it—you needed a job and this one opened up?"

Ben smiled. "Maybe a little more to it, Lars."

"I'm listening."

"I grew up on a small dairy farm in Clark County," Ben began. "When I was ten years old we started a 4-H club in our community. We named the club Busy Doers. About a dozen kids from our neighborhood joined. The county agricultural agent, I think his name was John something, came out to the community hall and told us about 4-H work and how we could sign up for projects such as dairy, field crops, and forestry, and for the girls, cooking and sewing. He gave each of us a little four-leaf-clover pin with an H on each leaf. He said the H's stood for head, heart, hands, and health. What caught our attention was his talk about the county fair. As 4-H members, he said, we could take our projects to the fair, where they would be judged and we'd get ribbons, a blue for first, a red for second, and a white for third. I thought that 4-H was just about the most interesting thing there was for a farm kid who spent most of his summer working."

Lars sat sipping his coffee and listening, the corners of his mouth turned up in a sly grin. "So being in 4-H was one of the reasons you wanted to be a county ag agent?"

"You know . . . I haven't thought about this for a long time, but that was surely one of the reasons. I also thought how great it was that the county agent would come out to the farm and talk to Pa. Imagine that. A teacher driving out to see his student—although I'm sure Pa didn't think of it that way. I'd listen in as they talked about new alfalfa varieties, or how Pa might put together a different feed mixture and get a little more milk out of our cows. I was impressed with how much the county agent knew about new approaches to farming, yet he was low key about making recommendations. What he was doing mostly was getting Pa to think about how he farmed and how he could do it better. The county agent didn't seem the least bit disappointed when Pa sometimes said, 'I don't think we can afford that right now.'"

"All that sounds kind of similar to what you've been doing these past twenty years, Ben," Lars said as he motioned to Mazy for a refill.

"I guess so. Does sound familiar, doesn't it? I've been so darn busy I haven't thought much about those sorts of things."

"You think the job with Osborne will be the same?" Lars asked.

"I don't know. Sounds pretty similar. One major difference, I suppose, is that people will have to pay for my services." Ben hesitated for minute. "Lars, what do you think I should do?"

"It's something you've got to figure out by yourself, Ben. I can't tell you what to do."

When Ben returned home that afternoon, Beth greeted him with "Well, have you called Osborne University yet and accepted the job?"

14

Hailstorm

A couple of days later Ben Wesley sat in his courthouse office looking out the window, a view he had enjoyed for twenty years. He had but a few more days left in his job as Ames County agricultural agent, and the reality of the office closing was beginning to sink in. He thought about the hundreds of men and women he had worked with over the years, mostly farmers and small-town people. He remembered the questions. Questions about feeding cattle and growing alfalfa. Questions about irrigating vegetable crops and improving cranberry yields. Questions about growing strawberries and pruning apple trees. Questions about staying in business despite increasing costs and decreasing income. He thought about the young people, 4-H members, who worked on projects that provided "learning by doing," the organization's motto.

And he thought about the job offer and what would be the same and what would be different if he decided to work for Osborne University. He considered Shotgun's advice—take the job, if it doesn't work out, find something else—and Lars Olson's rather lukewarm response to the offer.

Out his office window Ben saw a bank of dark clouds building in the west, over the rooftops of the mostly two-story buildings that made up Willow River's downtown. He remembered hearing the weather forecast: a 50 percent possibility of scattered showers. He thought little of the upcoming storm, as thunderstorms were common in Wisconsin in late June. A loud clap of thunder brought him back to the present. He got up from his chair, walked down the narrow courthouse hall, and stepped outside. The air was close and clammy, like it often was before a rain. He now could see and hear the full fury of the storm that was but minutes away. This was surely more than a scattered shower, he decided, as he thought back to the forecast for the day.

The dirty black clouds rolled over on themselves. In between two layers of black he saw a streak of white, a white cloud amongst the angry black ones. He remembered his father's words: "See a white streak in a thunderstorm and it usually means hail and wind." His father more times than not had been right about the weather.

The storm came in quickly, like an unwelcome visitor crashing a private party. Ben was thinking about the possibility of hail—a devastating weather event for farmers, especially this time of year, when the corn was growing rapidly and the oat crop was heading. High winds were always a problem, with resulting power outages, building damage, and flattened crops.

His worst fears were soon realized. He felt the first big drops of rain and then saw the hail—huge chunks of ice, some as small as marbles, others as large as golf balls, some even the size of baseballs. The ice pieces were grotesque, jagged, and irregular chunks of agricultural misery. Ben stood under the canopy that jutted out from the courthouse door and watched the ice accumulate on the lawn, watched it destroy the flower beds, saw it dent the roofs of cars parked in the courthouse lot. Like an ice storm in winter, the pieces of hail collected in the street until the black pavement had turned a slippery white.

And then came the wind, blowing out of the southwest, churning the clouds, and whipping the tree branches. As Ben stood watching, an enormous branch from a century-old oak tree cracked off and punched through the roof of a sheriff's squad car in the parking lot. The ruined car now appeared to have an oak tree growing out of its middle.

When Ben returned to his office, Delores was on the phone. "Lot of hail and wind damage west of here," she said. "Farmer just called to say his cornfield was ruined and what should he do, it being nearly the first of July."

Other calls soon followed—dozens of them. The storm had cut a broad sweep across much of Ames County, denting cars, ruining building roofs, breaking windows, but more importantly ruining thousands of acres of corn and oats and hay.

Ben had seen agricultural devastation in Ames County before, but this storm appeared to be one of the worst. Perhaps even more devastating than the tornado that touched down in the northern part of the county five years ago, essentially destroying three farmsteads. By late afternoon he'd gotten twenty-five calls and he knew what he must do. He called Joe Cramer, an agronomy researcher at the University of Wisconsin in Madison. "Choices are limited," Cramer said. "Could work up the ground and plant some eighty-day corn, but chances of it ripening are slim. Might make silage though."

Ben reserved the courthouse meeting room for a session he would hold tomorrow evening for all the farmers who had suffered losses in the storm. He called the radio stations in Berlin and Waupaca, asking them to announce the emergency meeting. He began poring over the research materials he had in his office.

This surge of activity took his mind away from losing his job. Although he suffered with the farmers and their loss, he also felt good about being in a position to help them. To share what he knew with them. To give them his best judgment after reviewing the research and other reports he'd accumulated as to what they could do.

One hundred farmers turned out for the meeting. Ben asked for damage reports after he called the meeting to order.

"My cornfield looks like a steamroller passed over it. The field's flat as a pancake. Ruined," said the first farmer to stand up. He had tears in his eyes as he spoke.

"I had thirty acres of the best oats I think I've ever grown. Nothing left. Absolutely nothing," a second farmer added.

One after the other, farmers reported on their crop losses; a few had also lost outbuildings to the wind. "Wind took our corncrib, moved it ten feet off its foundation, dumped it on its side, and smashed it to bits. Got nothing left except kindling wood," an older woman reported.

Ben also learned that few farmers had crop insurance because they couldn't afford it, so their losses were severe. Ben took notes as he listened to the devastating damage reports. Then he stood up to share his thoughts. The room immediately quieted.

He began, "For some of you, your corn might grow out of the hail damage, if it wasn't complete. You'll get a lesser yield of course, but you'll get something." Ben saw heads nodding in agreement. "If your cornfield is a complete loss, and that sounds like the case for a bunch of you, you might consider replanting with eighty-day corn and taking your chances on it maturing. At least you should get some silage out of it."

Ben paused briefly, as he saw several farmers taking notes. "Those of you with ruined oat crops, there's little you can do. One upside. If you planted the oats as a cover crop for alfalfa, the alfalfa should be fine; in fact with the oat crop gone the alfalfa should grow better than ever." He assured those concerned about their hay crop that it would come back, and they'd get some hay at least.

After the meeting, Ben got the most applause he'd ever gotten and several people even stood as they clapped. He knew their appreciation was for more than what he had just shared, as he had worked with many of these farmers for years. Ben felt good as he drove home. He knew how to work with farmers, how to help them, especially in times of great need. He was good at this, really good at it. He knew he could never manage a Wal-Mart department and receive the kind of satisfaction he'd gotten this evening. He'd made up his mind; he needed to keep working in agriculture.

The next morning Ben called Sara Phillips and said, "I'll take the job."

"Wonderful," Phillips responded. "I'll meet you this afternoon to go over your contract . . . would the Lone Pine restaurant be okay? Say one o'clock?"

"I'll be there."

She's already here," Mazy said when Ben arrived at the Lone Pine. "In the back booth."

When Ben arrived at the booth, Dr. Sara Phillips, dressed as she had been when Ben first met her, stood up and offered her hand.

"Congratulations, Ben. You've made a wise decision." She was all business. No small talk. No questions about family this time. "I'll go over your contract with you before you sign. We don't want any surprises." She placed a several-pages-long document in front of Ben. She had another copy in front of her.

Ben began reading, reviewing information that he already knew—what his title would be, the starting day of July 1. That he would be responsible for assisting farmers and other interested parties in understanding and applying various Osborne University research results, that the outreach office would be Osborne University's community link.

He carefully read the section titled "Compensation." "The Research Application Specialist will receive a percentage of the income from billable hours, speeches, workshops, and written materials sold. Additionally, during the first year, Osborne University will pay the Research Application Specialist a full salary; during the second year of employment, half-salary; and during the third year, one-quarter salary. For succeeding years of employment, compensation will be based on income generated by the office."

Ben looked up. "I have a question."

"Yes," Phillips said.

"About the compensation. Does this mean I receive no salary from Osborne after my third year?"

Phillips laughed. "It says that, but the language is almost irrelevant. By your third year with us, your office income will provide considerably more income than the modest salary Osborne is paying you as the office gets established."

Ben hadn't heard about this part of the contract before. It sounded like a salesman who worked on commission. He decided not to push the issue, but knew it was something he best not mention to Beth. He finished reading the document and signed it.

A day after his meeting with Dr. Phillips, the following announcement appeared in the *Ames County Argus*:

Ira Osborne University is pleased to announce the opening of an outreach office in Willow River, Wisconsin, beginning July 1. The office will be in the former Frederick Office Supply building in the Willow River Plaza.

Brittani Stone, long-time employee of Osborne University, will serve as office manager, and Ben Wesley, formerly with the University of Wisconsin Agricultural Agent Program, has been hired as research application specialist.

Hours: 9–5 Monday–Friday, by appointment only.

Mr. Wesley, who is highly trained and experienced in all aspects of agriculture, is available for field consultations, also by appointment. Additionally, Mr. Wesley will speak on agricultural topics to interested groups.

A first phone call or office visit is free of charge. Further consultations will be billed at a reasonable rate. Rate schedules are available by stopping in the office or calling 1-877-AGR-INFO.

The most up-to-date publications with information on new agricultural research and how to solve practical problems on the farm are available at the center for a reasonable charge.

Ira Osborne University is especially pleased with its decision to open this new office and kindly invites those with agricultural questions to contact the office using the above phone number.

Cranberry Red

*T*he following article appeared in the *Ames County Argus* on June 25:

Today, scientists at Ira Osborne University, a for-profit educational and research institution with headquarters in Oshkosh, announced the development of a new treatment for enhancing the antioxidant level of cranberries. Named "Cranberry Red," the new discovery, researchers claim, will increase the antioxidant level of cranberries by several times when the product is applied to cranberry beds during the growing season.

Dr. Quinton Foley, vice president for research at Osborne University, said, "We are on the cusp of modifying ordinary cranberries in such a way that they will become extremely important as medicinal food supplements. These specially treated cranberries will help prevent heart disease, reduce brain damage from strokes, and, perhaps most importantly of all, work toward eliminating Alzheimer's disease. Cranberry Red–treated cranberries will become more popular than drugs commonly used today to treat these diseases."

The research results, thoroughly tested in Osborne's laboratory and further tested in a field trial, are proving enormously promising. Gunnar Godson, leàd scientist for the project and former Rutgers University horticulture professor, explained, "The results of our work exceed our most optimistic hopes for this product. We are building on the work conducted at the famous Agricultural University in Wuhan,

Cranberry Red

People's Republic of China. The Chinese researchers used a pre-harvest salicylic acid–spray treatment on navel oranges with the intent to maintain the nutritional value of the fruit. We are applying some of the same theory to cranberries, with considerable modification of course."

Andy Cho, spokesperson for Osborne University's office of community relations, said, "We've been field testing Cranberry Red with a major cranberry grower in Ames County this past year. The results from the extensive testing of treated cranberries have exceeded our expectations, and this fall's harvest of these special cranberries will soon appear on the market for the first time. Osborne University has licensed the International Farm-Med Company of Cleveland to sell Cranberry Red as well as market the miracle fruit, which will be labeled "Healthy Always Cranberries" and marketed as a dietary supplement.

Part 3

16

Fred and Oscar

*W*hat you got there, Fred?" asked Oscar Anderson. Oscar sat in a rocking chair on the back porch of his farm house, enjoying the end of one of the first warm days so far this season. He had seen his friend pull up in his 1970 green and rusty Chevy pickup, stop, lean over, and pick up something from the seat, then step out of the truck and walk toward the old, fading farm house.

"What's it look like I got? Your eyesight leavin' you, too?" said Fred.

"Looks you got a couple quarts of strawberries. Where'd you get those?"

"Whattya mean, where'd I get 'em? I grew 'em, that's what I did. In my patch out back the barn," answered Fred.

"You still got a berry patch behind that barn of yers? Ain't you a little old for growing strawberries?"

"You want decent strawberries, you gotta grow your own. No way around it. Them berries you buy in the store, them big red ones they grow out in California, they taste like nothin'. They're all looks and no taste."

"So where you goin' with them berries?" asked Oscar.

"Whattya mean, where am I goin' with 'em?"

"Well, you're standin' there holdin' onto 'em like they're gold."

"I'm givin' 'em to you, Oscar. Somethin' to put on your Wheaties."

"I don't eat Wheaties. Stuff's too expensive. I eat oatmeal. Every day I eat oatmeal for breakfast."

"Well put 'em on your oatmeal then."

"I believe I will. Nice lookin' berries."

"They taste like strawberries, too. Not like those ones from California."

"You just told me about those California berries," Oscar reminded Fred.

"I did?"

"Well, set them berries down and have a seat," Oscar said. "Sit here in this spare rocker. Rest them old bones of yours."

"Believe I will," said Fred as he gently placed the two quarts of deep red strawberries on the side of the porch, climbed up the three steps, and sat down in the well-worn wooden rocker.

After a brief time, with both men gently rocking and the sound of the creaking filling the quiet evening air, Fred asked, "What's new?"

"What's what?" asked Oscar.

"New. What's new?" said Fred.

"Who?"

"Not 'who.' New," Fred said more loudly.

"Just readin' the *Argus*," said Oscar. "Readin' about this Osborne University. Says here in the paper they've come up with a new miracle chemical."

"A what?"

"Chemical. New miracle chemical," replied Oscar.

"Thought I heard right. What's it supposed to do? Ask me, we got way too many chemicals. Chemicals everywhere. Chemicals for everything."

"This here Osborne chemical is called Cranberry Red. Supposed to make cranberries more healthy than they are," Oscar explained. He reached over and picked up the newspaper from the floor, paging through it until he found the article. "Says here that Cranberry Red's gonna make guys like us live longer," said Oscar.

"Doubt that," said Fred. "Besides, if ever'body lives so damn long, there like as not won't be enough room for all of us. Damn country will be so cluttered up with old people, ever'thing will probably just come to a halt. One big people jam."

"Be kind of nice to be around to see if that's what will happen," said Oscar. He had a big smile on his face. He glanced over toward the strawberries and then began rocking again. He swatted a mosquito that lit on his bare arm. "Too bad they can't come up with a chemical to git rid of these bugs."

17

Brittani Stone

*B*rittani Stone got the news late Friday afternoon when she checked her e-mail before leaving her Oshkosh office:

> Congratulations, Brittani. You have been promoted to office manager for our new outreach office in Willow River, Wisconsin. You will be working with Ben Wesley, whom we recently employed as Research Application Specialist to work out of this new office.
>
> You will have complete responsibility for all office operations, keeping detailed records, filing weekly reports with the main office in Oshkosh, and, most importantly, scheduling Mr. Wesley's time, keeping a record of his billable hours, and sending appropriate invoices to the clients with whom Mr. Wesley has contact.
>
> We know you will do a great job, as you have in your previous assignments.
>
> Once again, congratulations.
>
> Sara Phillips, PhD
Director of Field Operations
Ira Osborne University

Brittani, who had just reached thirty, had let everyone with any authority at Osborne University know that she was ready for a new challenge. She was tall and thin—willowy, some might say. Her black hair, which she wore in a ponytail, contrasted well with her olive complexion. Her dark eyes flashed when she read the e-mail a second time. Office manager for an outreach office in Podunkville? What kind of promotion was that? And to work with some guy doing farm stuff. What did she know about farming? Nothing. What did she care about farming? Nothing. First thing Monday morning she must talk with Dr. Phillips about this so-called promotion and see if she could refuse it with the hope that something more exciting and prestigious might come along soon.

She spent the weekend in Milwaukee, visiting with friends, doing a little partying, and thinking about what she might say to Dr. Sara Phillips, whom Brittani thought was a jerk and was in way over her head. Phillips liked to be called "doctor." What kind of doctor was she? Just another PhD. And in what specialty? Educational administration. For God's sake, what kind of doctorate was that?

Brittani had met several other PhD's at Osborne University. They had degrees in biology, genetics, horticulture, subjects that made a difference.

What could she say to high and mighty Dr. Phillips? She'd come up with something; Brittani always did.

*F*irst thing Monday morning, Brittani appeared at Dr. Sara Phillips's office.

"Brittani, so good to see you. And congratulations on your promotion. The other officials here at Osborne met last week and we were unanimous. You'll make a great office manager."

"But in Willow River?" Brittani sputtered. "In tiny little Willow River, Wisconsin, that doesn't have three thousand people?"

"Britt, I remember our talk a few months ago, and how you said you were up to a new challenge. You make this satellite office work and you'll be on your way—surely a candidate for one of our top spots here at Osborne University." She looked coldly at Brittani, with little patience for her protest.

"But . . . but," Brittani stammered.

"No buts, Brittani. This is one great opportunity. No question about it. Oh, did I mention we are planning a 20 percent bump in your salary?

You'll also get a percentage of Ben Wesley's billed-hour income. And we'll pay for your commuting costs from here to Willow River for a month, to give you a chance to find suitable housing in Ames County."

Sara Phillips stood up from behind her desk, extended her hand, and shook Brittani's. "Once more, congratulations, Britt. We'll be in touch." The words were without emotion.

Brittani got up and left the office, not exactly sure what had just happened, except that she was getting a raise. So this new spot in Willow River must really be a promotion.

On Wednesday, the first of July, Brittani Stone drove her convertible Ford Mustang down Highway 21, through Omro, through Redgranite, and then into Willow River. When she arrived in town, she looked for the Willow River Plaza, where her new office was located. The first time she missed the sign and before you could say "only one street light in town," she was in farm country again. At the first farm drive, she drove in, backed up, and once more drove down Main Street. The place was worse than she imagined. A couple of taverns, a gift shop or two, what looked like a jewelry store, a lawyer's office, and not much else. *What a dump*, she thought as she drove east on Highway 21, looking for the Osborne University sign. This time she spotted it, a rather small one hanging beneath a cluster of competing signs.

She turned into the Plaza shopping center, scanning the various buildings for the location of her new office. She saw the Lone Pine restaurant, Ed's Small Engine Repair, an Ace Hardware, and an Amish furniture store. Between Ed's Small Engine and the Amish store, Brittani spotted what appeared to be an empty store front. In the window was a small sign that read "Osborne University, Outreach Office, Hours 9–5, Monday–Friday."

She parked her Mustang and walked inside. The outer room was bare except for a metal desk with a computer monitor, a chair, several file cabinets, and an empty publication display cabinet.

As she looked around, a man appeared from an interior office.

"Can I help you?" he said.

"I'm Brittani Stone," the young woman responded. She was wearing a tailored suit and spiked heels and carried a box.

"I'm Ben Wesley," the man said. "I heard you were coming. Welcome to Willow River."

"Is that my office, Dr. Wesley? This box is getting heavy." She nodded toward the office from which Ben had emerged.

"Your spot is right here. Let me help you." Ben reached for the box and set it on the desk in the outer room. "And by the way, it's just Ben. I have a master's degree, not a doctorate."

"Oh," Brittani managed to say.

"Tech services was in over the weekend and set up both our computers. I'm still trying to figure out mine, but they told me you have the same username and password you were previously using."

Ben heard the phone on his desk ring. "Pardon me," he said. "I'd better get that, first day and all."

Brittani turned on the computer monitor and the login screen appeared asking for username and password. In a moment she read "Osborne University, User Brittani Stone."

"Damn," she said under her breath. "I deserve that office. I'm going to get that office." She looked toward the open door where Ben was talking on the phone.

18

The Osborne Dream

Congratulations on the new job," Dr. Sara Phillips said when Ben appeared at her office door on Wednesday afternoon, his first day on the job. She stood up from behind her desk. Her office was on the first floor of an old furniture building in Oshkosh that Osborne University had retrofitted. The building had been built in the late nineteenth century and was on both the national and state registers of historic places. Besides being written up in the *Oshkosh Northwestern* and the *Milwaukee Journal Sentinel*, the National Trust for Historic Preservation had included an article in their magazine applauding the efforts of Osborne University in "maintaining the architectural integrity of a historic building, while at the same time adapting it to modern use."

"We're so pleased you've decided to work with us, Ben," Phillips said, smiling. "You've got all the skills we've been looking for. You're the first research application specialist we've hired, and your office is our first outreach office. By the way, did the furniture and computers arrive?"

"They did, thank you very much."

"And you've met Brittani, of course. She's one of our rising stars."

"Yes, we've met," Ben said. "But we really haven't had time to talk; I had to leave for my meeting over here."

"You'll like her. She's got a real business head on her shoulders. She'll be in charge of setting up your schedule and keeping all the records for our business office. And of course, she'll take care of all the billing, sending out the notices, that sort of thing, so you won't be bothered with such details."

"Thank you," Ben responded. He looked around Phillips's office. It was extremely plain—quite different from its occupant, who was as stylishly dressed as she was when Ben first met her. The office had but one picture on the wall, some modern piece of art, a gray metal desk holding a computer monitor, a small bookshelf crammed full of books and papers, and a couple of chairs. Venetian blinds covered the one tall window in the little room.

"I've worked out a schedule for your afternoon, Ben. We have a Power Point presentation for you to see, and then I've arranged brief meetings with several Osborne executives, a chance for you to see who's running the place." She smiled when she said it.

"Thank you," Ben said. He felt like an eighteen-year-old who had accepted his first job.

"Then tomorrow afternoon when you come over, I've set up a meeting with Joe Schneider, our business manager. Joe will explain the business side of our operation and how you fit in."

Together, Ben and Dr. Phillips walked down a narrow hallway to a small conference room with a screen on one wall.

"When you've finished watching, stop by my office and I'll answer any questions you may have." She pushed a button on the computer projector; the first image came up on the screen, and she left.

The background music was the theme from *Chariots of Fire*.

"It all began with a dream," a deep baritone voice intoned. A photo of an old bald guy with a red face and a white moustache appeared on the screen. "Ira Houghton Osborne grew up in Wisconsin Rapids, Wisconsin, where his father worked in the paper mill and his mother worked part time as a maid at the Mead Hotel. Upon graduating from high school, Ira Osborne began work in the paper mill, which was the expectation in his family, as his grandfather and his father had worked there before him."

Ben noticed that the music became a little louder as he looked at an image of a big paper mill factory on what he assumed to be the Wisconsin River.

"Ira Osborne also worked with the cranberry harvest each fall, raking cranberries by hand during the day and continuing to work the night shift at the paper mill."

Now Ben saw a black-and-white photo of a cranberry bog, with a line of workers raking cranberries by hand, an approach rarely used today, except for Shotgun Slogum, who insisted on doing things the old-fashioned way.

"The cranberry bog owner was so impressed with Ira Osborne's work ethic and his interest in cranberries that he recommended the Central Wisconsin Cranberry Growers Association hire him."

Ben remembered the Cranberry Growers Association. Ocean Spray bought it out about the time Ben arrived in Ames County.

"Ira Osborne became interested in the health benefits of cranberries, and soon expanded his interests to cherries, blueberries, and a host of other common agricultural crops, and he started the International Farm-Med Company, with headquarters in Cleveland."

Now the screen filled with the International Farm-Med Company logo, a cornucopia overflowing with fruits and vegetables—apples, cranberries, blueberries, cherries, broccoli, carrots, potatoes, onions.

The voice continued, "The IFM Company has grown into one of the largest suppliers of natural health foods in the world. They are dedicated to providing people with the healthful and disease-preventing ingredients found in common fruits and vegetables. With the IFM's products, one only has to take a garlic capsule or drink a teaspoon of concentrated cherry juice to receive benefits equal to eating a large quantity of a fruit or vegetable."

On the screen appeared a healthy-looking family—mother, father, and two children sitting around a dinner table. "This young mother," the narrator continued, "need not worry about her family's health because she supplements her meals with International Farm-Med products."

Now the image on the screen shifted to a photo of what appeared to be a university building—the name of the university was nowhere evident.

"Ira Osborne lamented that he did not have an opportunity to attend college. He knew that thousands of others like him, young and old, had longed for a college education but for a variety of reasons could not attend. He wanted to correct that situation and he has."

A photo of Osborne University's sign, the one that Ben saw when he entered the building, appeared on the screen.

"Many people today cannot attend traditional universities. They are working full time, they have families, and they have limited budgets. Ira Osborne's dream was for these people to have access to a high-quality university education."

Ira Osborne's image once more appeared on the screen. "When Ira Osborne retired from his position as chief executive officer and chairman of the board for the International Farm-Med Company, he wanted to leave a legacy that meant healthier lives for people and an opportunity for those who wished to earn a college education to do so. To achieve the latter, he provided a multimillion dollar gift to establish a new kind of university."

A series of photos of people working at computers appeared on the screen. Next to their computers were various written materials with the Osborne University logo on them. These people were young and old, African American, Latino, Asian, white.

The music faded and the voice continued, "With the advent of computers and the Internet, our students can work toward their college degrees wherever they live, whenever they want, and at a pace that is comfortable for them. Osborne University is designed around the needs of its students, not around the wants of its instructors and administration."

Ben then watched as another series of images appeared on the screen, illustrating the various degree programs available—educational administration, nursing, business, agriculture, liberal arts, creative writing, political science, economics.

An image of several modest buildings with the Tamarack River running behind them appeared on the screen.

"Though we surely are not the first university to offer degrees via the Internet, unlike other online universities, Osborne University has an onsite research program, complete with a research station in Ames County. There, some of the top scientists in the world are researching how to increase the health benefits of the foods we eat."

Ben sat forward in his seat. As he understood it, he would be working with farmers, helping them to apply the research results that Osborne was discovering.

A photo of a small cranberry bed appeared on the screen. "One of the newest discoveries at our research station involves an approach for increasing the health benefits of cranberries. This is but one of many projects our researchers are working on in order to improve the health of the people of the world."

The logo of Osborne University once more appeared. "For further information, write to the address on the screen, call us at the number you see, or check our website for complete contact information: www.osborne university.org."

Ben got up, shut off the computer projector, and returned to Sara Phillips's office.

"Well, what do you think, Ben? Impressive?"

"Quite," Ben said.

"There's someone I especially want you to meet. He's our vice president for research." Ben followed Phillips down the hall to a corner office with the name "Quinton Foley, PhD, Vice President for Research" on the door. She knocked gently.

"Enter," a voice said. Different from Sara Phillips office, this one had bookshelves from floor to ceiling on three walls. Books, journals, and papers were piled everywhere—on the chairs, on the floor, and tumbling off the bookshelves.

"This is Dr. Quinton Foley, our vice president for research," Phillips said. Foley, a tall, thin, intense man whom Ben took to be in his midfifties, stood up from behind his desk.

"I'd like you to meet Ben Wesley, our new research application specialist out in Ames County."

Foley came out from behind his desk and shook Ben's hand. "I've heard about you, Wesley, good things. You seem to be a good fit for what we're trying to do." Foley talked fast, almost machine-gun-like.

"I'm looking forward to the work," Ben replied, not able to think of anything more profound to say.

"Lots of work. Got to get the word out. Have to work on the cranberry growers in your area. We're onto something. Something big," Foley said, the words flying out of his mouth in rapid succession.

"Cranberry Red," Ben responded.

"That's it, Wesley. Cranberry Red. The greatest new research product to come out of a laboratory in a generation. We'll help save thousands of lives, maybe millions." As his excitement grew, so did the speed of his delivery. "And you'll be a part of it. On the ground floor. Right there on the front fighting for better health."

With that, he returned to his desk and resumed looking at his computer screen.

"Thank you, Dr. Foley," Phillips said. Foley raised his right hand from the keyboard, but said nothing. Phillips and Ben exited the office and quietly closed the door.

"Busy man," Phillips said admiringly. "Very busy man."

"Appears so," replied Ben.

They next made the rounds of several other offices, a "meet and greet" of the sort Ben never much cared for. He smiled his way through it as he shook hands, accepted congratulations, and tried but failed to remember the names of the important people at Osborne University. Ben had never been impressed by important people; he was more impressed by what people were able to do and what they had accomplished. So he smiled, said thank you when he was congratulated, and little else.

Soon he was on his way back to the quiet of Willow River. He wondered what Brittani had been doing in his absence.

19

Business Office

*S*o, how'd it go yesterday?" Brittani asked when Ben arrived at his office on Thursday. It was 8:00 a.m., and obviously Brittani had already been at work for some time, as her computer screen was glowing and she had a pile of papers beside it.

"Okay," Ben said. "Learned a lot about Osborne University. Ira Osborne was quite the man."

"Yes, he was," Brittani replied. "I met him once a few years ago. Nice guy. Made a pile of money in his business. Started out with nothing, too."

"Anything happening here?" Ben asked, expecting a "no."

"Lots going on. We'll be in the parade on Saturday—Fourth of July, you know. Then I've arranged for us to have a booth right next to the bratwurst and beer stand. Should have lots of customers stopping by." She laughed as she said it.

"I'm in the parade? Why?"

"We, Ben, we. We're both in the parade. I've arranged for a convertible from Link Lake Motors. I'll drive. You'll sit in the back, smile, and wave."

"Smile and wave," Ben said under his breath.

"People need to know about us. Need to know our office is open and that we're in business," Brittani said. She was the picture of efficiency as she talked and worked on her computer at the same time. "Nothing for you to worry about, Ben. I've got it all set up. I've also made several appointments for you, too. Starting next Tuesday, when your orientation meetings are finished. The schedule is on your desk."

Ben walked into his office. A big picture of Ira Osborne hung on the wall, next to a photo of the Osborne University logo. Brittani must have hung them up while he was gone.

Ben glanced down at the big appointment book that lay open on his desk. Starting Tuesday morning, nearly every hour of the day had a name written next to it. Brittani had been busy. What Ben didn't know was that Brittani received a percentage of the billable hours that Ben worked—she had plenty of incentive to fill up every hour she possibly could.

That afternoon Ben drove once more to Oshkosh, this time to learn about the business operations of Osborne University. Arriving at the business office on the third floor of the old refurbished building, he opened the door and found a room full of people working at computers.

At the counter he faced a serious young woman sitting in front of a glowing screen. She wore no makeup and had short, bobbed black hair. Her long fingers moved effortlessly over the keyboard.

"Can I help you?" she asked, looking up from her work and smiling.

"I'm Ben Wesley and I have an appointment with Joe Schneider," Ben said.

"Mr. Schneider is expecting you, Mr. Wesley. I'll let him know you're here. Please have a chair. Would you like some coffee?" The young woman smiled again.

"No, I'm fine," Ben responded. He looked around the office. Everyone was staring at a computer screen.

Before Ben could sit down, a youngish man wearing a white shirt and tie and wide blue suspenders came from the side office. He extended his hand.

"I'm Joe Schneider," he said. He was tall and thin. His handshake was firm.

"Dr. Phillips asked me to spend some time with you this afternoon. Let's meet in my office."

Schneider's office, not different from Sara Phillips's, had but two pictures on the wall, one of Ira Osborne, and the second of the Osborne University logo.

"First, welcome aboard, Ben. I can call you Ben?"

"Of course; everyone calls me Ben."

"Well, let's get right to it. You know of course that you will charge for your work?"

"Yes," Ben said. "It'll be different from my previous job."

"Actually, it's pretty simple. Brittani Stone will take care of the details, the actual record keeping and the sending of invoices to clients. I can proudly say I trained Brittani. You're fortunate to have her as your office manager."

"We're just getting acquainted," Ben said.

"Basically, our billing system is modeled after a law office. You will charge hourly rates, plus expenses."

"Yes," Ben responded.

"Additionally, the work you do with a large cranberry grower could be offered on a retainer basis."

"How would that work?" Ben asked.

"Like this. Let's say Joe Cranberry Grower has one hundred acres of cranberries and wants you to work with him for the entire season. He would pay you a sum of money up front. Of course you would keep track of the hours you spent with Joe Grower, and if you go over the hours agreed upon with the retainer, you would charge the regular hourly fee."

Ben spent the afternoon listening, looking at payment schedules, reviewing billing procedures, and learning about the weekly reporting system he was expected to follow.

"Of course Brittani will do all the detail work so you can spend your time working with clients. Every non-billable hour is down time," Schneider said with a serious look on his face. "After all, we are a for-profit company," he added.

"You have three other sources of income in your office, as I'm sure you are aware," Schneider continued. "The speeches that you give to groups, the workshops you conduct, and the bulletins and other written materials you sell. We have charge schedules set up for all of this." Schneider handed Ben yet another folder filled with numbers and examples of what to charge when the group size is fifty versus what to charge when it's over fifty.

"Do you have any questions?"

"I . . . I don't think so," Ben said. His head was filled with the examples of the various ways to charge people for the services he provided essentially for free when he worked for the University of Wisconsin Agricultural Agent Program.

"Of course the more hours you bill, the more talks you give, the more workshops you conduct, and the more bulletins you sell, the more money you'll make," Schneider said. "It's a wonderful incentive program, wouldn't you say?"

"Sounds that way," Ben replied in a noncommittal way.

Driving back to Willow River, Ben's head was filled with figures, schedules, and, above all, Osborne expectations. *How different it will be compared to my previous job*, Ben thought. He wondered if he should share with Beth the details of his compensation package. So far he hadn't.

20

Fourth of July

*B*en liked to sleep in on Saturday mornings. Except this particular Saturday happened also to be the Fourth of July.

"Ben, you up yet?" Beth called up the stairs. "You've got a parade to do, you know."

"I'm up, I'm up," Ben muttered. *Why should I be in a parade?* he thought. He'd never been in one before and people seemed to know about Ben and what his office was about. Whose goofy idea was this anyway? Brittani's? Doubt it. Idea probably came straight from Oshkosh.

Brittani's words came back to him when he had asked her about the parade. *"We're the new kids on the block, Ben. Got to let folks know about us."* *She may have been the new kid on the block and Osborne University may still be new to people, but me, I've been here for twenty years,* thought Ben. If people don't know about their county agent by now, when will they? Except now, Ben was no longer a county agent. He had to remember to say research application specialist. A "RAS," as Brittani said with a smile the other day. She pronounced it with a soft "a" so it came out as "roz." Better than a long *a*, producing "razz," which is something you do when you tease somebody. "Roz" or "razz"—either way Ben didn't think much of his title. You'd think Osborne would have come up with something better—yet the job does sound challenging. And important, too. He had to admit that Osborne University just might be setting the pace for the future of higher education in the country.

"Well, how's my research application specialist this morning?" Beth said. She was dressed in a bright red dress. She more cheerful than Ben had seen her for weeks.

"Okay, I guess," Ben muttered. The words "research application specialist" once more swirled around in his head.

"That what you're going to wear?" Beth commented when she noticed he was wearing his usual khaki pants with a blue shirt. "It's the Fourth of July. Got to wear something red, white, and blue."

"Not me, Beth. You won't see me dressed up like a clown."

"Aren't you the grouchy one this morning."

"Well, it is Saturday. Supposed to be my day off."

"Ben, Ben, you've got to get with the program. You are going to be in the parade, letting people know about your new job with Osborne University."

"I know," Ben said. "That's not all."

"What else?"

"Brittani has arranged for Osborne University to have a booth next to the beer and bratwurst tent. We're to sit there all afternoon talking to people."

"So?"

"Sit in a booth and talk to beer-drinking bratwurst eaters?"

"Ben, you don't get it. These are your potential customers. People who may one day need your help and be willing to pay for it. I have other news for you, too."

"And what would that be?" Ben asked. He had woken up grouchy and he was getting grouchier by the minute.

"I've enrolled in Osborne University's nurse-practitioner program."

"You what?"

"You heard me, Ben. I am a graduate student. And because you work for Osborne, my tuition is free. Besides, I don't have to attend any classes. None at all. Everything is on the Internet. Finally, you've done something right, Ben." She wrapped her arms around him and kissed him hard on the lips.

An hour later, Ben found Brittani and the new Ford convertible at the parade staging area. The car had a big "Osborne University" sign on each door, along with the logo for the college.

"Well, what do you think, Ben? Pretty fancy, wouldn't you say?"

"Nice car," Ben muttered. "Do I drive or do you drive?"

"I drive, Ben. You sit in the backseat and wave at the crowd. Smile and wave, that's all you need to do. Smile and wave."

"Smile and wave," Ben repeated, tonelessly.

Soon they were headed down Main Street, driving a short distance behind Willow River High School's band, which was gallantly attempting to play Sousa's "Stars and Stripes Forever," keep in step, and avoid the horse manure from the Ames County Quarter Horse Club and its six-horse contingent that pranced in front of them.

Ben hated parades. He avoided them whenever he could. Now here he was, right dab in the middle of one. People—young and old, fat and skinny, and mostly all smiling—lined the street on both sides. He was surprised by how many of them he knew. He smiled and gave a halfhearted wave when he recognized someone. He saw several of the farmers who had been at the emergency hail meeting just a week ago. He spotted Shotgun Slogum standing off to the side, wearing new bib overalls, a red straw hat, and a big smile. He gave Ben a thumbs-up when the convertible passed. Ben also spotted several members of the Ames County Fruit and Vegetable Growers Cooperative standing alongside the parade route with their families, little kids, bigger kids, all polished up for the celebration.

And standing in front of the pharmacy he spotted Oscar Anderson and Fred Russo, wearing bib overalls with red shirts and what looked like new straw hats. A pair of characters. He didn't know them well, but knew they loved fishing. Some day he wanted to spend some time with these guys to see if they'd share some of their fishing secrets. People who knew Fred and Oscar chuckled at their stories, for they were full of them; you just had to get them started. Mostly it was fish stories they told, but they also knew about the early days of farming in Ames County, when everyone worked the land with horses and life was a lot simpler.

Once the parade was finished, Ben sat in the little booth with Brittani, who gushed the virtues of Osborne University to whomever passed by, handing out little pins with the Osborne logo on them, and a brochure that outlined the services available in their new Ames County office. Ben was surprised at how many people stopped by the booth to congratulate him on his new job and just to pass the time of day. These were his friends, small-town and farm people, folks he had worked with for years. Larger farmers, smaller farmers, dairy farmers, fruit and vegetable farmers, hobby farmers, part-time farmers with jobs in town—they all stopped by.

"Looking forward to seeing more of you," almost every one of them said. "Sure glad you're still around."

By the end of the afternoon, Ben's old cheerfulness had returned. He liked people, liked working with them, liked hearing their stories. He began looking forward to the coming days.

When the *Ames County Argus* came out that week, it included a photo of Ben and Brittani riding in the new convertible. The caption read "Osborne University's entry in the Fourth of July parade." A rather grumpy-appearing Ben Wesley was waving his hand. A beaming Brittani Stone drove with one hand and waved with the other.

Further down on page 1 an unusual news item appeared:

On the Fourth of July, Ames Memorial Hospital reported the admission of two brothers, Jon, 10, and Joe Kingsley, 12, of rural Link Lake with strange bites on their legs and arms. The boys had been swimming in the Tamarack River when the incident occurred. The cause of the bites remains under investigation. A team of Department of Natural Resources fish biologists has been studying the stretch of the river where the boys were swimming, but uncovered no evidence of what happened. At first, doctors thought the boys might have encountered broken glass from a beer bottle someone had tossed in the river, but the nature of the lacerations clearly pointed toward something having bitten them. Local resident and world traveler Clarence Higgins, 82, suggested the bites had been made by red piranha fish that someone tossed out of his or her aquarium. Higgins explained, "Those fish are not to be fooled with. One time in South America, I came upon a school of piranha and watched a water snake devoured in front of my eyes. Those fish got teeth like razorblades."

The boys are expected to recover fully from their wounds, but young Jon said, "I think I'll do my swimming in Silver Lake after this."

21

Gunnar Godson

The third and last day of Ben's orientation involved learning about the activities of Osborne's research station, located on the Tamarack River on the western edge of Ames County. He stopped at his office to pick up his notepad and saw that Brittani was already hard at work.

"So, what'd you think of the parade?" Brittani asked, looking up from her computer screen.

"Okay, I guess."

"Just okay? Look at all the people we met. I passed out a hundred flyers and gave away that many Osborne pins. Lots of interest in our office, Ben."

"Seems that way," Ben replied.

"Admit it, you had a good time riding in that new convertible down Main Street," Brittani said, teasing. She was trying to get acquainted with her coworker and was having some difficulty understanding his rather bland approach to things.

"I did talk to a lot of people. Enjoyed doing that. That's always the fun part of this work. The people you meet. The problems you try to help them solve. I'll be at the research station all day. Keep the home fires burning," Ben said as he left the office.

"Bye," Brittani said. "Have fun."

In a half hour, Ben arrived at the entrance to Osborne's research station. There were no signs indicating such, just a big red one that said "No trespassing. Violators will be prosecuted." A second, somewhat smaller sign read "Guard dog on premises." The gate stood open.

Ben drove along an overgrown gravel driveway for nearly a quarter mile before he arrived at a small cluster of nondescript buildings in a little clearing. He recognized the buildings from the orientation video. Ben stopped his car next to a late-model Ford pickup, got out, and looked around for the dog. He spotted a small laboratory sign above a door in a brown steel pole building. Cautiously, he pushed open the door, still looking and listening for a bark or a growl. He'd had too much experience with mean dogs over the past twenty years. He had had a couple of torn trouser legs and even a bite on his leg that had required rabies shots. So he was wary.

"Anybody here?" he said in a not-too-loud voice.

"Is that you, Wesley?" he heard from the back of the building, where there was an enclosure with an open door. The voice had an accent.

"Yes," Ben responded. He was still wondering about the guard dog. Was it a Doberman, or maybe a Rottweiler?

Ben walked past some farm equipment, a John Deere tractor, a two-bottom plow, a rotary mower. A short, bald man stood in the doorway of the interior room. The light behind him reflected off his head. He wore a white lab coat.

"Dr. Godson?" Ben said.

"God morgan," Gunnar Godson responded. He spoke with a Swedish accent. Godson extended his hand and shook Ben's.

"I was wondering about the guard dog," Ben said.

Godson laughed. "No guard dog. But the sign works. At night we turn on our security system, and if something trips the sensor, a recording of a big, mean dog scares the bejeebers out of anyone nosing around the place." He had a lyrical way of speaking.

"Oh." It was all Ben could think to say.

"Come on into my lab," Godson said.

Inside this rather plain building, Ben saw a modern laboratory looking to be fully equipped with microscopes, computers, and a host of devices that were completely foreign to him.

"Here's where we discover things. Out there," Godson said as he pointed out the window to the experimental plots, "is where we find out if they work." Two lab technicians bent over microscopes. Godson introduced them to Ben, telling them briefly about Ben's new job. Ben and

Godson walked into Godson's small office at one end of the building. It had a window that looked out on the Tamarack River.

"Why all the mystery out here?" Ben asked Godson. He was accustomed to the University of Wisconsin Experimental Farms, where the research activities were mostly open to the public, with large signs and annual field days to show off the research results.

"Proprietary," Godson said. "We don't want the world to know what we're doing until we're ready. Don't want somebody stealing our ideas. Osborne is doing research to make money, plain and simple. It's a business."

"A little different from my old boss," Ben said.

"Before Osborne hired me I worked in cranberry research at Rutgers University. I've been where you've been. Got my PhD at Rutgers and just stayed on until they ran into budget problems."

"You, too," Ben said. He was certain that Gunnar Godson was well aware of the state budget cuts that eliminated the county agent program in Wisconsin.

"I'm lucky to have a job. Hard to find work at universities these days. Let me show you our test plots, give you a little background of what we're doing out here in the boonies."

Outside, they first walked past a strawberry bed. Fully ripe strawberries stuck out from beneath lush plants, some standing a foot or more tall. Ben then saw a long row of blueberries growing on a wire and wood framework.

"This is a new variety we've developed. Has twice the antioxidant level as ordinary blueberries."

Ben then saw what appeared to be a vegetable garden with rows of carrots, radishes, broccoli, sweet corn, cabbage, cucumbers, and green beans. Two Latino men were hoeing in the garden and smiled when Ben and Godson walked by. They did not stop working.

"What about potatoes?" Ben asked.

"The College of Agricultural and Life Sciences in Madison is doing great work with potatoes. Their Hancock Research Station is one of the top research centers in the world. We didn't see any need to compete with them."

They then arrived at a small cranberry marsh, one that had been abandoned several years ago, but was brought back to life by Gunnar Godson and his small crew of workers.

"This is the centerpiece of our work," Godson said. "This is what gets all the publicity."

"Cranberry Red," Ben said.

"Ja, Cranberry Red. We learned that when we spray Cranberry Red on cranberries while they're growing, it modifies the plant's hormonal status. Cranberry Red is a derivative of salicylic acid. The plant thinks it is under severe stress and produces more antioxidants as a natural protective response. The plant does the same thing when attacked by pests or suffers from drought. Of course with pests and drought the yield goes down dramatically. Spraying Cranberry Red on the plant appears not to affect the yield, just the antioxidant level."

"Very interesting," Ben responded. This was the first time he'd heard any explanation of how Cranberry Red was supposed to work.

"As you've heard, Ben—I can call you Ben?"

"Of course," Ben said. Despite all his training and brains, Godson seemed down to earth.

"For me, it's just Gunnar. None of this Doctor Godson stuff. That's for those back in Oshkosh who need to impress each other with their degrees."

"What's next?" asked Ben.

"Well, we've got this plot going plus one commercial grower. You know him. Jeff Johnson treated about an acre for us last year. This year he has about five acres of treated berries. Should have some treated cranberries on the market this fall."

"Have you seen any side effects, besides an increase in antioxidant level of the treated cranberries?

"No side effects whatever. We've tested the cranberries in every way we can think of. We also tested the cranberry plants. Nothing out of the ordinary. Maybe a little faster growth, but not much."

"One of my jobs is to promote Cranberry Red to the other cranberry growers," Ben said.

"I know. Off the record I wish Osborne would hold off until next year before promoting Cranberry Red. At least wait for after this fall's harvest," said Gunnar. "Wait until we can do a little more study."

"Sounds like they're ready to give Cranberry Red a big push," Ben said, a little surprised with Gunnar's reluctance.

"Ja, they're worried about China. Researchers there are moving right along with increasing antioxidant levels of various fruits. I always lean toward more testing before we do a lot of promoting."

Ben laughed. "I remember BST, a growth hormone and a supposed miracle chemical. Inject it in a cow and she gives more milk. BST was pushed hard and it backfired. Some people won't buy milk from cows that are injected with a chemical that forces them to give more milk."

"I know that story," Gunnar responded. "I studied it carefully. We don't want the same thing to happen to Cranberry Red."

"If I remember correctly," Ben said, "Canada and a bunch of countries in Europe have banned BST-treated products."

"That's right. People are concerned about their food, and they should be," Gunnar said. "That's why we're doing all this testing on Cranberry Red. We don't want to run into the challenges that Monsanto faced with BST."

"I should think not," Ben replied as he listened to Gunnar's concerns.

"International Farm-Med will be selling Cranberry Red–treated cranberries. I'm sure they don't want anybody raising questions about food safety," said Gunnar.

After these few minutes of conversation, Ben already liked Gunnar Godson. He sounded sensible, cautious, yet practical—and he enjoyed his Swedish accent; the way he talked had a melodic tone.

The two men chatted a bit more about possible comparisons between BST and Cranberry Red. "My hope is," commented Gunnar, "that Cranberry Red–treated cranberries will attract customers, not turn them away."

"I guess we all hope that," said Ben as he prepared to leave.

At the door, Gunnar said, "Any time you have a question about Cranberry Red or anything else about our research, just ask."

"Thank you," Ben responded. "Thank you very much. I'll be in touch."

The two men shook hands. Ben was certain he'd found a friend, some-one who thought along the same lines that he did.

"Be careful of the guard dog when you leave," Gunnar said, smiling.

22

Farm Visit

The first visit Brittani scheduled for Ben on Tuesday morning was with Joe and Julie Evans. Brittani took special care to write down their names, their address, including their fire number, and how many miles from the office to their farm. Ben smiled when he read the entry. He had known the Evans family for many years; in fact, both Joe and Julie had attended the emergency meeting just last week. The freak hailstorm had struck the Evans farm, along with many other Ames County farmers. Ben drove the ten miles to their farm, which was located straight north of Willow River and just west of Link Lake. The Evans family was part of a group of farmers in the area called graziers, which meant they allowed their dairy herd to roam free in their carefully managed pastures. Ben chuckled when he thought about what they were doing. Grazing cattle was considered an alternative idea to the more standard practice these days of confining dairy cattle and hauling the feed to them. When Ben was growing up in Clark County everyone pastured their dairy cattle; it was the way it was done from May until October in that part of Wisconsin. Now grazing was considered a new idea. It seemed to Ben that so much these days amounted to revisiting the past, hanging a new label on it, and calling it new.

As he neared Link Lake he began seeing the damage from the hailstorm, entire fields of corn ruined. The leaves stripped from the stalks, and sometimes the stalks, too, smashed to the ground. The trees growing along the road had lost most of their leaves, with the dry leaves, like in fall, accumulating on the sides of the highway.

He pulled into the Evans driveway and got out of his car. Joe and Julie had two kids, Joey and Melissa, and they maintained a neat and tidy farmstead, keeping their lawn cut and their buildings painted. Ben noticed their vegetable garden. It had clearly taken a beating from the hail. He also wondered about damage to the buildings' roofs and windows, a common result of hailstorms such as this.

"Hello there, Ben," Joe Evans called out. Ben had not seen him working near the barn. "Thanks for coming out." Joe spoke slowly and deliberately, as if he had to think about each word before he spoke it.

"Glad to do it, Joe. How are those kids of yours doing?" Ben knew that both of them had been enrolled in 4-H projects since they were nine years old.

"Oh, they're doing okay." Joe paused for a moment. "Melissa is around here somewhere," Joe said. He took a deep breath. "Joey is helping a neighbor today," he continued slowly, looking down at his feet. "Melissa is sure upset about 4-H closing down."

"Yup, it's gone, along with all the agricultural agent offices in the state. Dumb decision for the state legislature, but don't get me into that," Ben said.

"Didn't think 4-H would ever be eliminated. Just not right. Sure disappointing a lot of kids—mine included. No more 4-H at the fair either? That right?" Joe asked.

"Afraid you're right, Joe."

Just then Melissa Evans came from behind the barn.

"Hi, Mr. Wesley," she greeted him. Melissa wore bib overalls and her blonde hair was tied in a ponytail. She had a sprinkling of freckles across her nose. "Pa said you were stopping by this morning."

"How are your rabbits?" Ben inquired. Ben remembered that the twelve-year-old had bought a couple of rabbits with money she'd earned from selling produce at the farmers' market in Willow River and had been raising them as a 4-H project.

"Not so good," the thin, well-tanned girl replied.

Ben noticed that her bottom lip was quivering and tears were welling up in her eyes.

"It was the hailstorm," Melissa said, fighting back tears.

"What happened?" asked Ben.

"Both killed. Hailstones killed them. Let me show you."

Ben followed behind Melissa and her father to the now empty rabbit hutch with a little fenced area outside it. Melissa pointed to two little mounds of dirt, with a homemade wooden cross pushed into each of them.

"I buried them there," Melissa explained, her voice quivering. "Here is where I buried Mozart, and here is Beethoven." Ben remembered that Melissa also enjoyed music and played in her school orchestra.

"It's terrible," Ben managed to say. He noticed that Melissa's father was also fighting back tears.

"Melissa will get some new rabbits," Joe managed to say in a near whisper.

"Pa told me there's no 4-H at the fair anymore. That right?" The little girl wiped away some tears.

"That's right, Melissa," Ben said. He put his hand on her shoulder. The little girl continued crying.

"It's just not right," she sobbed. "Just not right." She turned and ran toward the barn where she'd been doing chores.

"She's taking all this pretty hard," Joe said.

"It's a terrible situation. No doubt about it. The 4-H program has been around for a hundred years," Ben responded.

"Let me show you my cornfield," Joe said, changing the subject. "See what you think I should do."

Ben followed Joe across the road, to one of the most devastated cornfields he had seen. It was completely flat, smashed into the ground. Destroyed. He could smell the drying corn, a particular smell associated with dead corn stalks.

"What do you think, Ben? Is the field a total loss?"

"Got to be honest with you, Joe. Looks like you've got to start over. I think there's still time to get some kind of crop if you work up the field and plant some early maturity corn. Won't yield as much and you've got to be a little lucky that frost holds off for a couple weeks this fall. If worse comes to worst and we do get an early freeze, you can put the crop in the silo. You'll get something out of it."

"Sounds like what I've got to do," Joe said. He took off his green cap with John Deere printed on the front and rubbed his hand through his head of thick brown hair. "I was hoping on making a little extra money with the corn this year," Joe explained. "And now this."

"You and a bunch of other farmers," Ben said. "Old Mother Nature dealt you a bum hand. Happens."

"Yup, sure does. Happening to me a little too often, it seems." Ben remembered that last year a couple of Joe's cows had died. They never did figure out what had happened to them.

Dealing with loss and setback was a part of farming; it was built into the very fabric of the enterprise. One thing about most farmers, though, is that when a catastrophe hits them, they don't stand around lamenting the loss. They know they must go on. When they're knocked down, and Ben knew Joe Evans felt as flattened as his cornfield, they know they must get up, brush themselves off, and keep going. Joe will do that. So will his daughter. Farm kids learn about loss by experiencing it, and by living through it with their parents.

"Ben, don't you have time for coffee and a cookie?" Julie Evans called from the open kitchen door.

"Never pass up a cup of coffee," Ben replied.

The Evans family and Ben Wesley sat around the kitchen table, drinking coffee, talking about the hailstorm and what it had done, and how farm families in the community were coping. Over the past twenty years, Ben couldn't count the number of times he had done this. He knew he sometimes accomplished more around a kitchen table than he did at one of the many meetings he held. Besides, it was when he was out on the farm, sitting at the kitchen table and looking a farmer in the eye, talking with a spouse, listening to what the kids had to say, that he really learned what was happening on a farm. Farmers were good at covering up bad situations; they tended to be optimists, had to be in order to survive. But when the county agent visited the place and talked to the people, he could see what was really happening. He could feel it, too, no matter what words the farmer might use to cover up a bad situation. With this more in-depth knowledge, he could usually help the farmer beyond handing him a self-help bulletin, or giving him a quick one-liner piece of advice or referring him to a website on the Internet.

When Ben got back in his car, he noticed it was nearly noon. Brittani had a few things to learn about working with farmers. She had scheduled his farm visits one hour apart. Ben was already an hour behind and he had three visits scheduled for the afternoon. He decided to drive back to his office. Working with farmers who had lost their crops and their animals was hard not only for the farmers. Ben felt drained after spending two hours at the Evans farm. He would try to explain this to Brittani.

Business of the Year

*T*he Office of Community Relations at Osborne University submitted the following news item to the *Ames County Argus*:

The Oshkosh Chamber of Commerce has selected Ira Osborne University as the Business of the Year for the greater Oshkosh area. The award will be presented at the chamber's annual recognition banquet in October.

Jason Jenkins, president of the chamber, said, "Osborne University represents everything we want to applaud and encourage in a new business. They are entrepreneurial, they are innovative, and they have a solid business plan that should ensure their success for years to come."

Dr. Delbert George, president of Osborne University, responded, "I am extremely pleased with the selection and the recognition given to Osborne University and our hard-working staff. We have been trying many new things here, including enrolling students from around the world in our online degree programs and noncredit offerings. The computer and the Internet are surely the future for education, and we believe we are on the cutting edge of innovation in this area. We offer bachelor's, master's, and doctorate degrees in disciplines ranging from nursing to business, from agriculture to the liberal arts. We also offer an array of noncredit courses ranging from basic piano and guitar instruction to flower arranging and photography.

Business of the Year

"I am pleased that the chamber recognizes the work we are doing in agricultural research focusing on the improvement of the country's food supply, and the development of extraordinary fruits and vegetables for the prevention and treatment of disease. Our work with Cranberry Red will likely revolutionize and expand exponentially the use of the common cranberry for medicinal purposes.

"And finally, we thank the chamber for noting the opening of our new outreach office in Willow River. We firmly believe that providing up-to-date research findings to the farmers, cranberry growers, and other food suppliers is an essential component of our mission. We have recently employed a Research Application Specialist who will work full time out of our Willow River office and who will serve the needs of those living in the greater Ames County area."

Accolades about Osborne University also came from the community and were published in the *Argus*:

Dear Editor:

I recently signed up for the three-session "How to Grow Giant Dahlias" course offered by Osborne University. I received the instruction on the computer that I have set up on my dining room table. My grandson has been showing me how to use it.

What a joy to learn right at home and not have to drive anywhere. The photos are clear. The teaching is down to earth, and my e-mail questions were promptly answered. And besides all that, the cost was less than buying gasoline to travel three times to Oshkosh.

How fortunate we are to have Osborne University.

And remember: We are never too old to learn, even with a computer.

Lizzie Hatliff
Link Lake

24

Ben and Brittani

All that July, Ben Wesley struggled to keep up with the schedule that Brittani Stone laid out for him each day. She was the picture of efficiency. Each morning when he arrived at the office, she had already placed on his desk an hour-by-hour plan for his day. Farm visits to make. Appointments with people to see him in his office. Speaking engagements. He hardly had time to go to the bathroom, to say nothing of trying to keep up with what was new in agriculture. He soon discovered that if he wanted to do any self-education he would have to do it on his own time, in the evenings (when he wasn't scheduled to speak to some group) and on the weekends when Brittani didn't have him scheduled.

When traveling to visit a farmer, about the only time he had left to think, he fondly considered his old job. The pace then had been challeng-ing as well, but nothing like now. He knew the motivation for the tight scheduling. The more farmers he visited, the more people he talked to in his office, the more speeches he gave, the more money Osborne took in. Of course he received a percentage of the income; that was the upside of his working so hard. Another upside was his marriage. Beth hadn't been so happy in years. She was thoroughly engrossed in the nurse-practitioner course she had enrolled in with Osborne and she enjoyed the extra money Ben was earning. She even planned a shopping trip to Chicago in the fall, so she could buy some clothes "that were fitting of someone married to an important person," as she said one day to Ben. Beth was clearly enjoying being a part of the "Osborne Experience," as she called it, and of course she delighted in telling all her friends and anyone else who would listen about the virtues of Osborne University and how she was a student there, and that her husband headed up their outreach office in Willow River.

Good thing that Brittani Stone didn't hear what Beth Wesley had to say because in Brittani's mind she, Brittani, was in charge of Osborne's outreach office and Ben Wesley was a mere functionary she kept scheduled, organized, and working on task. It continued to bother Brittani that Ben Wesley sat in the office that should be hers. She had complained a couple of times about that to Dr. Sara Phillips. Phillips had responded, "Patience, Brittani. Patience. In due course you will have your own private office." Brittani couldn't wait. She sat in the outer office, facing the outside door, and met everyone coming through it. Her spot left people with the impression that she was a receptionist, not the office manager. She tried to correct that impression as often as possible. When people said words to the effect "So, you're Ben Wesley's secretary," she would bristle and answer, "No, I'm the office manager."

What she wanted to say was "I'm the one who is in charge here. I'm the one calling the shots and setting the direction for this place. Ben Wesley, well, he's new and doesn't know diddly-squat about Osborne University, its history, and its goals." But she didn't. Sometimes she knew when it was best to keep her mouth shut and keep smiling.

Frosty would be the best way to describe Brittani's relationship with Ben. She had almost no understanding of what he was doing when he was out of the office on the many farm visits he made, or what he talked about with people who came into the office. Brittani's biggest concern about Ben was that he just wasn't efficient. He had a difficult time sticking to his schedule, and even worse, he made no apologies for it. "Sometimes it takes a bit of time to get a point across," Ben explained. But Brittani clearly didn't understand his meaning. Osborne University was in business to make money, clear and simple. Brittani had sent a bill to the Evans family "for services rendered" and had charged for two and a half hours. True, that's the amount of time Ben spent, from when he left the office to when he returned to his desk.

When Joe Evans got the bill, he thought there must be some mistake. He called the office and talked with Brittani.

"No, it's not a mistake," Brittani had replied to Joe's question of the possibility of an error in the billing. Joe explained that he was prepared to pay for an hour of Ben's time, which was about the amount of time they had spent talking about his destroyed corn crop and what alternatives he might take in replanting.

Using her most professional voice, Brittani explained that the charges began when Ben left the office and ended when he returned. Joe could understand paying for the travel time; he had to do that with his plumber. But he tried to explain that half of that time was when Ben shared coffee and cookies with the Evans family.

"Do you mean I have to pay for Ben's time when he's drinking our coffee and eating our cookies?"

There was a moment of silence on the line, and then Brittani responded, "Every company that wants to stay in business has rules. I'm sorry, Mr. Evans, but these are our rules."

That evening Joe Evans called Ben Wesley at home.

"What can I do for you, Joe?" Ben said when he answered the phone.

"We've got a problem, Ben."

Ben thought Joe had some further questions about figuring out what to do with his crops.

"That secretary of yours, Brittani somebody, is a piece of work."

"What'd she do?"

"Don't you know?"

"Joe, I don't know what you're talking about."

"Well, let me put it to you straight. Brittani billed me for the time you spent drinking coffee and eating cookies at my kitchen table."

"Really?" It was all Ben could think to say.

"Ben, it's one thing to pay for your services. But I'm not about to pay for the time you spend drinking coffee and eating cookies."

"Hold on, Joe. She charged you for the time we sat talking and drinking coffee?"

"Yes, she did. I think you'd better take her aside and talk to her or you're going to have a hard time finding any coffee to drink." Joe laughed when he said it, as he and Ben had been friends for many years, and he didn't want this little incident to cause a rift in their relationship.

"I promise you, Joe, I'll straighten this out. First thing tomorrow morning. Got to be some kind of mistake. Don't pay the bill."

"I have no intention of paying the bill. It's the dumbest thing I've run into in a long time."

"Thanks for calling, Joe, and you take care."

"Good luck, Ben. You've got a spitfire for a secretary, believe me."

Ben hung up the phone. He was furious. He wondered about the wisdom of leaving all the billing and record keeping to Brittani, and this was a good example of why he should sign off on every bill she sent. It was a good thing he had a night's sleep or he would have fired Brittani on the spot—of course he didn't realize that he didn't have the authority to do that anyway.

The next morning Ben asked Brittani if she would step into his office. He closed the door.

"Brittani," he began. He was trying to control his anger.

Brittani wasn't too happy about being called into Ben's office. She should be the one sitting him down and talking to him when there was a problem.

"Last night I had a phone call from a friend of mine, Joe Evans. He said you charged him for the time I was drinking coffee and eating cookies with his family. You shouldn't have done that."

"You were on a tight schedule. Osborne wants you to keep on schedule."

Ben took a deep breath. "Brittani, send the Evans family a new bill and charge them for one hour of my time. That's what they expect to pay."

"But we'll be breaking Osborne rules if we do that."

"To hell with Osborne rules." Ben's face was turning red. He stood up from behind his desk and glared down at Brittani, who sat with her hands crossed on her lap.

"I'll consider it," Brittani said.

"If you don't do it, I'll do it," Ben said. "We need to keep people like Joe Evans on our side."

"Okay, this once," Brittani said as she got up and left the office. Once at her desk she immediately sent an e-mail to Dr. Sara Phillips in Oshkosh.

Part 4

25

Fred and Oscar

*J*uly in central Wisconsin had been hot and humid. In the early part of the month, farmers complained that their hay just wasn't drying well, that it took an extra couple of days before they could bale it. Corn farmers not affected by the hail were happy because with the heat the corn was shooting up, way beyond knee high by the fourth of July.

Fred had driven over to Oscar's farm without any purpose other than to spend a quiet evening with his old friend on the back porch, sitting in a rocking chair, sipping lemonade, and sharing stories. Both men had long retired from the hard work of farming, but you couldn't drag either one of them off their farms to live in town or, worst of all, one of those new "assisted-living centers" that seemed to be springing up everywhere, even in Ames County, Wisconsin.

"You know, Fred, I been thinkin' about 4-H the last couple days," said Oscar.

"Forage, why you thinkin' about forage? You're too old to be makin' hay," replied Fred.

"Not forage; 4-H. You know, 4-H clubs. Like the 4-H club we both belonged to back during World War II," Oscar reminded him. "The Tamarack Twisters. That was the club's name."

"Oh, yeah, 4-H. The Twisters. I think about that, too. I remember the Victory gardens everybody was growin' in those days. Even the city people. Everybody had a little garden. Not a bad idea either. Wouldn't hurt if we went back to that," Fred mused.

"You 'member what them four H's stood for?" asked Oscar.

"Bet I do. Head, heart, hands, and health. Head for clearer thinking. Heart for greater loyalty. Hands for larger service. Health for better living," said Fred, confidently.

"Hey, you ain't losing your memory near as much as I thought you were."

"Course not. Memory's as good as ever," said Fred, touching a finger to the side of his head.

"Well, how about this? You 'member the 4-H meeting when we were at the Higgins farm and Henrietta Higgins said she wanted to show us their haymow?"

"Yup, I remember that well," said Fred, a big grin spreading across his wrinkled face.

"She had more on her mind than showin' off their big barn full of hay," Oscar said.

"She was a wild one, wasn't she? Whatever did happen to her?" Fred asked.

"Last I heard she retired from being a vice president of some big bank down in Chicago."

"Became a banker, huh? Just never know how people turn out. You just don't," commented Fred.

"Know what I liked best about 4-H?" asked Oscar.

"What was that? You're not goin' back to the haymow story?"

"Nah, it was the fair. The county fair. Staying there overnight with our project calves, sleeping in an old tent. You 'member that?" asked Oscar.

"Them was the days all right. County fair was a sweet time. Nobody around to tell ya what to do and what not to do. Ferris wheel to ride. Games of chance. Didn't have much money for that stuff, though," Fred said.

"Yup, good time all right," Oscar agreed.

"Too bad what happened to 4-H. It goin' away when all the ag agent offices closed," said Fred.

"Yup, too damn bad. That 4-H was a good outfit. Taught us farm kids lots of stuff, besides going up to a haymow with the likes of a Henrietta Higgins," offered Oscar.

Fred and Oscar

"Country's goin' to hell, Oscar. Just plain goin' to hell. Most of the little farmers have all disappeared. What's gonna happen next?" said Fred. He took a long sip on his lemonade and commenced rocking once more.

26

RFD

*T*he following article appeared in the *Ames County Argus* on July 30:

A new Wisconsin youth organization officially began this week. The organization will be called the Wisconsin RFD and seeks to replace Wisconsin 4-H clubs, which were eliminated when the legislature slashed the state budget and closed all county agricultural agent offices on July 1. Although affiliated with the University of Wisconsin–Stevens Point's environmental program, the organization will receive no tax dollars and will be funded entirely by member dues, a modest grant given by an anonymous donor, and fund raising.

"Wisconsin RFD is named after rural free delivery, which began in 1896 in West Virginia and soon spread across the country. With rural free delivery, farmers for the first time could receive mail delivered to their farmsteads. It was a revolutionary idea in its time, just as the RFD program for young people is revolutionary in our time," said Henry Hopkins, executive director of the new organization.

Hopkins, former agricultural agent and one-time 4-H and youth agent for Portage County, further explained, "We intend to follow in the footsteps of the 4-H program that served Wisconsin's young people, both rural and urban, for more than a hundred years. Our program will emphasize taking care of the land, growing one's own food, and various aspects of nature study. The core of RFD is the local club, led by a volunteer leader. We accept members eight years old to sixteen, no matter where they live—cities, small towns, or in the country. Our symbol is a barn, a long-standing icon for Wisconsin agriculture and rural living."

When asked about this recent development, Gladys Swendryzinski, Link Lake, commented, "It was a colossal mistake for the legislature to eliminate the University of Wisconsin Agricultural Agent Program and the long-standing and highly respected 4-H program. I will certainly be a supporter of this new RFD program for our young people. The Boy and Girl Scouts have done and continue to do wonderful work. But there is a need for a youth program with environmental education and food self-sufficiency as its goal, which is what RFD purports to do."

RFD club members, according to Executive Director Hopkins, can enroll in a series of projects ranging from gardening to prairie restoration, from nature photography to the study of endangered species, from home preservation of fruits and vegetables to quilt making.

Hopkins said many will want to enroll in a special project called "Climate" in which RFD members study the effects of climate change by noting when area lakes freeze in winter and thaw in spring, when they see the first migrating birds in the spring, and when the last ones leave in fall.

The Wisconsin RFD has begun a comprehensive fund drive to provide the necessary money to support the main office, train volunteers, and assist local communities and organizations that may wish to sponsor a local RFD club. For further information, go to www.wisconsinrfd.org.

27

Rules

*B*en Wesley was not aware of the fiery e-mail Brittani Stone sent off to Sara Phillips in Oshkosh, in which she asked for a transfer and suggested she could not work with Ben Wesley one more day. "The guy doesn't pay any attention to the rules, and besides he treats me like I'm his secretary. I came to this godforsaken outpost of civilization to manage this office, not to babysit an incompetent."

And of course Ben did not see the reply Brittani got back saying, "Relax, Brittani, take a deep breath and let this pass. Remember, Ben Wesley has lots to learn about our operation. You know Osborne University well. Don't forget we put you in our new Willow River office because we wanted someone who could make it work. We have confidence in you."

"There's a note on your desk, Ben. We need to talk about it," Brittani said when Ben arrived at the office the next day. "A fellow dropped it off late yesterday."

Ben saw the handwritten page on his desk. It read:

Ben,

Trust the new job is going well. Glad you're still working. We cranberry growers need you and have appreciated your work in the past.

I suspect you know that Wisconsin will soon celebrate 150 years of commercial cranberry growing in the state. We are organizing a special Sesquicentennial Celebration for next year and would like you to chair the committee. Our first meeting is scheduled for next week. Give me a call and I'll give you more details.

Jeff Johnson

"You had a question about this note?" Ben asked as he walked into the outer office where Brittani was working at her computer.

"I think you'd better call Dr. Phillips before you agree to chair this committee," she said.

"Why?" Ben was a bit perplexed by her question.

"This sort of activity comes under the category of public service work."

"Public service work?"

"Work that you are not paid for."

"Oh," Ben responded.

"We have rules about how much public service work our employees can do," Brittani said, holding Osborne's employee manual up for Ben to see. He didn't admit it to Brittani, but he hadn't cracked the cover of this thick, three-ring binder apparently chock full of rules and procedures.

"A maximum number of hours per quarter of public service time is allowed, as you will note on pages 246 to 255 of the employee manual. You'd better call Dr. Phillips and discuss this request with her."

"Why would she care?" Ben said.

"She cares," Brittani assured him rather sarcastically, as she turned back to her computer.

Ben was scratching his head as he returned to his office and looked up Dr. Sara Phillips's number in his Rolodex. Brittani suggested he keep his phone directory on his computer, but he had never quite figured out how to do that. As he looked for her number he thought about his previous job as a county agricultural agent working for the University of Wisconsin. The university had rules, and lots of them, but it let its employees make decisions about who they worked with and when. He would not have needed to ask permission to chair a festival committee for cranberries, in fact he would have been applauded for doing it. One side of Ben thought,

To hell with what Brittani says, she's beginning to get on my nerves, and besides, one of these days I've got to let her know who is boss around here. The way she's been acting lately, you'd think she was in charge.

But the practical side of Ben prevailed and he decided not to rock the boat anymore than it was already rocking. Ben had not forgotten the fuss Brittani had made over billing the Evans family.

He punched in Sara Phillips's phone number and soon heard, "This is Dr. Phillips; how can I help you?"

"This is Ben Wesley over in Willow River."

"Ben, how are you? Good to hear your voice. How are things going?"

"Okay, I guess. Lots of work."

"Glad to hear it. I'm pleased people are finding our outreach office and asking for your services."

"I've got a question for you."

"Question away." Sara Phillips seemed especially friendly this morning.

"I've been asked to chair a cranberry festival planning committee. Next year we'll be celebrating one hundred and fifty years of commercial growing of cranberries in Wisconsin."

There was silence on the other end of the line.

"Dr. Phillips, are we still connected?"

"Yes, yes, we're still connected." Her voice had switched to the professional tone he had heard many times before.

"This is public service work, you know," she said.

"I know that," Ben answered. Thankfully, Brittani had pointed this out to him a few minutes ago or he wouldn't have even bothered to call her.

"You've checked the employee manual for the guidelines for this sort of thing."

"Yes, I'm aware of the guidelines." Ben thought it best not to admit that he hadn't opened the manual. He'd been so busy working he hadn't taken time to check on the rules.

"Tell me a little about this committee," Phillips said. "How many times will they meet? How many hours will you spend meeting and preparing for the meetings?

"They haven't met yet, so I don't know. I've chaired other committees like this over the years; they do take a good bit of time."

"Do you have a rough estimate of the hours?"

"I don't know. Can't know until the committee starts its work."

"You know why I'm asking these questions, don't you?"

"Frankly, no. In my other job I would chair committees like this without question."

"Must I remind you, Ben? This is not your other job." Her voice was curt and cold.

"When you are doing public service work, and that's what this would be, you are cutting into the time that you can bill. When you are not billing hours, we are not making money, and you aren't either."

"I realize that," Ben said.

"I hope you do, Ben. Too much public service time can kill your program. Dry it up for lack of finances. Remember, Ben, Osborne University is a business. We're here to make money. Like any other business, unless we can show a profit, we're finished."

"I understand," Ben said haltingly. He wasn't accustomed to being chewed out by a supervisor.

"Do you think it's important to chair this committee?" Phillips asked. Her voice had gone from curt and cold to frosty.

"Yes," Ben said firmly. "I think it's important that I chair this committee. After all, we've got to stay on the good side of the cranberry growers if we expect them to use Cranberry Red."

"Point taken," Phillips responded with an annoyed tone to her voice. "Go ahead and do it, but keep me informed. In fact send me copies of the meeting minutes."

She hung up before Ben could explain anything more about this new assignment.

Ben took off his glasses and rubbed his hand over his eyes. Every day it seemed he was learning some new wrinkle about his job. What just happened he had never expected. He was accustomed to working with people, helping them without worrying about some profit motive behind what he was doing.

28

Promoting RFD

*T*he several hundred former 4-H members in Ames County, their parents, and the volunteer leaders hadn't yet fully understood the elimination of the long-standing 4-H program. The day after the article about RFD appeared in the *Argus*, phone calls began pouring into Ben Wesley's office; he had been the professional in charge of 4-H programs in Ames County since an earlier budget cut had eliminated the former 4-H and youth agent position.

Of course Brittani Stone, office manager, took the calls and knew little if anything about 4-H clubs, what they did, what they stood for, and their more than one-hundred-year history in the United States.

"I'm sorry," she said. "We have nothing to do with this 4-H program for kids. We work only with college-age students and adults interested in our programs. Our position is that educating young people is the role of parents, the schools, churches, and scout organizations." The latter part she made up. The thick employee manual made no mention of working or not working with children.

Callers wondered where they should turn. "I suggest you contact the local Girl Scout or Boy Scout office," she would answer rather brusquely. She saw the calls as a nuisance and a distraction from what she considered more important work.

"Do you have a number we can call?"

"I don't," she would say and hang up.

Promoting RFD

Ben Wesley was out of the office, on one of the many farm visits that Brittani had scheduled, so he didn't have a chance to check his voice mail about the phone calls concerning 4-H, but he had read the notice in the *Ames County Argus*:

A special meeting to discuss the organization of RFD clubs in Ames County will be held Thursday, August 6, at 7:00 p.m., in the community room of the Willow River Library. All young people ages eight to sixteen and their parents are invited. Refreshments will be served following this informational meeting.

Henry Hopkins, executive director of RFD, will make a presentation and answer questions. Former 4-H members and their parents are especially invited to the meeting.

The afternoon before the meeting, Ben ran into Joe Evans on the street.

"Hi there, Ben. How you doin'?" Joe spoke in the slow, deliberate manner characteristic of him.

"Doing okay. How's that new crop of corn coming along?" Ben asked. He was remembering the advice he had given Joe when he visited his farm back in July, after the big hailstorm.

"It's comin' right along; hot weather and rain really gave it a boost. Surprised how fast it's growin'. Of course ground was pretty warm when I planted it. That sure makes a difference in germination time."

"You bet it does," Ben answered.

Ben hesitated to bring it up, but he did anyway. "Are we straight in that billing mistake the office made about my visit to your place?"

"Yeah, finally it's all taken care of. What's going on in your new office anyway?"

"Oh, the new girl has a bit to learn about farm folks. But she's bright. She'll learn."

Joe laughed. "Lot of that going around these days. Folks not understanding farmers, I mean."

"That's for sure," Ben agreed.

"Say, did you see the notice in the *Argus* about that new RFD organization coming into Ames County?"

"Yup. I saw it."

"What's that all about?"

"This new organization, the RFD, is apparently trying to step in and do what 4-H used to do."

"I think the family and I will attend the meeting, see what it's all about. Kids would sure be disappointed if they couldn't take their 4-H projects to the fair this year. By the way, will your new office be involved with RFD?"

"Nope, not at all. I'm out of it. No work with school-age kids is Osborne's rule."

*E*arly August can be hot in Wisconsin, very hot. But no one complains much, leastwise farmers, for they know that they need hot weather to make a corn crop, to push the soybeans along, and to move the canning crops such as sweet corn, green beans, and cucumbers toward higher yields. By early August, the peas and green beans had been harvested, and the cucumbers were just coming into full production. It would take several more weeks before the sweet corn and potato harvest began. And of course the cranberry harvest wouldn't begin until October.

By 6:30 p.m. on Thursday evening, the community room at the Willow River Library had filled to capacity. It was a hot evening, with high humidity, so everyone appreciated the air-conditioning. No one mentioned how contentious putting in air-conditioning had been when the new community room was planned and submitted to the taxpayers of Willow River for approval. Some of the old timers spoke up and said they had no air-conditioning in their homes and why should they have it in the library. But cooler heads prevailed and tonight, with a room full of former 4-H members, their leaders, and parents, everyone appreciated the much maligned "air-conditioning for books."

Various pieces of literature were displayed on two long tables: brochures described the RFD program and its history, membership application forms were available, a pamphlet outlined the role of volunteer leaders, and finally a series of single sheets provided details of the several

RFD projects for children. A big red barn, with the letters RFD painted along one side of the structure, appeared on every piece of literature.

Promptly at 7:00 p.m., Henry Hopkins, a balding, red-faced man, stood up and began speaking. "Thank you all for coming," he began. Hopkins had a deep, resonant voice that carried to the far corners of the room without the need of any amplification.

"First, how many of you were 4-H members?"

Nearly every young person's hand shot up.

"You all know, I'm sure, that 4-H was eliminated on July 1, at the same time the university's agricultural agent offices were closed?"

Everyone nodded, indicating they knew the fate of 4-H.

"How many of you had planned to take your 4-H projects to the Ames County Fair?"

Again almost every youngster's hand flew in the air.

"Well, I'm here to tell you about a new program that will allow you to take your 4-H project to the county fair, even though 4-H is no more. I have already talked to the Ames County Fair board, and they said they would be happy to allow former 4-H members to exhibit at the fair, as long as they belonged to some youth organization."

Hopkins surely knew how to capture the attention of a group. Everyone was anxiously waiting for what he had to say.

"The answer is RFD," Hopkins said. He held up a poster containing the barn symbol with the letters RFD prominently displayed. Also, each piece of literature included the words "Affiliated with the University of Wisconsin–Stevens Point Environmental Education Program."

"If you join an RFD Club here in Ames County, this year you'll be able to take your projects to the fair, no matter what they are—woodworking, photography, dairy, field crops—it doesn't matter. For this year, we in RFD are willing to grandfather in all the current 4-H projects, so you can take them to the county fair."

Somewhat to Hopkins's surprise, a round of applause greeted his last statement. It was obvious that 4-H membership and going to the fair had been very important to these young people, their parents, and their volunteer 4-H leaders.

Hopkins went on in some detail to discuss the various projects sponsored by RFD, and indicated that an RFD club would operate like a 4-H club. A volunteer leader, called a general leader, would be in charge of each club. He or she would be assisted by project leaders—a leader for gardening, a leader for nature photography, and so on. He stressed that all the RFD projects fit into a theme of respecting the land and restoring the environment.

"The goals of RFD are three-fold," Hopkins explained as he held up a poster with the following words listed:

Self-sufficiency
Respecting the land
Improving the environment

"All of RFD's projects and activities relate to these goals."

He had scarcely gotten the last words out of his mouth before a young man in the front row, one of the older former 4-H members, held up his hand.

"Yes," Hopkins said. He did not want an interruption, but thought it best to take the question.

"My favorite 4-H project is dairying," the young man said. "My family and I live on a dairy farm, and I've had the dairy project since my first year in our local 4-H club. Will I be able to have a dairy project if I join RFD?"

"That's a very important question," Hopkins responded as he turned directly to the young man. "Remember what I said earlier? For this year you can continue your 4-H dairy project, and even take your project animal to the fair, if you'd like."

"But what about next year?" the young man asked. "Can I have a dairy project as a part of RFD?"

Hopkins hesitated for a moment. He turned and picked up a collection of RFD project brochures from the table behind him.

"We have many related projects that I think will interest you. I know anyone with as much experience as you've had caring for dairy animals has many other interests, and is surely interested in preserving farms and farming," Hopkins said. "I'm sure one or more RFD projects will interest you."

Another hand shot up from the back of the room. "Is there a cost to join RFD?"

"Very minimal. About the same a young person would spend to participate in certain school sports or other activities. It's fifty dollars a year per child, with a maximum of one hundred dollars per family. So if a family has five children in RFD, it will still only cost them a hundred dollars to belong."

Hopkins noticed a little whispering of children to parents when they heard about the costs.

Hopkins continued, "Our hope, once we are well organized, is to have RFD scholarships available for members who find the fifty-dollar-per-person fee a little too difficult to handle. We want every young person who is interested in RFD to have an opportunity to join."

"Where do we go from here?" a former 4-H leader standing in the back asked. "Can our 4-H clubs become RFD clubs?"

"Yes, of course," Hopkins replied. "That would be the easiest way. Keep the same leaders, keep the same members, keep the same name if you want. Just replace 4-H with RFD."

Further questions came up about leader training, and the availability of special programs such as public speaking, music, and field trips. Hopkins said all were a part of RFD thinking and would be possible.

"Before you go, be sure to have some free ice cream and lemonade, and pick up the RFD literature that interests you."

Before you could say "hot summer day," the ice cream and lemonade had disappeared and the crowd dispersed into the humid night, many with mixed thoughts about RFD and what it would mean for the young people of Ames County.

RFD News

*J*ust a week after the RFD informational meeting, a variety of letters were printed in the *Ames County Argus*:

Dear Editor:

I was one of about one hundred former 4-H parents, members, and leaders who attended the special meeting at the Willow River Library to learn about a new organization called RFD. As everyone knows, 4-H clubs were eliminated when the legislature cut the budget for UWAAP and closed all the county agricultural agent offices in Wisconsin.

I am happy that this new organization is available to the young people of Ames County, no matter where they live. And I am also pleased with the mission of RFD, that of promoting self-sufficiency, respecting the land, and improving the environment.

I will be one of those supporting RFD in Ames County, and encouraging our young people to become members of this new organization.

Ethyl Emerson
Link Lake

Dear Editor:

I attended the recent meeting at the library in Willow River where a new youth organization called RFD was discussed. RFD was described as an alternative to the recently eliminated 4-H program, which had been taxpayer supported. At first I was impressed with RFD, because it is a nonprofit organization and not one penny of hard-earned tax dollars appears headed in its direction. But when I learned of its mission and examined the youth projects it promoted, I was appalled. RFD appears to be another liberal knee-jerk environmental group trying to brainwash our young people into believing such nonsense as global warming, protecting endangered species, and spending time worrying about saving the environment. This is a dangerous organization, clearly out to capture the minds of our young people.

Wake up, citizens of Ames County. RFD is another end run by the wacky environmentalists who will stop at nothing when it comes to advancing their liberal agenda. This organization must be stopped in its tracks, before it has an opportunity to gain a foothold in Ames County.

Felix Swenhold

Willow River

Dear Editor:

My name is Melissa Evans. I'm 12 years old and a former 4-H member. I have a rabbit project and I am so happy that even with 4-H gone, I will still be able to take my rabbits to the fair as a member of RFD. I joined RFD right after the meeting the other night. I am so happy I had a chance to do it.

We must all thank RFD for coming to the rescue of many Ames County 4-Hers who would otherwise not have been able to take their projects to the fair.

Melissa Evans

Link Lake

Celebration Planning

After making sure he notified Dr. Phillips at Osborne headquarters in Oshkosh, Ben Wesley set up the first planning meeting for the 150-year celebration of cranberry growing in Wisconsin. On a Wednesday afternoon in August, the planning committee—consisting of cranberry grower Jeff Johnson; Shotgun Slogum, representing the Ames County Fruit and Vegetable Growers Cooperative; William "Billy" Baxter, editor of the *Ames County Argus*; Hector Cadwalder, president of the Ames County Bank and Trust; Lars Olson, retired county agricultural agent; Cindy Jennings, realtor and member of the county board; Megan Fritz, Willow River librarian; and of course Ben Wesley, chairman of the group—held their first meeting. Before the meeting, Ben asked Billy Baxter to serve as secretary and he agreed.

It wasn't Ben's idea to have Cindy Jennings on the committee, but he felt it necessary to ask for a representative from the county board and the board chair suggested Cindy. Ben still remembered well her supporting the budget cuts and closing all agricultural agent offices in the state.

"Thank you all for coming and agreeing to serve on this committee," Ben began. "It should be interesting, and besides, we are doing something very important for the cranberry industry."

"I surely can agree with that," said Hector Cadwalder. Hector stood six feet two, was thin as a fence post, and had thick, graying hair he combed straight back. As one of the prominent bankers in Ames County, he knew how much the cranberry industry contributed to the economy not only of Ames County but of the entire state of Wisconsin.

"Let me second Mr. Cadwalder's comment," said Cindy. Cindy, forty-five, was short, thin, and quite nervous in her actions. "As a member of the Ames County board, I want to be first in line to applaud the good work of cranberry growers and give them some of the publicity they so much deserve."

"When are we going to hold this shindig?" piped up Shotgun. He was one for getting right to the point. He had little patience for people prone to making speeches, calling attention to themselves, and not being able to stick to the task at hand. Shotgun had developed a fundamental dislike for Cindy Jennings after he had read her letter to the editor and her support for eliminating Ben Wesley's office along with all the other county agricultural offices in Wisconsin.

"I have a calendar," said Ben. "Looks to me like the ideal time next year would be the second weekend of August, that's a week ahead of the Ames County Fair and a week after the big pickle festival they have every year in Link Lake. And we should still have lots of tourists in the county and thus would be assured of a crowd."

"Well, that's not a good weekend for me," said Jeff Johnson, one of the largest cranberry growers in Ames County and a site for Cranberry Red field trials. Jeff was forty-five years old, slim and tall, with balding red hair and a red moustache.

"What's the problem?" asked Ben.

"My only daughter is getting married that Saturday."

"I think we can excuse you long enough to march your daughter down the aisle that Saturday," said Billy Baxter. He chuckled when he said it, as he had three married daughters and knew the importance of the event. Billy was sixty years old, fairly rotund, and had a thick head of graying hair that he almost never combed.

"I suppose I can make it work," grumbled Jeff. "It's the wife that's going to be a problem."

"Easy now, Jeff," said Cindy. "Let's be careful about blaming these wedding plans on the mothers. I've heard fathers get pretty wrapped up in weddings, too, especially when it's their daughter."

Jeff smiled, but didn't say anything.

"All right, let's move along," Ben said, walking to a flip chart with a magic marker in hand. He wrote on the top of the flip chart paper, in big red print: "Cranberry Celebration—second weekend in August."

"Okay, what do we call the event? Got to have a catchy name for it."

Ben wrote several suggestions on the flip chart. "Cranberry Sesquicentennial," "150 Years of Cranberries," "Celebrating Cranberry's History."

"How about 'Cranberry One-Fifty'?" suggested Megan Fritz, who had so far said little during the meeting. Megan was middle-aged, with short, graying hair, and she spoke with a soft voice.

Ben wrote her idea on the board along with the other suggested names.

It took but a few minutes for the committee to unanimously agree on Cranberry One-Fifty for the name of the celebration.

"What else?" asked Ben as he circled the event's title.

"Need a parade," said Shotgun.

Ben wrote "parade" on the sheet.

"Got to have a cranberry queen," offered Cindy.

"Street dance, got to have a street dance," said Lars Olson.

Ben wrote "queen" and "dance" on the paper.

"Art and craft show, should have an art and craft show. Good place for Ames County artists to show off their work," Cindy added.

"Well, I think we must have a historical pageant," offered Billy.

"A fine idea, indeed," said Lars. "But who's got the moxie to put one together? They are a heckuva lotta work."

After a brief pause, when everyone looked at each other and it was clear no one had a suggestion as to who could put such an idea together, Billy said, "What the heck. I suggested it. I'll give it a go at putting it together. I'm sure I can get the drama department over at the high school to help out."

"We'll all help out, won't we?" Cindy said as she glanced around the room. The response, from the looks on people's faces, amounted to something like "Speak for yourself, Cindy," but no one said it.

Ben had chaired meetings like this for twenty years; it was one of the duties of a county agent to organize things. He had forgotten how much he enjoyed doing it, watching the eyes of people light up as they brainstormed possible events and activities, watching how people interacted with each other and built on each other's ideas, watching how old relationships faded into the past as a group of people worked toward a common task that all thought important. Celebrating one hundred and fifty years of cranberries in Ames County quickly tied the group together.

"I have an idea for something we should do," said Megan. "I will volunteer to prepare a series of bookmarks that we'll give out to our customers announcing the event. On each one we should also include some factual information about cranberries."

"That's a great idea," Billy said. "Ben, I think you're the one to do the factual information."

"Sure, I'll do that," Ben said. So far, he had not volunteered to do anything specific outside of chairing the committee. When he offered his help, he didn't think about what his supervisor, Dr. Phillips, would say of yet one more "public service" activity, as she would refer to it.

"I'll bet there isn't one person in a hundred who knows how Wisconsin got started in cranberries, and very few know much about them today," said Hector, who had been mostly quiet during the meeting. "And people should know that the cranberry is Wisconsin's state fruit."

By the time the meeting ended, several sheets of flip chart paper had been filled with suggestions and names of organizations and individuals to contact, and assignments of committee members to get it all started.

Ben felt good about the meeting, better than he had felt in a long time. Most of his work for the last month and a half had been with individuals and on the clock. People knew they were being charged for every minute they spent with Ben. Since his trip to the Evans farm, there was no time for small talk, no time for stories, no time for coffee, just questions and answers. Ben felt like an information machine, spewing out answers on command. Not too different from a human computer.

The celebration planning meeting was clearly different. No rush to finish within a given period. Time for people to discuss, think, and consider.

This was how Ben liked to work, whether it was with an individual or a group. For him, this was what it meant to be a teacher and not merely an information giver. Draw ideas out of people, ask questions, offer suggestions, help people consider alternatives, push them to look for deeper answers, but then let them decide what is best for them.

This is the strategy he used with the cranberry celebration planning group, the same strategy he had used with hundreds of groups before this one. Today's meeting helped Ben see what was troubling him in his new job with Osborne University. They were not allowing him to teach. Somehow he had to work at changing that. It was teaching that drew him to county agent work in the first place. If he was to be at all happy, he must return to teaching in spite of Osborne University's thick book of rules, and Brittani Stone's compulsion toward billing someone for every minute of his time.

Ames County Fair

*O*f all the various activities Ben Wesley had been involved in when he was county agricultural agent, the Ames County Fair stood high on the list of those he enjoyed most. He liked the excitement surrounding the event; the Ferris wheel with its seats swinging high above the fair grounds, giving riders a bird's-eye view of Willow River and points beyond; the merry-go-round with its carved horses moving up and down in a circle, with spirited music playing; the games of chance lining both sides of the blacktopped midway: "Knock over the milk bottles." "Dump the politician," a game where you bought a ticket and tossed a baseball at a target; if you hit it your favorite, or not, politician—the mayor, county board chair, assembly person—fell into a round tank of water about four feet deep with a big splash and considerable cheering by those gathered around.

Ben liked walking through the livestock barns, watching 4-H members prepare their animals for the show ring, talking with their parents, many of whom he knew personally from many years working with them. His strolls through the horticulture building delighted him: 4-H members' garden project exhibits, with freshly dug carrots, beets, potatoes, rutabagas, cabbage, and sweet corn. And of course cucumbers because Ames County, as it had been since the 1930s, was a major producer of cucumbers in Wisconsin. Ben knew the stories going back to the 1950s, long before he became a county agricultural agent, when the cucumber growing competition was not only among 4-H members with garden projects, but also among cucumber growers who competed for the title of Ames County Cucumber King. He remembered the story that several old timers told him about what had happened at the 1955 Ames County Fair when two old farmer friends competed for the title. It was the year that Jake Stewart began growing vast acreages of cucumbers for the H. H. Harlow Company, while his neighbor, Isaac Meyer, like many other farmers in Ames County, grew but one half acre. Jake was certain his cucumber exhibit would best Isaac's; after all, Jake had thirty acres of cucumbers from which to choose. And he was certain the ones he put in the exhibit would outshine any other cucumbers in Ames County, especially those of his old friend and neighbor Isaac Meyer.

The judge, a county agricultural agent from Portage County, discovered that Jake Stewart's cucumbers were diseased, had what was called "spot rot," and the judge disqualified the entire entry. Of course Jake Stewart had a fit about it, to the point that the 1955 fair seemed to be the one that everyone talked about when someone mentioned Ames County fairs from the past.

As county agricultural agent, Ben Wesley had been essentially in charge of the fair, rounding up volunteers, hiring judges, lining up a carnival for the midway, helping write the publicity (of course the Ames County Fair board made all the policy decisions). But this year much had changed. All 4-H signs had been removed or painted over and replaced with the emblem for RFD, the new organization that had recently arrived in the county and had the blessing of the fair board to allow RFD members to show at the fair. The red barn with the letters RFD superimposed on it was not an unattractive sight. But Ben missed the popular and longstanding 4-H symbol, a four-leaf clover with a block letter "H" on each leaf.

As per a temporary arrangement with the RFD organization, former 4-H members could bring their projects to the county fair, if they joined RFD. Many did, but not all. The cattle barn appeared to be about a third empty, one entire long table in the horticulture building stood empty, and the former 4-H woodworking display had about half as many entries as in previous years. It was clear that many former 4-H member families didn't have the money necessary for the membership fee to join RFD, and thus their projects stayed home along with many unhappy young people.

Ben, rather than making sure everything at the fair ran smoothly from night security to project judging, had none of these responsibilities this year. He, along with office manager Brittani Stone, sat in a little booth underneath a huge banner that read OSBORNE UNIVERSITY. Their booth was between the Watkins products booth and the booth for the Ames County Republican Party. Ben and Brittani's task at the fair was to hand out brochures proclaiming the virtues of Osborne University and especially the outreach office, and sign up people for appointments.

Brittani loved the assignment. Ben hated it. He wanted to stroll around the fairgrounds, meet and chat with people he knew, encourage and thank volunteers, talk to young people and comment on their various projects. But now, he felt like a lion on display in a zoo. Ben sat behind a table and handed out pieces of paper to passersby, many of whom tossed the brochure in the nearest trashcan.

"Smile, Ben," Brittani said as she observed Ben's grumpy demeanor. Brittani was her bubbly self, chatting up people, young and old alike, telling them the high points of Osborne University.

Joe Evans and his wife, Julie, stopped by the booth. Ben introduced them to Brittani. "Joe and Julie, this is Brittani Stone, our office manager."

"How do you do?" said Joe. Julie said, "Hi." Both of them remembered the bill they'd gotten from Brittani for Ben's services, and how they had been charged for serving Ben coffee and cookies.

Joe, Julie, and Ben chatted for some time, talking about everything from the weather to how much they missed their 4-H club, and wondered aloud if the new RFD organization could ever replace 4-H. Meanwhile a number of people stopped by the booth. Brittani, in a very professional style, chatted briefly with all who stopped by, handing each person a brochure.

When the Evanses moved on, Brittani said quietly, "Ben, we've got work to do here. There is no time for visiting with old friends. Remember, the reason we're here is to bring in more business for our office."

Ben bit his tongue but before he could respond another person came up to the booth.

"Say, weren't you our county agricultural agent?" asked an older woman. "Sure sorry to see your old office close. Shame what's going on these days. Budgets being cut everywhere. Just a darn shame. Glad you found other work." She thrust out her hand and shook Ben's, then she moved on. She didn't even glance at Brittani, who had a brochure ready to hand the woman.

32

Cranberry Red Meeting

*I*t was the Monday after the Ames County Fair had ended, and Ben was looking over the schedule of appointments that he and Brittani had gotten from sitting in their little booth and promoting Osborne University. Ben was having difficulty adjusting to the hard-sell approach of his new employer. True, when he worked as a county agricultural agent, he let people know what programs he had available, what new bulletins had come to his office for distribution, and what new workshops he had planned. But he did all this quietly and mostly through a weekly newspaper column he wrote, his regular radio program, and direct mail pieces to folks he knew might have an interest in the office's educational programs.

This morning Ben hadn't gotten through the pile of phone messages that had been left on his voice mail, when the phone rang.

"This is Ben Wesley," he answered.

"Ben, this is Dr. Phillips over in Oshkosh. How are you this morning?"

"Little tuckered after spending three days at the fair."

"I heard from Brittani that it went quite well, that you got several appointments and some workshop requests."

"Yup, we did," said Ben.

"Ben, let me get right to my reason for calling. Do you have any workshops on your calendar for cranberry growers? We've got to get them acquainted with Cranberry Red."

"Not yet, but it's on my 'to do' list."

"Better push it to the top of your list. Gunnar Godson over at the research station has early results to share, and Dr. Foley, our vice president for research here at Osborne, is anxious to get the word out."

"Shouldn't we wait until this fall's crop from Jeff Johnson's bog comes in, so we can see if the results hold up under regular growing conditions?"

"Ben, Ben. You're thinking like a land-grant university person. Researchers take forever to release their findings. Testing, checking. Testing again. Holding something off the market way too long. In our business, we strike when the iron is hot. And the iron is hot. The cranberry growers need to know about Cranberry Red."

Ben was silent for a moment, but he was thinking.

"Ben, you still on the line?"

"Yeah, I'm still here."

"Well, are you planning to organize a workshop? I'd suggest you do it at the research station, give the cranberry growers a chance to see our research operation."

"Okay. I'll get on it," Ben responded. He hoped his voice didn't convey what he was thinking.

"Thank you, Ben. Have a nice day."

Ben pushed back in his chair. He knew why his employer was in such a hurry to promote Cranberry Red. It had little to do with education and much to do with selling the product. Ben surmised that if Cranberry Red was as good as early research suggested, cranberry growers would jump at the chance to buy the product.

Ben wondered about the arrangement between Osborne University and the huge International Farm-Med organization that would be making and marketing Cranberry Red. Could it be that Osborne University was really a front for the gigantic IFM Company? Likely millions of dollars were involved. He didn't like what he had to do, didn't like it all. What he was doing was a long way from being an educator. Plain and simple, under the guise of teaching about better agricultural practices, he was hired to sell a product. True, Cranberry Red appeared to have enormous health benefits, from reducing heart attacks to preventing strokes, according to research findings so far, as reported in the media by Osborne officials. Maybe he should climb off his high horse and join with those trying to improve people's health. Perhaps Osborne University's approach was the way of the future. Discover something new, do some brief testing, and then try and convince people to use it. Still, Ben's many years of training and experience raised flags. And Osborne University's close ties with International Farm-Med were an even more serious concern.

Ben walked out to the front office, where Brittani sat with a smile on her face. She had obviously overheard the conversation with Dr. Sara Phillips.

"Got to organize a workshop for cranberry growers at the research station," Ben announced. "I suggest we invite the growers here in central Wisconsin. Besides Ames County, I'd suggest we include Portage, Wood, Adams, Jackson, and Monroe County growers. I imagine we should use our regular fee schedule for the workshop," Ben said.

"Workshops for Cranberry Red are free," Brittani replied. "And I've already prepared a list of cranberry growers we should invite."

From the expression on Brittani's face, Ben knew that she had already talked with Phillips in Oshkosh and had discussed every aspect of the workshop, including who would be invited, who would speak, and that no fees would be charged. Ben didn't let on that he knew what was going on between Brittani and the Oshkosh office. But it irked him. He felt like a small cog in a big machine.

*O*n a cool September afternoon, about fifty cranberry growers from a half dozen central Wisconsin counties gathered at Osborne's research station in Ames County. As they arrived, Gunnar Godson's assistants organized groups of eight or ten and toured them around the facility. They saw the vegetable plots, looked at the strawberry bed, and learned about the work with blueberries.

At 2 p.m. the growers assembled on chairs set up near the cranberry bed, one that had been abandoned some years ago but had now been renovated by Osborne University's research staff.

The day was clear with the sun in a cloudless sky warming the site. Some of the maple trees to the south of the station had just begun turning color, providing a backdrop to the cranberry beds. The blue waters of the

Tamarack River were clearly visible in the distance, forever mysterious, as rivers tend to be. An early frost had killed off the last hatch of mosquitoes, so sitting outside was a pleasant experience.

A cedar fence post with a board nailed to its top served as a podium. Ben walked to the makeshift podium and began, "My name is Ben Wesley. I'm with Osborne University and work out of the outreach office in Willow River. Welcome to Ames County and to Osborne's research station. I know many of you, especially the growers here in Ames County who I worked with for many years when I was county agricultural agent. I have always been impressed with our cranberry growers in this state; you are on the cutting edge of technology and new approaches for enhancing the production of your crop. Today, we have something even newer to share with you. Let me introduce Dr. Quinton Foley, vice president for research at Osborne University."

Foley, wearing a navy blue sport coat and light blue shirt, but no tie, walked quickly to the podium and began speaking. Tall and thin, with thick brown hair, he commanded respect by his very appearance.

"Welcome to Osborne's research station. As you likely already know, we are new here in Ames County. Our headquarters is in Oshkosh, but this station is the center of our research activities that focus on fruits and vegetables." Foley spoke rapidly, pausing only long enough to take a breath. "We wanted you to see the breadth of our operation before we turn to the matter at hand, the research we are doing with cranberries and more specifically the research we are doing with Cranberry Red. How many of you have heard of Cranberry Red?"

Every hand went up. Cranberry growers had obviously read the reports in the newspapers and heard about Cranberry Red from their friends and neighbors.

"We at Osborne and our partner in the Cranberry Red project, the International Farm-Med Company, are thrilled with what we have discovered here at this almost primitive research station. You all know about cranberry's medicinal qualities. Your customers and you have known this for years. But now, we are about to make the simple cranberry, when it is treated with Cranberry Red, an even more desirable enhancer of health and preventer of many common diseases." Foley paused once more to take a breath.

"Before we go on, I want to introduce you to one of your own. I'm sure many of you already know Jeff Johnson. He has a cranberry marsh here in Ames County, and he has agreed to treat five acres of his cranberries with Cranberry Red this year. Last year, he treated about a half acre. We want to make sure the solution performs in an actual bog situation. Jeff, would you hold up your hand?"

A smiling Jeff Johnson, sitting near the front of the group, raised his hand.

"Some of you will want to talk with Jeff before you leave this afternoon, to get a take on his experience with Cranberry Red."

Foley continued, "It is my distinct pleasure to introduce Dr. Gunnar Godson, director of our research station and the person who developed Cranberry Red. He's prepared to tell you more about an invention that could change the cranberry industry forever, and improve the lives of thousands, if not millions, of people in this country and around the world."

Slowly, Gunnar walked up to the rustic podium. Wearing thick glasses and looking rather frail, he shuffled through some papers he carried.

"Thank you, Dr. Foley," Gunnar said. His speech pattern was slow and deliberate, as was often the way of those for whom English was a second language. His speaking style directly contrasted with Foley's rapid-fire delivery.

"Let me also welcome you to our modest research facility. I hope you enjoyed your little tour of the place and now know a bit more about what we are doing here."

Gunnar paused and shuffled through his papers a bit more after adjusting his glasses.

"We have developed something that should interest every cranberry grower in the country," he continued. "We have developed an application that when sprayed directly on your cranberry beds during the growing season . . . will at least double the antioxidant levels of the harvested fruit."

Even with his Swedish accent and his slow and deliberate way of talking, he had everyone's attention.

"I think most of you know what that means, yes? Cranberries will become the food of choice to prevent all sorts of serious diseases ranging from stroke to heart disease."

Gunnar went on to explain, in as simple terms as possible, that the product he and his research team had developed was related to salicylic acid, and that when they sprayed it on the cranberry plants during the summer growing season, it stressed the plants. The cranberry plants responded by increasing the antioxidant level of the berries. He described the procedures he and his researchers used in applying the material, and then asked for questions.

"What will Cranberry Red cost?" someone asked.

"We don't know yet. Osborne University's partner in this research is International Farm-Med. They will be selling the product as well as marketing the Cranberry Red–treated cranberries."

"What is this International Farm-Med Company—where they located?" called out a voice from the front row.

"I'll take that question," said Dr. Foley. "The International Farm-Med Company has its headquarters in Cleveland, and they are one of the largest suppliers of natural health foods in the world. Cranberry Red–treated cranberries will be one more health food they will add to their arsenal of powerful natural health foods."

"What are the side effects when this Cranberry Red chemical is used?" a voice boomed from the back of the group.

"We found none," responded Gunnar Godson, who once more stood at the podium. "We have tested cranberries from our test plot and from Johnson's experimental plot. The berries look exactly the same as regular cranberries. They also taste the same as berries from untreated plots, but they have a considerably increased level of antioxidants."

After a few more questions, the group walked a short distance to the experimental cranberry bed. The group agreed, as they talked among themselves, that these cranberries looked just like the cranberries they were growing in their bogs.

"When can we buy some Cranberry Red?" someone asked.

"Very soon," replied Dr. Foley. "At least that's what the folks at Farm-Med are telling us."

Before the group left, they were invited to add their names and addresses to a sheet if they wanted to receive information on how to purchase Cranberry Red when it became available. Everyone signed up.

33

The Day After

Back in the Willow River office the following day, Brittani and Ben met to discuss Ben's upcoming schedule.

"How'd the workshop go yesterday?" Brittani asked.

"Okay, I guess. Had about fifty growers show up. Good crowd."

"I heard they were all pretty excited about Cranberry Red," Brittani said.

"I suppose so. They're all looking for a way to increase their income; can't blame them for that."

How did Brittani know what happened at the meeting? Ben wondered. It didn't conclude until four yesterday afternoon. And why did someone think it necessary for her to be kept up to date on everything that went on in their office? After all, she was only the office manager, responsible for scheduling, billing, and record keeping. He chose not to say anything, but Ben was sure she noticed the perplexed look on his face when she commented on the meeting.

"What's on the docket for today?" Ben asked, trying to be noncommittal. He knew he had to get along with Brittani, but every day was a struggle. Something about her just grated on him, but he couldn't put his finger on what it was.

"This afternoon I have you scheduled for two hours at the Clarence Higgins farm. Higgins said he just expanded his dairy operation and wants to landscape the grounds around the new buildings. Wants you to draw up a plan and suggest the plantings he should use. Oh, he had no problem with the consulting fee. He said he expected to pay it. You usually get what you pay for, he told me."

Ben knew Higgins was one of the few dairy farmers remaining in Ames County, and quite a successful one at that. Last he heard Higgins was milking around seven hundred and fifty cows and planned to expand further. Ben also remembered that Higgins was one of those who wrote a letter to the editor applauding the legislature for eliminating the county agricultural agent offices. He was somewhat pleased with the request for assistance; at least Higgins had nothing against him personally.

"Anything else?"

"Don't forget tonight you're speaking at the annual banquet of the Willow River Flower Club. They called a few weeks ago and said you speak at their banquet every year and that you are quite the storyteller. Didn't know that about you, Ben. Didn't know you were a storyteller," Brittani added, smiling.

"What time?" Ben asked.

"Let's see." Brittani scanned the big schedule book that she kept on the side of her desk. "The meeting begins at 6:30 at the Lone Pine restaurant."

"Got it," Ben said as he scribbled a note in the pocket calendar he always carried, had in fact carried for the past twenty years. He remembered that some of the younger county agricultural agents had fancy electronic gizmos where they kept their schedules. Ben preferred a calendar that required no batteries and didn't need to be charged.

"Oh, this week's edition of the *Ames County Argus* just arrived. Nice story about yesterday's meeting."

Ben returned to his office and unfolded the paper. On the bottom of the front page, he saw a photo of the cranberry growers listening to Gunnar Godson. Ben had noticed Dr. Quinton Foley snapping some pictures while the meeting was going on, but he didn't guess a photo would find its way into the newspaper so quickly. He saw himself standing in the back of the group, with arms folded. Ben began reading:

The Day After

Area Cranberry Growers
Attend Osborne University Workshop

On a sunny and warm Tuesday afternoon, area cranberry growers learned about Cranberry Red, a new product developed by Osborne University. The "breakthrough" application, as university officials describe it, is purported to increase the antioxidant level of cranberries by several times. The new discovery and the cranberries treated with it will be promoted by the International Farm-Med Company, a nationally known marketer of natural health foods. More than fifty cranberry growers from as far away as Tomah and as close as Willow River gathered for a field day at Osborne University's research station on the Tamarack River, west of Willow River. They toured the grounds and saw the various vegetable and fruit studies that were in progress there. But the centerpiece of the meeting was inspecting the experimental cranberry bog that had been treated with the Cranberry Red solution.

Ben Wesley, research application specialist for Osborne University, with an office in Willow River, welcomed the group to the research facility and introduced Dr. Quinton Foley, vice president for research at Osborne University. Dr. Foley summarized the health benefits of cranberries and said that Cranberry Red "could change the cranberry industry forever, and improve the lives of thousands, if not millions, of people in this country and around the world."

Dr. Gunnar Godson, director of the research station and lead scientist in charge of the Cranberry Red project, spoke next. Godson explained how the product works and what could be expected from its application on cranberry beds. He said that Cranberry Red was a salicylic acid relative, and when it was sprayed on cranberry beds during the growing season, it stressed the plants and caused them to produce more antioxidants, thus increasing the health benefits to those who eat the treated cranberries. Cranberry growers seemed impressed with Cranberry Red and its potential. For further information about the new product, contact Ben Wesley, research application specialist at Osborne University's outreach office in Willow River.

Ben sat back in his chair. The public relations office for Osborne University surely knew how to get the word out. He expected to hear essentially the same story on the area radio stations, and he wouldn't be at all surprised if the TV stations in both Green Bay and Wausau carried the story. His thoughts were interrupted by a phone call from one of the cranberry growers who had attended the meeting.

"This is John Edwards, over in Monroe County," the caller began. "I was at your meeting yesterday. Say, this Cranberry Red stuff sounds too good to be true."

"Powerful stuff," Ben said.

"You sure the chemical is safe? Doesn't do stuff we don't know about?"

"Appears to be okay," Ben replied. "Researchers are doing lots of testing."

"You don't know for sure if it's safe?"

"Do we know for sure if anything is safe?" Ben replied, but he knew his voice lacked conviction.

"What do you think? Your personal opinion?" the caller prodded.

Ben paused for a moment. He wanted to say that Cranberry Red needed a lot more testing before IFM put it on the market, but he knew if he did there would likely be hell to pay. Someone from Osborne in Oshkosh would call faster than you could say "Ben Wesley, you're fired."

"You'll want to contact Osborne University directly about the testing they've been doing with Cranberry Red."

"I believe I'll just do that," the caller said curtly. "Thank you for your time."

Several more calls came in with similar questions.

Ben's enthusiasm for Cranberry Red continued to wane. One of his major assignments was to promote the material along with helping cranberry growers learn how to use it. Somewhere back in the recesses of his mind, his conservative and often skeptical view of everything new came back to him. Many times over the past twenty years when he worked as a county agricultural agent for the University of Wisconsin, he heard about breakthrough research, new plant varieties, new types of fertilizers, new tillage strategies, new weed control chemicals, new computer applications.

Each time he asked the same set of questions. Is this an improvement over what we have now? Does this new idea have unintended consequences, things that will happen that no one thought would occur? How expensive is this new thing? How difficult is it to use? Some of his colleagues called him a Luddite, someone who was hopelessly stuck in the past. But Ben held his ground, and more times than not, he was correct in being deliberate and thoughtful before promoting something new.

When Ben arrived home that evening, Beth greeted him at the door.

"Isn't it exciting?" she said. She was beaming.

"What's exciting?"

"For heaven's sake, Ben, didn't you read the paper?"

"I did read the paper."

"Aren't you excited about Cranberry Red?"

"A little, I guess."

"Ben, Ben, what will I ever do with you? Cranberry Red is the most exciting thing to come our way in a very long time. And just think, you're in the middle of it. You, Ben Wesley, research application specialist for the great Osborne University. You are in charge of spreading the word."

"Beth, there's a lot more to it than just spreading the word."

"Huh," Beth said. "You're not a teacher. You're a research application specialist." She emphasized each word as she spoke it.

34

Office Problems

*B*en wasn't one to notice such things, but he couldn't miss the big, new, lighted sign that greeted him when he turned into the parking lot. "Osborne University Outreach Office" it read, in huge red letters. On the outside door of the office was another new sign, also with red letters and lighted.

"How do you like the new signs?" Brittani asked when Ben entered the office.

"Impressive," Ben responded. "Impressive."

"Well, the signs *are* impressive," Brittani said, using her bubbly voice. Sometimes Ben couldn't tell if she was teasing him, making fun of him, or simply putting up with him.

"No excuse for people not finding us now. New signs will help," Brittani said.

As best he could, Ben Wesley tried to carry out the wicked schedule Brittani Stone established for him each day. He traveled the width and breadth of Ames County and even into neighboring counties, as there was no restriction on where he worked. Ames County did not contribute to his salary nor to the maintenance of his office, so he was free to work and travel as far as his time and energy allowed. It had taken Ben a while to realize that he was no longer confined by county boundaries.

Ben met with farmers in Portage County and discussed potatoes; he met with cucumber growers in Waushara County, with sweet corn and

143

green bean growers in Wood County, with lettuce and carrot growers in Marquette County, and with several strawberry growers in Adams County. And of course he met with cranberry growers all through the region. Unfortunately, few of the smaller market gardeners contacted the office. Ben knew they couldn't afford his time, and he was concerned about that. Last week he'd been invited by a Hayward cranberry grower to visit his northern Wisconsin bog, but Brittani put a kibosh on the request. "Too much time wasted on the road," she said.

"Got the bill back from the Willow River Flower Club," Brittani announced. "They said it must be a misunderstanding. They said you have spoken to them for free each year for as long as they could remember."

"How much did you charge them? I only talked for forty-five minutes."

"Three hundred dollars, which is the standard speaking fee."

"Didn't you tell them ahead of time there would be a fee?"

"Yes, I included our fee schedule along with the speaking contract I sent them," Brittany responded.

"I used to speak to them for free," Ben said, perhaps a little too abruptly.

"What are you going to do about it?" Brittani asked.

"I'll talk to them. See what we can work out," Ben replied.

"Got another problem. It's the Ames County Fruit and Vegetable Growers Cooperative's workshop."

"What's the problem?" Ben asked. In his old job, he conducted a workshop each year for this group from the time they first organized. Attendance ranged from fifty to seventy-five and more.

"Only three people signed up. Got to have at least a dozen before we can go on."

"Only three people signed up? Seventy-five people used to come," Ben said, disappointed.

"Not anymore."

"When did the announcement go out?"

"Three weeks ago today. Workshop is next week."

"Got a copy of the flyer we sent out?" Ben asked.

"Sure, it's right here." Ben looked at the folder and immediately recognized the problem.

"It's the hundred-dollar-per-person fee. That's the problem."

"That's our usual fee for a workshop like this. It's spelled out right here in Osborne's rule book," Brittani said, pointing at the thick tome.

"These growers don't have a hundred dollars to pay for a one-day workshop, especially when I did the workshop free for many years."

"Ben, you've got to quit comparing what you're doing now with what you used to do. This is a new day. People don't get valuable information free. They expect to pay for it."

Ben could feel the color rising on the back of his neck. "Brittani, not everyone has money to pay for information and sometimes the people who need the information most are the ones who can least afford it."

"Well, that's just too bad," Brittani said breezily. "We have rules to follow."

Ben decided he'd wait for another day to continue this conversation. He had a job to do and she had a job to do. He hoped one day they might better understand each other.

"Well, if we have to cancel, we have to cancel," Ben said.

Rules, rules, rules, Ben thought. I've never seen so many rules. This will not look good to the folks in Oshkosh, canceling workshops that should attract substantial enrollment. But people are people. If they are accustomed to getting something for free, they expect the practice to continue.

35

Fish Survey

Gus Caldwell slowly backed the lime green Department of Natural Resources truck down the public boat landing on the Tamarack River. Gus, a long-time DNR employee, had a neatly trimmed beard, now mostly white, and a pair of shoulders like a football halfback. His deeply lined face was weather worn from years working in the fishery unit of the DNR. He'd gotten his start working at the Wild Rose Fish Hatchery thirty years ago, when he had just finished a biology degree at Stevens Point State University. Now he was in charge of the fish census unit, which was responsible for doing fish census counts on Wisconsin's many lakes, streams, and rivers.

Kirsten Leary, a University of Wisconsin–Madison biology student, was helping Gus today. As part of her internship, she worked with the DNR to learn about fish management and develop some skills for doing fish counts.

"Far enough, Kirsten?" Gus shouted out the window of the pickup as he continued backing the boat trailer down the ramp.

"I think so," Kirsten said. Though well trained in all aspects of fish biology, Kirsten lacked practical knowledge for doing the work—how to back a boat trailer down a boat ramp, how to operate the generator on the fish-shocking unit, even how to hook a boat trailer to a pickup.

Kirsten, who was twenty, with short brown hair, stood about five feet tall. What she lacked in stature and practical information she made up for in her knowledge of fish, their habits, their diseases, their growth patterns, and the kind of habitat most conducive for their survival and reproduction.

With the boat unloaded, both Gus and Kirsten pulled on rubber waders that came above their waists, on Kirsten nearly to her chin because she was so short. Then they both waded into the river, pulling the little flat-bottom boat containing the generator and the fish-shocking equipment behind them.

The Tamarack River was only as much as four feet deep along this section, so wading was relatively easy. Gus carried the electrically charged wand, which emitted just enough current to temporarily stun fish and cause them to rise to the surface. Kirsten's task was to net each stunned fish and measure it, clip a fin to mark the fish, note the information in a notebook, and then release the fish to the water none the worse for the experience.

Three brown trout came up first, all over eighteen inches.

"Nice fish," Gus said as he continued working.

Kirsten measured, recorded, and clipped one fish after the other.

"When were these browns put in here?" Kirsten asked.

"Last year, I think," Gus replied. "But I'll have to check the records."

"Phenomenal growth," Kirsten said. "Absolutely outstanding growth."

"Tamarack's a good river," Gus said. "Lots of natural food."

"Don't the cranberry growers around here use some of this river water?"

"They all do, but they're pretty careful these days. Haven't had a pollution case against the cranberry growers. Nothing like the paper mills along the Fox River south of Green Bay. Talk about pollution—those mills did a number on the Fox. But that river is on its way back now—after we got after the mills a few years ago."

The two-person crew had continued on for fifty feet or so when Gus said, "Whoa, what have we got here?"

A huge northern pike came to the surface. It measured fifty-five inches.

"The biggest northern I've ever seen," Kirsten commented.

"Don't see many this big, no matter where you go in the state. I've been in this job thirty years; I've never seen a northern this big."

"Wonder what he's been eating," Kirsten said. "Whatever it is it sure has agreed with him."

That afternoon, on their way back to the ranger station, Kirsten thought about what she had seen. Something about these big fish just didn't seem right.

Gus was thinking, too. He made a mental note to return to this site next year and do some more census work. He wondered what it was about this stretch of the Tamarack River that made it such an ideal habitat for fish.

36

Fishing with Lars

*T*he weather had been pleasantly warm for late September in Wisconsin. The trees had begun turning color: brilliant red maples, bright yellow aspens. The sweet corn harvest was in full swing; semi-load after semi-load rolled through Willow River on the way to Markesan and the big canning plant there. Potato farmers hurried to dig their hundreds of acres of potatoes and haul them to the huge potato warehouses scattered throughout western Ames County. Farmers, those with beef or dairy cattle, were cutting field corn for silage and filling long white plastic tubes that several years ago began replacing upright silos.

Home gardeners busied themselves picking the final crop of green beans, cutting broccoli, slicing the heads off cabbage, digging late potatoes, gathering up squash and pumpkins, and otherwise preparing for frost, which, if the season was like other years, might come any night now.

When Friday night arrived, Ben Wesley was exhausted, both physically and emotionally. Slowly he had adjusted to the heavy schedule of field visits, office calls, and speaking engagements. But the work tired him, wore him down to a frazzle.

Beth was not sympathetic when he came home complaining about how tired he felt. "Now you know a little of how I feel when I come home from the hospital after standing up all day," she said when he arrived home and commented on the challenges of his week. "You should be so pleased you have such a good job and with such a prestigious university."

"I am glad I have a job," Ben said. "And I work hard, too, if you haven't noticed," Ben remarked, a bit put-off from his wife's nagging.

Ben opened the fridge, pulled out a Point Special, and settled down in his favorite chair. He flipped open his cell phone, scrolled his contact list, and punched the number for his old friend Lars Olson.

After Lars quickly answered, he said, "Lars, this is Ben. How are ya?"

"Fair to middling. How are things with you?"

"Could be better. But I'm muddling through," said Ben.

"Yup, what I always say is you do the best you can with what you got," Lars said.

"Say, Lars, the reason I'm calling. What do you say we go fishing tomorrow? The bluegills ought to be biting on Mt. Morris Lake. A mess of bluegills cooked on the grill would sure go good."

"Well, let me check my busy schedule," Lars said, laughing. "Sure, let's go fishing. You gonna pick me up?"

"I will. How about, say, 7:30 tomorrow morning? I'll hitch my old boat to the pickup and bring along a bunch of worms and little minnows. All you need to bring is yourself and your fishing poles."

"Deal," said Lars. "See you in the morning."

Like the several days before, Saturday dawned clear and warm, an ideal day for fishing or doing just about anything else. Ben backed his old twelve-foot Sears Aluminum boat down the concrete ramp at the Mt. Morris Lake boat landing, while Lars Olson, with hand signals, directed the exercise.

With the battery, electric motor, fishing rods, life preservers, fishing boxes, and bait in place, the two old friends pointed the boat toward what the locals referred to as the second lake in the chain that made up Mt. Morris Lake. Some years ago Ben had purchased an electric motor. Although it was much less powerful than the gasoline models, and considerably slower as well, Ben appreciated the motor's light weight, its quiet operation, and its nonpolluting qualities.

"Should be a good day for bluegills," Lars said as he readied his spinning rod with the new Johnson reel he had gotten for his birthday. He carefully knotted a hook on his line and dug through his rather messy fishing box for a red and white bobber, which he snapped on the line. He then threaded a fat night crawler on the hook.

They motored by mostly empty cottages owned by folks who spent summer vacations on the lake, people from Milwaukee and Madison, from Oshkosh and Fond du Lac, and several from the Chicago area as well. A handful of people lived full time on the lake, maybe three or four families, among the more than fifty cottages that lined the banks.

"I remember when there were only a half-dozen cottages on this entire lake," Lars remarked as he waited for them to arrive at what they considered the ideal spot for bluegills.

"Not very many when we moved here twenty years ago, either," agreed Ben as he slowed the boat and steered it through the narrows that separated the two lakes.

"Yup, don't know where all this is going, Ben. Just too darn many people wanting to spend time at a lake. Can't blame 'em, I guess. Hotter than hell in the cities in the summer. Can't blame 'em for wanting a little lake air."

"I guess," said Ben as he shut down the electric motor and allowed the boat to drift toward a patch of pond lilies that grew from shore well into the lake.

Two bobbers sat on the glassy smooth surface of the lake as the two fishermen sat quietly for a time, neither saying anything but both enjoying the quiet of the morning and the natural beauty that was all around them.

"See that big blue heron over there?" said Lars. "Just as still as a statue. Not moving a feather."

"Keep watching him, Lars. The heron sees a fish and that long-legged bird becomes a killing machine," said Ben.

"Guess the heron's having about as much luck as we are," replied Lars. "And that's no luck at all."

"We'll get some fish, Lars, just got to wait. I can feel it. This is a fishing day," said Ben, smiling. It had been weeks since Ben had been this relaxed.

"How's that new job treating you, Ben?"

"I'm surviving."

"Only surviving?" Lars had a serious look on his face.

"That office manager of mine, Brittani Stone, is one heckuva go-getter. She's got me working every hour of the day it seems, running here and there, talking to this group and that. Some days I hardly have time to think."

"You're making good money, aren't you?"

"That I am. I get a percentage of everything the office takes in, plus my salary. I can't complain about the money part."

"Then what's to complain about?" said Lars as he kept an eagle eye on his bobber, which had seemed to move not at all since he last tossed it near the closest pond lily.

"You know, Lars, there is a fundamental difference between being a research application specialist for Osborne University and a county agricultural agent for the University of Wisconsin."

"Well, I guess I know what that is. Osborne pays you a heckuva lot more money than you ever got as a county ag agent," responded Lars, smiling.

"More than the money, Lars. It's taken me a while to figure this out, and maybe I haven't got it right yet. But it's sure causing me to lose sleep."

"Well, spit it out Ben, I'm a good listener."

"All I'm doing in this new job is handing out information. That's it. Plain and simple. I feel like a walking computer with a hard drive filled with facts that I'm supposed to offer on demand."

"So, what's wrong with that? Didn't you do that when you were a county ag agent when the state sent you 'research-based' information?"

"Yes, I did do some of that. But I did more. And here's where the difference comes in. When somebody has a problem, a question about something—let's say they want to set up a farmers' market for their vegetables. When I was an ag agent, I'd have on hand all the information on how to set up a farmers' market, how to staff it, how to display the vegetables, what income to expect, and how to make it attractive to passersby."

"So, what's your point, Ben?" Lars asked.

"When I was an ag agent, I wouldn't give the information to the person until I'd asked several questions: Why do you want a farmers' market? How much money do you want to invest in this project? Do you know how much time it will take? Do you have enough produce to keep it stocked? Do you have a marketing plan? How much do you already know about doing this sort of thing? I'd push them on the last question, to find out if they had their facts straight or they had a head full of wrong ideas. I'd get the person thinking about what they planned to do and whether what they already knew fit. I'd push them to consider their idea in ways they hadn't before."

"Sounds to me that you were being a good teacher," said Lars.

"That's it, Lars. With this new job, there's no time to be a teacher. I'm an information spreader, plain and simple. I have to charge people a hundred bucks an hour just to meet with me. For that kind of money, they expect information, clear and quick, with no questions about why they want it, or how they use it. It's a darn shame, Lars. I'm selling facts without a user's manual."

Just then Ben's bobber began bouncing on the water near the lily pads, and then dipped beneath the surface.

"Got one on, Lars. Feels like a good one, too," Ben said as he began reeling in the fighting fish.

"Hey, Ben, I got one on, too!" exclaimed Lars. Both men were now reeling in fish, their thin spinning rods bending as they cranked on their reels.

By eleven they each had their limit of bluegills, along with a couple of perch, three or four crappies, and a half-dozen sunfish.

"Told you this would be the day," said Ben, once more smiling. "Say, why don't you and Margaret come over tonight? I'll grill the fish—just like the old days. What do you say? For once we can show our wives that we really can catch fish."

"Sometimes, anyway," said Lars as they pulled up to the boat landing. A mother mallard and her brood, strung out in a straight line behind her, paddled away from the boat.

37

Family Cookout

*W*hen Ben arrived home with the fish, his daughter, Liz, met him at the door.

"Hi, Daddy," she said. Liz was now a junior at the University of Wisconsin–Madison in a pre-med program. She graduated second in her class at Willow River High School and had earned several scholarships. Both Ben and Beth were more than proud of their daughter, who at age twenty looked very much like a younger version of her mother, with red hair and green eyes. Except she was taller. She wrapped her arms around her father.

"Daddy, you smell fishy," Liz said.

"That's because I've been fishing and haven't had a chance to wash up. How did you get here?"

"A friend of mine was on her way to visit her folks in Waupaca and I asked if I could ride along, and so here I am."

"It's so good to see you," said Ben. "We miss you around here, you know."

"I miss being here," replied Liz. Beth Wesley stood back from her daughter, beaming. She was as proud as any mother could be about her daughter's accomplishments.

"Before I forget," Ben said. "I've invited Lars and Margaret over for a cookout tonight, just like the old days. I'll fix the fish on the grill."

Beth wrinkled her nose, as she sometimes did when Ben made a decision without asking her, but she didn't say anything.

After Ben had washed up, the three of them sat down for lunch at the kitchen table.

"How is school going?" Ben asked. He was famished after a morning on the lake.

"Every semester is tougher," Liz said. "I never thought learning could be such hard work. Some days I think my brain will explode."

"If you're going to be a doctor, you've got a lot to learn."

"How's your new job, Dad?" Liz asked, changing the subject as she reached for another tuna sandwich.

"Okay, going okay," said Ben.

"Liz, your dad is being your dad. His new job is so more than okay, you can't imagine. Besides earning a lot more money, which we surely need with the two of you in college, your dad is a part of something so big it's hard to describe."

"Now, Beth," Ben said. "Don't exaggerate."

"I'm not exaggerating. And you, Liz, with your interest in becoming a physician, will appreciate even more what your dad is doing."

"Geez, Dad, why didn't you tell me about this?"

"I meant to, Liz. But we're still in the testing stages."

"For heaven's sake, Ben. Tell her about Cranberry Red, probably the biggest breakthrough in preventative medicine in a hundred years."

"Well, I wouldn't go that far," replied Ben. "But it could be important, no question about it."

"*Could be* important?" said Beth as she raised her voice a bit. "It *is* important."

"So what's so special about this Cranberry Red? We haven't talked about it in any of our classes," said Liz.

Ben began to explain the many potential health benefits of the new product, especially how it increased by several fold the antioxidant levels in field treated cranberries.

"You know about antioxidants and disease prevention, I'm sure," said Ben.

"I do. We had an entire unit on antioxidants in a pre-med course I'm taking this fall. We learned that cranberries, blueberries, and, must I say it, broccoli, get high points."

"Well, what your dad isn't telling you is that his new job makes him one of the most important people in Willow River," said Beth.

"Easy now, Beth," said Ben as he fidgeted in his chair. One of these days he must share with his wife his misgivings about this "important person" job.

"Don't be modest, Ben. Just a few weeks ago your dad had his name in the paper again, as the go-to guy to learn more about Cranberry Red."

"Yes, and the phone's been ringing off the hook ever since," responded Ben, without much enthusiasm.

After lunch, Ben cleaned the fish, spiffed up the garage a bit, and dragged out the gas grill in preparation for the evening cookout. Beth shared with Liz some of the course work she was studying online at Osborne University.

"I'm proud of you, Mom," said Liz. "Look at you, doing advanced graduate work on the Internet. You are way ahead of me and my classmates—we spend most of our time listening to some professor drone on in a stuffy classroom."

Ben, who had come in the house a few minutes earlier for a drink of water, overheard the latter part of the conversation between his wife and daughter.

"Still can't beat face-to-face learning," said Ben. "Something about looking your teacher in the eye seems to make a difference."

"Ben, how old-fashioned can you be? I'm sure I can learn better in front of my computer. I can log on when I want to. I can participate as fast or slow as I feel like, and besides, I can do it wearing pajamas."

"Mom, you wear pajamas when you study online?"

"I don't, but I could. I could wear nothing at all and still be participating."

"Oh, Mom," said Liz.

Ben left to continue his preparations for the cookout and picnic with their long-time friends, something the family had not done since he started his new job.

"I'm concerned about your father, Liz," Beth continued in a hushed voice. "He seems to be stuck in the past. I worry about him. I don't think he knows what a great job he has, and how what he is doing has boosted his reputation in the community way beyond what it was when he was merely a county agricultural agent."

"Dad's never been one to brag," Liz said. "He always seemed to enjoy working in the background."

"It still bothers me. He's in a position to really make a difference, and he seems to be dragging his feet. Osborne University is a university of the future. In every respect. From their Internet classes to the research program your dad is a part of. But what does he do? He keeps talking about the days when he was a county agricultural agent, and how he enjoyed his work then."

"He'll do just fine, Mom," Liz said, touching her mom on the shoulder. The two of them had begun preparing potato salad and an apple crisp dessert for the evening picnic.

Just as the day had been sunny and warm, the evening was also pleasant. Lars and Margaret Olson brought with them a six-pack of Leinenkugel's Red, a bottle of Chardonnay, and a fresh loaf of bread Margaret had baked that afternoon.

Ben prepared a platter of pan fish, grilled to just the right crispness.

"Nothing better than bluegills; they have a sweet taste to them, not fishy at all. Something like walleye, but maybe even better," Lars commented when he sat at the picnic table in the Wesleys's backyard.

"Just like the old days," Ben said. "Except we've gotten older and Liz here has grown up. Remember the picnics we had when Liz and her brother were little tykes?"

"Now, Dad," Liz said as she reached for a piece of fresh-sliced bread and slid a couple of crispy bluegills onto her plate. "Some stories are best forgotten."

Ben held up his bottle of beer. "I want to make a toast," he said. "To the two most good- looking students in Willow River, Beth and Liz Wesley."

"Here, here," said Lars as they clinked wine glasses and beer bottles.

It had been a long time since Ben had such a pleasant day with family and friends. He was a lucky man, he thought. Perhaps luckier than he even imagined. Why let this new job get under his skin? Learn to live with it.

Maybe even enjoy it. He decided he must work on changing his attitude. Attitude was his problem. He took another bite of bluegill.

"Say, Dad, sitting here eating fish reminds me of something I meant to tell you before."

Ben looked up from his plate and wiped his mouth with his napkin.

"My lab partner in chemistry this semester, Kirsten Leary, has an internship with the DNR. She's interested in fish biology. One day a couple weeks ago, she was working on a fish survey team on the Tamarack River."

"Every couple of years they do a fish count on the Tamarack, at least that's what somebody told me," Ben said.

"Kirsten said they turned up some of the biggest northern pike anybody on the team had ever seen. They measured one northern that was fifty-five inches long. Several others were over three feet."

"Whew, never saw a northern that big," said Lars. "Guess we're gonna have to give the Tamarack a go one of these days, Ben."

"Well, I thought you'd be interested, Dad. I know you like to fish."

The two families continued talking about old times and how Ames County had changed in the past twenty years. They discussed county agent work and farming, fishing and deer hunting, all the things the two men had in common.

"Thanks for a great day," Ben said as Lars and Margaret walked to their car. A cold breeze from the northwest had begun to blow, a reminder of much colder weather to come.

38

Celebration News

On September 30 the *Ames County Argus* published an update on the cranberry celebration:

The committee planning the 150-year celebration of cranberry growing in Wisconsin met this past week. As announced earlier, the celebration is planned for the second weekend in August next year in Willow River. "We're calling it 'Cranberry One-Fifty,'" said Ben Wesley, research application specialist for Osborne University and planning committee chairman. Wesley announced that young women in the community interested in competing for the title of Ames County Cranberry Queen should submit their applications before February 1 of next year. Application forms are available at the Osborne University Outreach Office in Willow River.

The planning committee announced the involvement of several community organizations. The Farm Bureau Women have agreed to sponsor a cranberry baking contest open to anyone. Categories include desserts, breads, appetizers, and miscellaneous. The group will also hold a bake sale of cranberry products on Saturday and Sunday of the event. The Ames County Artists Association (ACAA) has planned an art fair on Saturday of the celebration. The ACAA is encouraging local artists to create paintings with some aspect of cranberry growing as their main subject.

Celebration News

The Ames County Scribblers, a group of local writers, will hold a writing contest in conjunction with the festival. They are especially interested in submissions featuring cranberry poetry, short stories, and memoirs of early days in the cranberry industry. Committee member Amos Slogum added that the Ames County Whittlers, a group of retired men who meet once a week at the Ames County Historical Society museum, have agreed to display samples of their work and to demonstrate whittling techniques during the festival.

Cranberry One-Fifty is shaping up to be a most interesting festival.

Part 5

39

Fred and Oscar

*E*very week or so Fred and Oscar met at the Lone Pine restaurant for coffee. They didn't belong to the regular coffee group that met there every day, six days a week.

"Bunch of old guys, those daily coffee drinkers," Fred said. "About all they do is gossip and invent rumors."

"That about sums it up," agreed Oscar.

Fred and Oscar drove to Willow River together, in Fred's old pickup. Mazy saw them when they came through the door.

"Your regular booth is available," she said to the two men, pointing with her pencil.

Once they settled in, Mazy came by with her pad.

"What are you guys up to today?" she asked.

"Oh, let's see . . . I'm up to about five nine and I suspect Oscar may be an inch or so more," said Fred.

Mazy rolled her eyes and smiled.

"The usual?"

"Yup, coffee and a chocolate doughnut," replied Fred. He glanced at Oscar.

"I'll have the same as Fred," said Oscar. "Coffee and a sweet roll."

Mazy scribbled some notes on her pad and hustled off.

"You heard about the cranberry party they got planned for next summer?" asked Fred.

"The what?"

"Cranberry party. Celebratin' one hundred and fifty years of growin' cranberries in Wisconsin," said Fred.

"Yeah, what about it?"

"What do you mean what about it?" Fred asked.

"What I mean is, what about it?"

"Well, you plannin' to write some poetry for it?"

"I just might, just might write a poem," said Oscar quietly.

"You plannin' to write a poem? You gonna write a poem about cranberries?"

"I know how to write poems," said Oscar.

"Since when?"

"Since I was a little kid."

"I didn't know that," said Fred.

"Lots you don't know about me," said Oscar. "Let's see, 'Under the spreading chestnut tree, the village smithy stands.'"

"You didn't write that," said Fred.

"I know that. But I wanted to show you that I know about poetry."

"I don't think you know a damn thing about poetry, Oscar."

Mazy came by with the coffee, doughnut, and sweet roll. "Let me know when you need more coffee," she said. "Got some more doughnuts and sweet rolls if you want 'em," she added.

"We'll let you know," said Oscar.

"So, Oscar, you're gonna write a poem for the cranberry celebration?"

"What was that?"

"A poem, you're gonna write a poem for the cranberry shindig?"

"When is that?" asked Oscar.

"It's next summer, next August," said Fred. "You writin' a poem for it or not?"

"Figured I would. Got a start on it. Been thinkin' about how I'd string the words together," responded Oscar.

"You wanna try her out on me, get my opinion?" asked Fred.

"You don't know nothin' about poetry, Fred."

"Know a good poem when I hear it."

"I doubt that," said Oscar.

"Give her a go. I'll tell ya what I think," said Fred.

"Okay. Here's what I got so far."

Oscar cleared his throat and began, "Roses are red, violets are blue, cranberries are red, what color are you?" He smiled and took another sip of coffee.

Dead silence at the booth. Oscar took another sip of coffee. Fred took a sip of coffee.

"That poem is no damn good," said Fred.

"How do you know?"

"It just ain't. Besides, it's racist."

"Racist? How the hell is it racist?" said Oscar, a bit miffed by his old friend's comments.

"You can't ask, 'What color are you?'" said Fred.

"Why not?"

"'Cause it's not the right thing to do these days."

"Who says so?" asked Oscar.

"Just about everybody."

"Name one. Name just one damn person who'd be put off by that question."

"Some Chinese person."

"Chinese person. How many of them we got here in Ames County?" asked Oscar. "How many Chinese people?"

"Don't matter," Fred replied. "Don't matter how many."

For a long time the two men just sat drinking their coffee. Mazy had come by to fill the cups.

"What do you think of celebrating cranberries?" Fred finally asked.

"Pretty good idea," said Oscar.

40

Harvest at Shotgun's

October in central Wisconsin is the most beautiful time of the year, at least to Ben Wesley's way of thinking. The trees—maples, aspen, birch, tamarack, and oaks—seem to pulse with color, starting with the maples in late September and ending with a magnificent display of oak color by mid-October. After the first killing frost, usually in mid- to late September, the days are often filled with brilliant sunshine and bright blue skies providing a backdrop to the fall color display. By now the mosquitoes have given up their mission of human torture, so hiking in the woods is once more pleasant, along with most other outdoor activities.

Skeins of Canada geese fly over in long-tailed V's, sometimes stopping briefly on local lakes and ponds before they continue journeys to their winter homes, honking loudly as if to brag that they know better than to winter in the north. The northern ducks arrive on their migration route and spend a few weeks on local waters: big green-headed mallards, little blue-winged teal, and even smaller widgeons, wearing their camouflage brown. Sandhill cranes gather in farmers' fields, congregating before they wing south to their winter haunts. Their prehistoric trumpeting fills the air on clear October days, their overhead flights impressing people with just how large these long-legged cranes are, standing four feet tall and boasting wingspans exceeding six feet.

Crop farmers guide giant combines across acres of field corn, collecting the yellow kernels in the machine's bin before off-loading the corn to semitrailers that haul the crop to nearby grain elevators for drying and sale.

Potato growers hurry to lift the last of their harvest from the ground. And the cranberry growers are in the midst of their fall harvest, gathering up the fruit from the bogs and hauling the berries to nearby processing centers.

The Willow River Farmers' Market was a popular place each Saturday all summer for out-of-town as well as local buyers who wanted home-grown vegetables and fruits. The market surrounded the courthouse on the city square with vendors from throughout Ames County and beyond. By early October buyers had picked up the last of the fresh broccoli and turned to rutabagas, onions, carrots, potatoes—red, white, and russet—pumpkins for Halloween and for pies, squash—acorn, buttercup, butternut, old-fashioned Hubbard—apples of many varieties—Honeycrisp, Gala, Red Delicious, Yellow Delicious, McIntosh, Cortland, and old-fashioned Wealthy and Northwestern Greening. Apples for eating. Apples for pies and apple crisp. Of course apple cider, gallons of apple cider. And, not to be forgotten, fresh-harvested, deep red cranberries. Directly from Shotgun Slogum's bog.

Shotgun, as his father before him, raked his cranberries by hand. No fancy equipment for him. Not that he was necessarily against more modern ways, but he felt compelled to do things the old-fashioned way. "Something special about raking cranberries by hand," Shotgun said to Ben Wesley some years ago.

Ben respected Shotgun for his decision not to go modern. But he also knew that Shotgun's smallish cranberry bog—he only harvested about five acres of cranberry vines—wouldn't lend itself well to the big equipment that most cranberry growers used today.

For many years, Shotgun Slogum sponsored an open house at his cranberry bog the first Saturday in October. He invited everyone who wanted to experience raking cranberries to find some hip boots and join him in the bog. He provided the rakes. For their efforts, everyone who raked would receive ten pounds of fresh cranberries and a story they could share with their kids and grandkids.

All comers were welcome, men and women, no matter their experience, but fifteen was the minimum age. "A little too difficult for kids," Shotgun explained.

Ben Wesley never missed the opportunity to participate; in fact he was quite proud of his skills as a cranberry raker. He remembered his first time, when he couldn't get the hang of swinging the two-handled rake just deep enough in the flooded marsh to capture the cranberries, but not so deep as to snag something else, like the side of one of his boots.

Ben asked Beth if she would like to join him raking cranberries. This had been ten years ago or so. Beth had said, "Anybody would have to be crazy to wade around in that cold water swinging a dumb-looking box with spikes on one end." Ben didn't ask her again, but he never missed Shotgun's open house.

The temperature was in the fifties when Ben arrived at the marsh, but it felt warmer as the sun shone from a cloudless sky, making Shotgun's cranberry bog a picture-perfect place on an autumn day.

Ben parked his car at the end of a row of about ten others, opened his trunk, took out his hip boots, and pulled them on. He then walked the fifty yards or so to the bog where a row of people were lined up across it, each wearing hip boots, and each attempting to swing an old-fashioned, double bow-handled cranberry rake. A wooden bushel crate floated behind each person, tied to the raker with a short length of thin rope.

Shotgun worked at the far side of the bog, the first raker in the line of a half dozen or so wading in the bog. "Come on in," he greeted Ben. "Take a spot at the end; we've been waiting for you." Shotgun Slogum, in his seventies, worked like a fifty-year-old. Those half his age were obviously having difficulty keeping up with him, as the nearest raker was at least a dozen or more feet behind him.

Several people, young and old, lined the banks of the bog, watching the novice rakers and chatting among themselves. Ben grabbed a spare rake, picked up a wooden crate, carefully walked the wooden plank across the water-filled ditch that surrounded the bog, and stepped into the water. It was cold as ice; he was glad he remembered to wear wool socks and long underwear under his waders.

Ben tied the floating box to his belt, and took his place at the end of the line, next to a young women Ben guessed to be in her early thirties. She wore what appeared to be a down-filled jacket, with a stocking cap pulled over her ears, and heavy, now quite wet, leather gloves.

"Morning," Ben said. "How's it going?"

"Not so good," the young woman replied.

"What's the problem?"

"Just can't get the hang of this thing." She pointed to the rake. "When I got here, Mr. Slogum demonstrated how to do it; he made it look so easy. It's not so easy."

"Old Shotgun's been doing this for fifty years; of course he makes it look easy. Here, let me show you a little of what I know."

Ben, without admitting that he'd been raking out here every year for more than fifteen, took a couple of swings with the rake.

"Geez, you make it look easy, too," the young woman said. "Maybe it's a man thing."

"I doubt that," Ben said, smiling. "Mostly it's a matter of catching onto the rhythm of it, swinging the rake just deep enough to catch the cranberries, and then lifting it so they tumble to the back of the rake."

Ben watched as the young woman took a couple of swings; he offered a suggestion and then went about doing his own raking. Slowly the young woman began to figure out how to do the work.

At noon everyone enjoyed a big potluck lunch; people coming had been invited to bring something to share—sandwiches, baked beans, an apple pie, whatever they wanted. Now the group lined up, filled their plates, and sat around on empty crates, enjoying each other's company, the autumn day, and an opportunity to rest their tired backs. What each person had learned quickly was that hand raking, no matter how well you do it, can be backbreaking work.

With the noon lunch finished, Shotgun stood off to the side, welcomed everyone to his bog, and said he hoped they were having a good time. Then he began to tell cranberry stories; he was filled with them. His favorite, Ben couldn't remember how many times he had heard some version of it, was about the year Shotgun went on strike while raking in a bog near Wisconsin Rapids.

"Back in the early 1950s, a good many Wisconsin bogs still raked their cranberries by hand," Shotgun began. "I'd finished helping Pa rake this bog, and he said that if I wanted to earn a little extra money, I could hire myself out. So that's what I did."

Several people were still eating dessert when Shotgun began talking; most of them stopped to listen, for he had a compelling storytelling manner. Besides, his white beard, long white hair, and tanned and deeply wrinkled face added to his mystique.

"So I hired myself out to this guy who had maybe twenty-five acres to rake, quite a lot. About fifteen or twenty of us worked for him. He paid us a buck an hour, which was pretty good money in those days. But his bog had a big problem."

Shotgun stopped for a moment, picked up his coffee cup, and took a long sip.

"What was the problem?" asked someone in the front row.

"Weeds. Too many weeds. Try to rake in a weedy cranberry bog and before you know it your rake is tangled, you're spilling berries, and having a dickens of a time.

"Besides that, this cranberry guy had a foreman who was the meanest cuss I'd ever run onto. He walked up and back alongside the ditch, yelling at us to keep going, to keep up with the guy in front of us.

"Couple other guys and I went up to the foreman at noon one day and said the bog was just too weedy, and we should be paid more than a buck to rake the cranberries there. The burly foreman laughed at us, said we hired on to rake cranberries, plain and simple. Either rake or find a different job.

"Well, that did it. I got together with a bunch of the boys that night after we crawled out of the bog and we talked and decided we deserved better." Once more Shotgun stopped and sipped his coffee.

"The next day, just before noon, we took action. Without saying a word to the foreman every last one of us splashed out of the bog and sat down on empty crates. All except one. Guy we called 'High Pockets' because he was so tall. This guy said we could strike if we wanted to, but he didn't want nothin' to do with it, so he kept on raking. I wanted to drown him, a scab he was.

"'What do you guys think you're doin'?' the foreman asked. He smoked a big cigar that he held in the side of his mouth so his words came out as a kind of growl.

"'We're on strike,' I said.

"'Whattya you mean you're on strike?' the foreman growled.

"'Your cranberries are too damn weedy. We want a buck and a quarter an hour to rake them,' I said. Old High Pockets was out there raking away and I worried that another couple weak-kneed guys might join him any minute, step back in the bog, commence raking, and spoil everthin'. But they didn't.

"After a few minutes, the foreman, who was a little on the dense side, said, 'Well, by gawd, I'm gonna get the boss.' He stomped off, climbed into his pickup, and disappeared. He weren't gone more than fifteen minutes when the boss, driving his big blue Caddy, pulled up alongside us.

"'What seems to be the trouble?' the boss asked. This was the first time we'd met him, and I must say he seemed like a pleasant enough fellow. Nothin' like that tail-ender he had for a foreman. He wore a suit and tie, not the kind of outfit you see much in a cranberry bog.

"I explained about the weeds and the trouble we were havin' rakin' his berries, and how we expected the job ought be worth at least twenty-five cents more an hour.

"'Hmm,' he said, scratching his head. He walked over and looked into the bog and could plainly see that where we was rakin' was weedy as all get-out.

"'Guess you're right,' he said. 'This bed's sure a lot more weedy than it ought to be. Tell you what I'm gonna do.'

"Well, right now everybody perked up and listened close, even the weak-kneed guys that I figured would fold and end the strike just to keep their jobs."

"'Here's what I'm going to offer. Your hourly pay will stay the same. But starting tomorrow, I'm offering a bonus of ten cents a bushel for every bushel you rake after the first fifty. What do you think of that?'

"Without giving it the first thought, everybody's hand went up in agreement with the deal. But the guy wasn't finished. 'Of course I'll have to dock each of you for the couple hours you've been resting here in the sun.'

"We all grabbed up our rakes, thinking about the success of our strike. But the more I thought about it, the more I knew the boss outfoxed us—expect that's why he was the boss. Now we worked harder than ever, and most days we never got to that magic number of fifty that would mean we'd get extra for each bushel we raked after that. In the end, we each lost three hours of pay. And besides, because we all worked so hard to reach the quota each day and some bonus bushels, we finished the job at his bog a week ahead of time. Lost an entire week's pay. Live and learn, I say."

Shotgun went on telling stories for another half hour or so; then, those who wanted to do a little more raking got back in the bog. Like every other year, it was a good day. For Shotgun, for the rakers, for the bystanders, and for Ben Wesley.

41

Gunnar's Discovery

Gunnar Godson had come to the United States from Sweden when he was a teenager. His family settled in New Jersey, where he grew up attending public schools and then, after winning a scholarship, graduated from Rutgers University. Gunnar, from the time when he was a child, found science fascinating. He enjoyed all his science courses, especially those where the teacher presented a problem and the students had to work out an answer, and there could be more than one solution. From the first time a high school science teacher introduced him to the scientific method, he was hooked. Science not only provided a wealth of subjects to study—from physics to astronomy, from biology to geography—it also offered a rock-solid method for inquiry: identify the problem, collect data by observing and experimenting, develop a hypothesis, test the hypothesis. The process was clean, required careful attention to detail, and depended on objective thinking (keeping one's prejudices out of the process) and constant testing. Almost all scientific findings continued to be subject to further testing, as new evidence on a topic developed.

Gunnar wished more people understood the power of science and made more decisions based on the scientific method. Too often ideology and politics clouded people's decision-making, leaving science behind, Gunnar thought. For instance, he simply couldn't understand politicians and other community leaders who treated science and the scientific method as some kind of a cult, rather than a solid, facts-based approach to problem-solving and decision-making.

Gunnar pulled his Toyota pickup into the parking lot next to the modest building at the Osborne Research Station. A warm, drippy rain, especially unusual for early October, had stopped an hour or so before dawn. The sky had cleared and the morning sun was rising above the tree line to the east of the station. Gunnar, as he did each morning, looked to the west, across the station's small cranberry marsh, and to the Tamarack River that was shrouded in early morning mist. He'd come to love the river. He watched its moods and appearance change as each day passed. The river was forever a mystery to him. Just when he thought he understood it and could predict what it would do, the river did something different. For instance, this past spring it gouged out a new channel after heavy spring rains, and it flooded acres never before flooded. But with all its quirks and mysteries, the Tamarack River was a constant in Gunnar's life. It was always there, day after day, week after week. Moving, always moving, its water on a relentless journey to the Wisconsin River, then the Great Mississippi, and finally mixing with the waters of the Gulf of Mexico.

Gunnar felt good this morning. He had a job that paid well and allowed him to do what he wanted to do. As he often did these days, he thought about his years at Rutgers, where he eventually earned a PhD in genetics, found a wonderful woman, and married. He appreciated the position the Department of Horticulture at Rutgers gave him when he completed his graduate work. He became part of the university's research team charged with developing new varieties of cranberries and seeking new cultural approaches to enhance the production of this important crop.

Soon the Godson family included three little girls, the joys of his life. When Gunnar thought he could relax and enjoy his family and his work, New Jersey, like so many states, faced a budget crisis and before you could say "cutback," Gunnar Godson had no job.

When he saw the ad in a national journal for the new position at Osborne University, he immediately applied and was elated when he received a call from Dr. Quinton Foley, vice president for research at Osborne, saying that they would hire him to head up their new research station in Ames County, Wisconsin.

Although the facilities were modest, Gunnar had sufficient equipment, budget, and staff to conduct the kind of research that interested him. He was especially pleased that the station had a small, abandoned cranberry bog, which he and his staff quickly restored.

What pleased Gunnar most was Cranberry Red. Soon after Gunnar began work at the research station, he read about the Chinese research projects that were attempting to enhance the antioxidant level of several kinds of fruits. Of course he already knew that cranberries had high levels of antioxidants and had been used as a health food going back to the Native Americans, who had discovered the health benefits of the tart fruit.

He tried several different chemical combinations in his laboratory, testing them on cranberry vines that he grew in the little greenhouse attached to the laboratory. When he thought he had the correct formula, which had at its base a salicylic acid–like compound, he divided the station's bog into two, applying the chemical to one segment and leaving the other segment untreated. Gunnar was pleasantly surprised to learn, after he harvested the two plots, that the treated plot's cranberries had nearly double the amount of antioxidants as the untreated ones.

Of course he was elated and reported these preliminary findings to his boss, Dr. Foley, at Osborne headquarters in Oshkosh. Gunnar stressed that the results were preliminary. Nonetheless, Osborne quickly began announcing the findings. When Gunnar told Dr. Foley more testing was necessary and they should wait a few years before announcing the findings, Foley scoffed and said, "You've spent too long working at a land-grant university. Those state universities take forever to announce their research results. By the time they do, the need for their findings has often passed." Gunnar didn't reply.

On the way to his office, Gunnar walked by a small patch of lawn that led from the parking lot to the office door. One of his staff kept this area mowed. Something moving on the still-damp grass caught his attention. At first Gunnar thought it was a snake, but when he stopped to look more closely, he noted that it was a night crawler, the biggest one he'd ever seen, for it was more than a foot long and nearly as big around as his little finger. Then he saw the others, dozens of them, writhing, twisting, turning, crawling under and over each other—monster night crawlers emerging from the wet soil. He remembered back in mid-September, when they were applying the last treatment of Cranberry Red to their experimental cranberry bog, that one of the workers spilled some of the chemical on the lawn. At the time he thought nothing of it. But now this.

It was immediately clear to him that a connection likely existed between the spilled chemical and the monster night crawlers. But of course he didn't know for sure; he would have to run some tests in his laboratory to confirm his hunch.

Gunnar was immediately caught in a dilemma. His scientific and ethical side demanded that he quickly call Osborne University and tell them what he had just observed, and strongly encourage them to hold off further promotion until he had conducted more tests. His practical, I-need-to-keep-my-job side told him to keep quiet. He knew how much Osborne University and the International Farm-Med Company were counting on sales of Cranberry Red. They surely didn't want to hear about some previously unknown side effect of Cranberry Red, which could put the entire project in jeopardy.

Gunnar walked out of his office and down to the river, where he sat on a little bench that he had placed there shortly after the research station opened, a place where he had often come to do his thinking. It was a quiet, peaceful place, and the river ran quietly by with scarcely a ripple on this windless morning. The early morning October sun warmed his back; he heard a sandhill crane call from the distance. The fall colors of the maples and the aspens reflected from the water's surface.

He sat for an hour, trying to decide what to do. He thought about his wife and daughters and how much they depended on his income. He considered what Osborne University's reaction to this new information would be, and how his job might be in jeopardy when they heard. But his thoughts always came back to his integrity as a scientist, and how he and he alone had developed Cranberry Red and thus must assume responsibility for both its positive as well as its less than positive features. He thought about the giant, grotesque night crawlers and he wondered what other creatures might be affected by Cranberry Red. He felt his body shudder as he considered this possibility.

He decided he must do what was right. He hurried into his office, picked up the phone, and called Dr. Quinton Foley in Oshkosh.

42

Budget Shortfall

*B*en was back in his office the Monday following the field day at Shotgun Slogum's cranberry bog. He whistled a little tune as he came though the office door and greeted Brittani, who was already hunched over her glowing computer screen.

"Good morning, Brittani," he said. "And what a fine morning it is. This autumn weather is outstanding."

"Just off the phone with Dr. Phillips. We've got a problem," Brittani said with a serious tone to her voice.

"What problem now?" asked Ben. With Brittani it seemed there was always some problem, some complaint to deal with—mostly from people feeling they were overcharged for Ben's help.

"We're way off on our projected earnings," Brittani responded.

"How so?" said Ben. He remembered seeing the pile of papers that had come from headquarters in Oshkosh, a new pile every week it seemed. He vaguely remembered that one document was titled "Quarterly Projected Earnings." He'd piled it on his inbox along with the other Osborne documents. He thought, *If they want me to get something done, the least they could do is let up on the paperwork.* But of course they didn't.

"Have you read our earnings report for the first quarter?"

"Nope, haven't had a chance," Ben said. "Too busy."

"Well, here's a copy and it's not good." She shoved the paper with its many numbers in front of him.

Ben glanced at the number-filled sheet of paper. On the bottom of the sheet, he noted a line in boldfaced type: "Actual earnings are 50 percent lower than projected earnings."

"So, what does this mean?" said Ben, not accustomed to such detailed cost accounting.

"It means we're in trouble," Brittani replied. "We're not meeting our budget, and when we don't meet our budget, we have some tall explaining to do. I had a heart-to-heart talk with Dr. Phillips."

Brittani had an I-know-things-that-you-don't-know look about her. Ben could feel his blood pressure rising. He had known from the first day on the job that Brittani would be a problem. He didn't like her; he was certain she didn't like him, but he had decided to keep his mouth shut and do his job. Now she was once more acting like she was in charge of things, and besides that she had apparently gone around him to talk with his supervisor in Oshkosh.

"Why are you talking about this with Dr. Phillips?" Ben asked, in a voice that was a bit too loud and probably threatening.

Brittani, no shrinking violet, jumped up from her computer and stood toe to toe with Ben, which somewhat surprised him. He backed up a step.

"Mr. Ben Wesley, I am the office manager and in charge of what goes on around here. You act like you're the boss. You are not, you have never been, and you will never be. Oshkosh hired me as office manager, and I intend to manage, by God, whether you like it or not." She had her hands on her hips and her eyes were flashing.

Now it was out in the open. It was what Ben had suspected all along. This young thing who didn't know beans when the bag was open thinks she's in charge of this office. She doesn't know a cranberry from a blueberry, wouldn't know a Jersey cow from an Angus steer, couldn't tell a John Deere from a buck deer, and she thinks she's in charge of this office.

"Dr. Phillips believes you are spending way too much time doing public service work and not enough time tending to business," Brittani added.

"She does, does she?" Ben said. "Well, let her tell me that."

"Oh, she will, Ben, she will," Brittani said. "She said you're too involved with planning this one-hundred-and-fifty-year cranberry celebration."

"Geez, I spend only a few hours a week doing that. Besides, it's one of the most important things I do these days. These cranberry growers deserve some recognition and this is one way of doing it."

"Dr. Phillips said you're too concerned with history and don't spend enough time worrying about right now. Our job is convincing these cranberry guys to buy Cranberry Red."

"Is that right?"

"Well, that's what she said. Besides, that committee work gets in the way of your billable hours. You don't have enough billable hours." She was pointing a finger at the sheet of paper in front of Ben.

"Not enough billable hours? Not enough billable hours. Hell, I've got something on my calendar four or five hours a day." Ben was furious and on the verge of losing his temper. He could feel his face getting red.

"We gotta up that, Ben. Gotta add at least a couple hours a day."

"When am I supposed to keep up with what's going on in agriculture, for God's sake?"

"That's what evenings and weekends are for, Ben. Phillips also said to tell you how disappointed she was that all your planned workshops had been cancelled because of low attendance. She wants to talk to you about that. And she also reminded both of us that the office hasn't even sold twenty-five bulletins since we opened. That's one of our profit centers, you know. If we don't make money, we go out of business. Simple as that."

"What's gotta happen is we got to make some changes around here. Simple as that," Ben muttered. He was beginning to regain his composure. He had to call Oshkosh and straighten out who was boss at this place. Wherever did Brittani get the idea that she was in charge? It couldn't go on this way.

Paul and Gloria Mayer

*T*hat evening Ben was home alone because Beth had a hospital meeting. He was busy reading his latest edition of *Horticulture Magazine*, trying his best to keep up with what was new with gardening and gardening practices. With his heavy work schedule he had no time to read during the day. Brittani had him on the go every hour of every day. From the report he'd just read, he would be spending even more time doing "billable hours." Those infernal "billable hours," as he began to think of them.

He jumped when the phone rang. His nerves were on edge; this was something new. Ben had always prided himself on taking what came his way in a quiet, confident way. It surprised him that he was startled.

"Hello," he answered.

"This is Paul Mayer," replied the voice on the other end. "You don't know me, but Professor Carlson in the Department of Horticulture at UW–Madison said I should talk to you."

"Yes."

"Well, here's the situation. My wife, Gloria, and I bought this little farm just out of Willow River; it was the old Maurice Jennings place, as people around here call it."

"Yes, I think I know the place," Ben said. "Maurice died last year, I believe. I used to work with him."

"That's the place. Anyway, Gloria and I and our three kids moved out here last month, in time for Gloria to start her new job as Spanish teacher at Link Lake High School. We've been living in Madison, but we wanted to raise our kids in the country. When Gloria landed the teaching job, we looked for a farm and bought this one."

"How can I help you?"

"We were wondering if you could stop out to the farm, talk to us, give us some ideas about how to start a home market garden project?"

"You may know that I have to charge you for the visit."

There was a brief silence on the line.

"We didn't know that."

Ben hesitated. He wanted to explain how he was no longer county agricultural agent and was working for a different university, but he didn't. He wanted to say how much he missed working with people like the Mayers, but he didn't.

"Well, that's the situation. You should call my office and our office manager will set up an appointment for a visit." Ben gave the office phone number.

Silence again on the line.

"We . . . we're pretty strapped for money these days," Mayer said. "Got about everything we have in this farm."

"I understand. These are tough times for most farmers, especially those just getting started."

Ben had a soft spot for farmers wanting to get started. He was trying to figure out a way of helping the Mayers without violating Osborne University commitments and rules.

"Professor Carlson said he couldn't think of anybody around who knew more about how to set up a market garden program than you."

"Thank you. I've done lots of work with Rudy Carlson over the years. He's a good researcher."

"I realize that this may be asking way too much. But is there any chance you could maybe just stop out for a few minutes sometime, to look over what we've got planned? We'd really appreciate it."

Ben hesitated. He thought of the recent conversation with Brittani about more billable hours and knew if Brittani found out he was making gratis farm visits she'd have a conniption fit, to say nothing of what Dr.

Phillips would have to say. But on the other hand, this was what he missed about his new job, the opportunity to work with farmers who truly needed help.

"I'm not supposed to do this, but how would it be if I stopped out to your place next Sunday afternoon for a few minutes? No charge."

"That would be wonderful," Mayer said. "Thank you so much."

*B*eth had to work the Sunday shift at the hospital. Ben didn't tell her he was making a farm visit that afternoon, and he certainly had no intention of telling her that he was going behind Osborne's back to do free farm visits. Still, Ben felt some compulsion to help people with problems and questions. The Mayer family surely seemed to fit this description.

Ben always enjoyed the drive to Link Lake. The village, once a farm service center, had transformed itself into a tourist destination with many little shops, antique stores, an active historical society with a museum, and even an upscale restaurant that had once been a bowling alley. But what he enjoyed most about Link Lake was the lake itself, one of the deepest lakes in the state and so blue this time of year. About half way between Willow River and the Village of Link Lake, after going over a little rise in the road, Ben could begin glimpsing the lake in the distance.

As he drove past harvested corn fields, he spotted Canada geese, huge flocks of them feeding on the corn the combines missed. And in the open fields, near the Pine River that ran into the lake, he counted as many as twenty sandhill cranes, once an endangered species but now increasing in numbers each year. Ben knew these big, long-legged, gray birds could be a problem for farmers, especially corn farmers. In the spring of the year, these hungry cranes would dig up the newly planted corn seeds before they had a chance to germinate.

Ben remembered the Jennings farm as not being especially prosperous; the land was sandy and in some places quite hilly. But Maurice Jennings and his wife had raised five kids there. All of them had gone on to either the university or to vocational school and were now doing well. When Maurice died, his wife, Mable, moved into a nursing home in Link Lake.

Ben stopped his car near the house, a large, old, two-story, early-twentieth-century farm home that could use a coat of paint. A faded red barn with a fieldstone wall stood beyond the house, its barnyard overgrown with weeds. Ben remembered when Maurice Jennings sold his small herd of dairy cows, some ten years ago.

A big, brown collie dog barked a couple times and trotted out toward him, its big tail wagging. A tall, slim, black-haired man wearing bib overalls came out of the house followed by his wife and three children.

Ben introduced himself as he petted the collie, who bumped into him as he walked.

"Paul Mayer," the man replied, extending his hand. Mayer appeared to be in his middle forties. "This is my wife, Gloria."

"Hi," she said. She was blonde, tan, and smiling.

"And these are our kids," Gloria said. "This is Jake, he's seven, Jennifer is eight, and Jackson is nine." Each of the children stepped forward to shake Ben's hand. They were all as blond as their mother, and each wore bib overalls.

"Well, what a fine family you have," Ben said.

"Thank you so much for coming out to see us," Gloria said. "I have something for you before you leave."

"How can I help you?"

Paul Mayer explained how he and his wife had long wanted to have their kids grow up in the country so they could get acquainted with nature firsthand. "We want to start a market garden operation and we need some advice," he said.

"On the positive side," Ben began. "This is a good time for market gardeners. We've seen the interest in people buying homegrown, local vegetables increase dramatically in the last few years. And you are close to several markets: Stevens Point, Oshkosh, Appleton, Neenah-Menasha, Wisconsin Rapids, and of course the very popular farmers' market in Willow River."

"Yes, that's what we thought. We've been buying locally for several years, as much as we can, anyway."

"On the negative side, market gardening is a lot of work, and you've always got the weather to contend with. You just never know what old

Mother Nature will throw at you—late spring frost, early autumn frost, not enough rain, too much rain."

Mayer smiled. "That's some of the challenge. Never knowing what to expect."

"Just wanted you to be aware of some of the unexpected, which usually, in one way or another, becomes the expected."

Ben quickly warmed to the subject. He talked with the Mayers for nearly two hours, discussing the feasibility of constructing a small greenhouse, vegetable varieties that do well in central Wisconsin, and what equipment Mayer would need. They discussed what he could do yet this fall, in preparation for next year's growing season. Ben explained how plowing the garden plot and planting it to winter rye might be something to do. "The rye will get started this fall. You plow it down in the spring to add organic matter to the soil." Ben went on to explain how the sandy soils in this area generally lacked organic matter and anything a farmer could do to increase it would enhance crop production.

"Before I forget," Ben continued, "I'd encourage you to join the Ames County Fruit and Vegetable Growers Cooperative. The group has farmers who've been in the business for many years and are more than willing to answer questions and share their experience with you."

"We've already joined," Paul said, smiling.

The time flew. Ben was doing what he most enjoyed doing, helping people who needed help and had limited resources. When he was about ready to leave, Gloria Mayer slipped into the house and returned with two loaves of recently baked bread and an apple pie.

"A little something for all your trouble," she said. "We sure appreciate your time. More than you know."

"Thank you," Ben said. "Thank you very much." As he returned to his car, he wondered how he would explain to Beth where he had gotten two loaves of fresh-baked bread and a big homemade apple pie.

Research Problem

*B*efore Gunnar Godson called Osborne's vice president for research at the headquarters in Oshkosh, he captured four of the giant night crawlers, put them in a plastic bag, and stored the bag in a freezer.

"This is Gunnar over at the research station," Gunnar said when he heard the rapid-fire greeting on the other end of the line. "Can you and Dr. Phillips come out here to the research station? I'm afraid we've got a situation."

"Can we talk about it on the phone?" asked Dr. Foley.

"No, I've got something to show you. We've got a problem. Got a big problem," Gunnar said in his accented voice. "President George probably should see this, too."

"I'll talk to him, but it better be serious," Foley said. His words came like bullets from an automatic rifle. "President George is a busy man these days."

"He needs to know about this," said Gunnar. "What's happened can affect the direction of our research program."

In early afternoon the top officials from Osborne University arrived at the research station: President Delbert George; Vice President for Research Dr. Quinton Foley; and Director of Field Operations Dr. Sara Phillips. They had stern looks on their faces as they marched in single file from the parking lot to the modest building where Gunnar Godson and his assistants conducted their research. Gunnar was waiting for them.

"This better be important," Foley said. He talked even faster when he was nervous. There were no "hellos," handshakes, or anything. All business.

"So, what've you got?" Foley glanced around the spotless lab where several assistants sat huddled over their work.

Gunnar held up the plastic bag containing four frozen, giant night crawlers.

"What've you got there?" snarled Foley.

"Look for yourself," replied Gunnar.

The three officials stepped up to look at the bag and its contents. Gunnar held the bag so the light struck it.

"Geez, looks like you got a bag of frozen snakes. You brought us all the way over here to look at stiff snakes?" said Foley. They were indeed stiff; he had that part right.

"Look a little closer," Gunnar said. "They're not snakes."

"What do you mean, 'they're not snakes'?" said Foley.

"Looks to me like you found four of the biggest, meanest-looking night crawlers I've ever seen," offered President George.

"Biggest night crawlers I've ever seen," agreed Gunnar.

"So, what's the point?" an ever-impatient Foley asked. "Big night crawlers, so what?"

"The 'so what' is I believe we created these monsters," said Gunnar.

"What?" said a surprised Phillips, finally joining the inquiry.

"I think we did it," Gunnar responded.

"All right, let's slow down," said President George. "You found four of the biggest night crawlers I've ever seen, and you think you had something to do with how big they are?"

"I know we had something to do with it," Gunnar assured him.

"How do you know that?" Foley, who was fidgeting, was ready to dismiss the entire episode as a researcher's overreaction.

"A few weeks ago a worker spilled some Cranberry Red on the ground where I found the night crawlers this morning," said Gunnar, still holding the bag of night crawlers where the group could seem them.

"Cranberry Red," repeated an astonished Quinton Foley.

"Yes, Cranberry Red. I believe the chemical caused this to happen to the night crawlers," said Gunnar.

"Are you absolutely sure? This all sounds quite unusual to me," said President George.

"I'm quite sure," said Gunnar. "What happened to these night crawlers is a side effect of Cranberry Red."

"Can't be," said Foley. "Can't be. You, yourself, Gunnar, have been testing Cranberry Red from the very beginning. You never found anything like this."

"I didn't test Cranberry Red on night crawlers," Gunnar pointed out.

"And why should you? Cranberry Red is for cranberries, not for worms that crawl in the ground. What do we care about worms, about giant night crawlers?" said Foley.

"If Cranberry Red does this to night crawlers, how might it affect other creatures?"

"We don't care about other creatures," insisted Foley. "It's cranberries we're concerned about."

"I think we should put a hold on Cranberry Red until we do further testing," Gunnar said quietly.

"What!" an incredulous Quinton Foley cried out. "We can't do that."

"We must do more testing," said Gunnar. He said it forcefully and with conviction. "It wouldn't be ethical to sell Cranberry Red until we know what is happening."

President George looked like he was going to be sick. Dr. Sara Phillips stood speechless. Dr. Quinton Foley stared at his shoes.

"Godson, under no circumstances will you breathe a word of this to anyone," said President Delbert George.

Gunnar Godson held the plastic bag with the frozen night crawlers at his side. The red-faced George shook his long, thin finger in Gunnar's face.

"First," said George, "we don't know for sure that Cranberry Red was responsible for what happened here. Second, we've got too much money and too much of our reputation invested in Cranberry Red to put a hold on its development now."

"But, Dr. George," Gunnar persisted, "it is not ethical for us to sell Cranberry Red without further testing. I firmly believe that the spilled Cranberry Red likely caused these monstrous night crawlers." He spoke the words slowly and distinctly.

"I don't care what you believe," said George, raising his voice. "You say a word of this to anyone and you are fired. And if you say anything to the press, our lawyers will make sure that you are the one who gets the blame. Do you understand what I'm saying?"

"I . . . I hear you," said Gunnar. He hesitated before saying anything else, because he knew that his job hung by a slender thread. "Can you give me a month to do some further testing?" asked Gunnar, who refused to back down to his boss.

"No. No testing. We're harvesting Cranberry Red–treated cranberries right now at Johnson's bog. The berries will be on the market in two weeks. What you found here with these night crawlers is a fluke. Something else must have affected them."

"What if it is Cranberry Red?" asked Gunnar.

"Well, I say it's not. Our treated cranberries are going on the market, no matter what."

"If I find out for certain that Cranberry Red did it?"

"Dammit, Godson, aren't you listening? I don't want you fooling around with night crawlers. No testing. You got that?"

"It's not right," said Gunnar.

"Not *right*!" an angry George blurted out. "What's right got to do with it? We know these cranberries will prevent disease, big time. What the hell do we care if it might cause a night crawler to grow a little bigger? We're interested in helping human beings, helping people. Who the hell cares about a worm?"

Sara Phillips stared at the floor, Quinton Foley looked off in the distance, and President Delbert George, veins pulsing in his neck, continued to shake his finger in Gunnar Godson's face.

"You tell a living soul about this and you will be looking for work. Do you get that?"

"You are perfectly clear," said Gunnar.

"And for God's sake, don't tell this guy Ben Wesley. He's got a tough enough job convincing cranberry growers to buy Cranberry Red as it is. These cranberry growers like to do things like they always have. Wesley doesn't need this information. You hear me?"

"I hear you," said Gunnar.

The threesome stomped out of the laboratory, jumped in their car, and roared up the driveway. Gunnar Godson put the big night crawlers back in the freezer.

RFD Collapses

*O*n October 23 the *Ames County Argus* reported some unexpected news:

Harry Hopkins, executive director of the new Wisconsin RFD youth program, this week announced the program's suspension. The program became available to Ames County youth earlier this summer. RFD was designed to replace the much-loved 4-H program, which had been eliminated this past July 1 when the state legislature cut the budget and closed all the county agricultural agent offices.

Hopkins explained, "We simply were not able to enroll enough former 4-H members and other young people to provide the financial foundation we needed." Hopkins went on to say how much he regretted the decision to shut down the program, and how disappointed he was that Ames County youth would not have the opportunity to participate in such a noteworthy activity. He added, "Somehow, someway, our young people need to learn about self-sufficiency, respecting the land, and improving the environment." These three goals had been the centerpiece of the RFD program.

Clarence Cartwright, 42, Willow River, a one-time 4-H leader and father of three 4-H members, remarked, "After serving as a volunteer 4-H leader for ten years, and with my three kids in 4-H, I looked forward to the RFD youth program. But it was too expensive, and besides, my kids had been in the 4-H horse project and the 4-H beef project. As RFD members, these animal projects would not have been available."

Abigail Clarkson, 14, of Link Lake, said, "I had really begun to like RFD. I was signed up for the climate change project and we were learning lots of neat things. I'm sure sorry to see RFD disappear."

Jimmy Jones, 10, of rural Plainfield, added, "I'll sure miss RFD. This was the first time I had a chance to show something at the fair. I took my pet rabbit and I got a red ribbon. It was sure fun being at the fair."

Ben Wesley, former Ames County agricultural agent and county director of the former 4-H program, said, "Any time a youth program disappears, it's a loss to the young people and to the community. I am sorry to see RFD disappear. I was even sorrier to see the 4-H program closed down."

At the present time, no new youth programs for Ames County appear in the offing. A few people the *Argus* interviewed said they planned to protest the closing down of the former 4-H program, but no specific actions were noted.

46

Ben and Dr. Phillips

*H*ow does my schedule look today?" Ben asked when he arrived at his office and greeted Brittani. Over the past several weeks, Ben and Brittani had reached an unspoken truce. Neither of them said anything to the other about who was boss in the office, although the issue remained in the background of everything that went on. Ben did his job; Brittani did hers.

"Every hour filled this morning with appointments," Brittani said. "And you're booked for a noon lunch meeting with Dr. Phillips. She said she'd meet you at the Lone Pine restaurant."

"I didn't know anything about a meeting with Phillips," Ben sputtered.

"It's Dr. Phillips, Ben. Dr. Phillips." Brittani was smiling, as she had no great love for Sara Phillips, whom she considered pompous, arrogant, and way over her head in the job she had.

"Well, what does Dr. Phillips want?" Ben said with a sarcastic tone to his voice.

"She didn't say. She called late yesterday when you were out and asked for the time—so I penciled it in."

"So I should jump anytime the good doctor calls?"

"Ben, you are working for a business. You bet you jump when the good doctor calls. It's the way business works. You're in the pecking order; we're all in the pecking order. Somebody pecks on you, somebody pecks on me, somebody pecks on Dr. Phillips."

Ben let the statement pass. He wondered if Brittani had any idea where the phrase "pecking order" originated—with poultry, of course, where the pecking was literal. He walked into his office and prepared for his first appointment, a cranberry grower who had some questions about Cranberry Red. Though he didn't spend much time looking at the paperwork, Ben had noticed that when cranberry growers stopped by, they were billed at only half the rate as the other "customers," as Brittani liked to refer to them.

The morning passed quickly. After his last appointment, with a fellow east of town who wanted to establish a pick-your-own strawberry operation, Ben walked over to the Lone Pine restaurant.

"She's sitting in that back booth," Mazy said when he entered the place. She pointed with her order pad. The Lone Pine was nearly filled with customers, those who had come for lunch, and the ever-present retired men's coffee group that started drinking coffee around nine and most mornings stayed on until noon. Ben wondered if one day he might be part of such a group, something for geezers to do in the autumn days of their lives.

He walked past several people he knew, said hello, and moved to the back booth.

"Hello, Ben," said Dr. Sara Phillips. No smile, no handshake. "I haven't ordered yet."

"Hello," Ben replied as he slid into the booth opposite her and glanced at the menu. Phillips had an unopened leather-covered pad in front of her.

"What's good here these days?" she asked.

"Most everything. I like the Turkey BLT sandwich myself."

"How's the family?"

"Doing well."

"Your daughter is a pre-med student at UW–Madison, right? She like it?"

"I think so," said Ben. "She gets good grades, likes her professors, and she's made some good friends."

"That's the way it should be. What about your son, what was his name again?"

"It's Josh. He's going to the technical college in Wisconsin Rapids. Wants to be an auto mechanic."

"Nothing wrong with that. Sure can use some good mechanics these days. Cars have gotten so complicated. And your wife, Beth. How is she?"

"She's fine. Having a good time with her correspondence course at Osborne."

"We call them online courses these days, Ben. She's in our nurse-practitioner program, I believe."

"That's right. And loving every minute of it. Best thing to happen to her in a long time."

"Glad to hear that. Always good to hear about a happy customer. And you, Ben, how's the job going?"

"Pretty good," Ben said. He was wondering what Phillips wanted, and why she was asking all the questions.

"Just pretty good?"

"Some days better than others."

"And the not-so-good days, you want to tell me about them?" Phillips was all business, from her tone of voice to her body language.

"First off, there's never enough time."

"I know what you mean," responded Phillips. "That's a common problem in our business. We've all got to work on time management. Got to get the most out of every minute—I read that some place."

"It seems I'm booked for about every minute of every day. When am I supposed to have time to keep up with what's new in my field?" Ben said it a little louder than he intended.

"Takes a little getting used to, doesn't it?" she said. "One of the things you just have to learn how to adjust to."

"Not easy to do," replied Ben as he saw Mazy approaching, her pencil and order pad at the ready.

"What'll it be today?" she asked. "Kind of nice out, ain't it? Gotta take advantage of what's left of fall. Don't much like winter. Just too long."

"I'll take the turkey BLT and black coffee," said Phillips, "and put both of these on my check."

"Turkey BLT and black coffee for me, too," said Ben.

Mazy scratched something on her pad and left. Ben wondered how, in the midst of what appeared chaos at the restaurant at noon, Mazy seemed to keep it all together, remained friendly, and even had time to comment on the weather. Maybe he should use Mazy as a model and he wouldn't feel so stressed out most of the time.

"How are you and Brittani getting along?" Phillips asked.

"Well . . ." Ben hesitated. "We're getting along, sort of."

"Sort of?"

"Some days she drives me right up the wall," Ben admitted. As soon as the words left his mouth he wished he hadn't said them. They sounded too harsh, yet they had more than a little truth to them.

"How so?"

"I expect we are just two different personalities," Ben said. He was fidgeting with his spoon.

"Any problem with Brittani being office manager?"

"Brittani thinks she's the boss. Says she is in charge of everything that goes on in the office," Ben blurted out. He began to perspire.

"Ben, she *is* in charge of the office," Phillips said firmly.

"But, but . . . I thought I was in charge of the office."

"Ben, this shouldn't be something to get worked up about. You are the professional in the office. You're our research application specialist. We don't want you worrying about day-to-day office operations. That's Brittani's job."

"Oh," Ben said. Now he realized that it was Brittani who had called Dr. Phillips and asked if she would talk to Ben. Brittani was a manipulator, no question about it. And she was going to put Ben in his place, no matter what it took.

"Work on this, Ben. Let Brittani do her job. You do your job, okay?

"Okay," Ben said quietly.

"We've also got some other problems to talk about, Ben."

"Yes." Ben pushed himself back and sat up straight in the booth.

"Here're your orders," said Mazy, appearing out of the din in the restaurant. She placed a cup of coffee and a sandwich in front of each of them. "Anything else you need right now?" she asked.

"No, this should do it," said Phillips, who now opened the leather portfolio and glanced briefly at it. Mazy disappeared back into the crowd.

"Ben, this is a rather stressful time for Osborne University," Phillips said quietly.

"Stressful time?"

"I'm not able to share all the details, but we need all our employees doing their very best. As you know, the first Cranberry Red–treated cranberries come on the market later this month. We especially need your help right now, Ben."

"Doing what?"

"First, keep talking to the cranberry growers. Take time to visit them. Drive out to their cranberry marshes and talk to them about Cranberry Red. Here's one package of the treated cranberries you can show them."

Phillips reached into her briefcase and took out a one-pound plastic bag of fresh cranberries. In bold, green letters were the words "Healthy Always Cranberries."

"Take these cranberries with you, show them to cranberry growers, show them that they look no different from the cranberries they're growing now. But then explain that what's *inside* each berry is what's different. Tell them that these cranberries can, and will, save lives. Thousands of lives."

"Cranberry growers are asking hard questions about Cranberry Red," said Ben.

"Such as?"

"Well, they're a smart bunch of folks. And pretty darn practical, too. They want to see the research reports on how Cranberry Red increases antioxidant levels of cranberries. And they want cost-benefit figures. If they use Cranberry Red, how will it affect their bottom line?"

"Good questions. I'll see what I can do in pulling together some materials that you can give to the growers," said Phillips as she scratched some notes on her pad.

"Something else. Growers want to know about the side effects of Cranberry Red, any possible dangers in using it."

Sara Phillips hoped Ben didn't notice her reaction to his question, for she immediately thought about the grotesque night crawlers she had seen recently at the research station.

"Apparently none," she lied. She had remembered President George's admonition to not tell Ben anything about the night crawlers.

"Well, that's good," Ben replied. "Cranberry growers can't afford to have anything go wrong when they try something new. They're a cautious bunch, and I can't blame them." Ben paused for a moment before he asked the next question. "Seems like Cranberry Red is coming on the market awful fast after its development. Are we sure there's been enough testing?"

"There's been plenty of testing, Ben. Plenty of testing," Phillips responded. But she didn't sound as assured as she usually was. He'd long ago learned how to read people by paying attention to not only what they said but also their tone of voice and their body language. What was she not telling him?

After listening to Phillips, Ben wondered if he could come close to, or even wanted to mimic, his boss's passion for Cranberry Red and these newly treated cranberries. He had come to the lunch meeting expecting to be reprimanded for not having billed more hours, for not earning more money for the company, and what he was getting was a lesson in sales strategy. At this point Ben wondered if he would ever become a salesman. He had always considered himself a teacher, and yet he had often heard that teachers had to be salespeople, too. Unless people paid attention to what you were teaching, you didn't succeed. As a salesperson, unless you got people to listen to your sales pitch and accept what you were saying, they didn't buy your product. Ben was perplexed—just where did he fit in this teacher-salesperson dichotomy? If it was a dichotomy at all.

Healthy Always Cranberries

*B*en Wesley always liked October. But this year he was not enjoying the month at all. Each evening he arrived home from work exhausted. He had no time to gaze at the fall colors that were in full peak by midmonth and beginning to wane as the days ticked by. No time to go fishing with Lars Olson. Fishing in October, on a sunny warm afternoon, was usually outstanding, and besides, the fish bit more often than they did during the dog days of summer. It's not that he wasn't outdoors, because he had been driving from cranberry grower to cranberry grower throughout western Ames County, and into Wood, Portage, Adams, and even as far as Monroe County, where cranberry acreage had been expanding in recent years. He visited with cranberry growers, one after the other, without invitation. Sometimes he felt he was intruding, getting in the way. These October days were busy ones, as cranberry growers were in the midst of their fall harvest. But it had been his instruction from Dr. Phillips to talk with the growers, tell them about Cranberry Red, show them the treated cranberries, explain to them the tremendous health benefits of the new Healthy Always Cranberries brand. He handed out a recently printed Osborne publication that used a question-and-answer approach to Cranberry Red and its benefits.

The common response went something like this: "We'll wait to see how these Healthy Always Cranberries do on the market. We don't want to buy any of this Cranberry Red stuff and then be stuck with another cost and no return for our investment." That was the gist of what he heard and he heard it often. He would return home each evening totally spent, but not surprised at the growers' response. He had worked with cranberry growers in Ames County for twenty years. He knew them, knew their families, knew how they made decisions. They weren't going to jump at something new, something like Cranberry Red, until they knew a whole lot more about the product.

On his way home from the office one of these late October afternoons, Ben stopped at the Buy It Here grocery in Willow River, where his family had shopped for years. He couldn't miss the huge sign in the window. "Arrived today: HEALTHY ALWAYS CRANBERRIES. A new health food from the International Farm-Med Company and developed by Osborne University researchers. Cranberries with twice the health benefits of regular cranberries." Pictured was a cranberry bog, Ben couldn't recognize which one, with children holding a pail of cranberries and their smiling parents standing behind. Everyone the picture of good health.

When he stood in line to check out with his basket of purchases—a gallon of milk, a bag of lettuce, a loaf of bread, and some peach yogurt (low fat, Beth said to buy)—Ben saw people in line with bags of the new cranberries. The fact that the berries cost nearly twice as much as traditional cranberries didn't seem to deter them in the least. The store had earlier put a two-bag limit on purchases. With one or two exceptions, everyone in line had two bags.

On his way home from the store, Ben continued to wonder about these new cranberries and the possibility that they had been rushed to the market too quickly. He had been reminded by his superiors at Osborne University, more than once, that he was still thinking like a state university person. "Problem with those state universities," said Dr. Quinton Foley, and he said it often, "is they take way too long to share the results of their research with the public. By the time a state university's findings become available, most people have lost interest in what they were researching."

Ben knew better than to argue with Foley, but every time he heard Foley say something like this, he bit his tongue. Most new research findings deserve more time, more thought, and a lot more testing, was Ben's position. He wondered if maybe Cranberry Red and these newly treated cranberries shouldn't fall into that category.

Only a week later, the *Ames County Argus* began to receive letters applauding Osborne University and their new research product:

Dear Editor:

    I want you to know how wonderful these new Healthy Always Cranberries are. I began eating them the day I bought them, and I have never been more regular. For a long time I've had problems along these lines. No more.

Lizzy Hatliff

Link Lake

Dear Editor:

    I bought me some of these here new cranberries that are supposed to make old guys like me live longer. I only been eating them for a week, and you can't begin to know how good I feel. How young I feel. All of us older folks ought to fall on our knees and thank that Osborne University for what they come up with. Also, I'm gettin' all these benefits from these new cranberries and they don't taste no different than the other ones I been eatin'. Imagine that, a medicine that tastes good.

Ollie Winters, age 87

Link Lake

Ben Wesley chuckled when he read the letters. He wondered if Ms. Hatliff and Mr. Winters knew what the health benefits of Healthy Always Cranberries were supposed to be. And further, he wondered how much people in general really knew about the health benefits of regular cranberries, before they were treated with anything.

County Fair Eliminated

*O*n November 5, less than a month after the RFD program was suspended, the *Ames County Argus* published the following report:

> In a surprise move yesterday, the Ames County Fair board voted five to
> two to permanently eliminate the Ames County Fair. When asked why
> they had made such a radical and far-reaching decision, Ed Stormer, fair
> board president, said, "It's because the legislature voted out the county
> agricultural agent office and eliminated the 4-H program. The county
> agent's office essentially ran the fair. They managed the exhibits, found the
> judges, signed up the grandstand events, contracted with the carnival—
> they did it all and they did it well. And without 4-H members, what is
> there to exhibit? We have but a handful of adults entering in open class.
> It was the 4-H members who made the fair."
>
> The Ames County Fair was one of the oldest institutions in Ames
> County, going back to 1858. A county fair has been held every year
> since, although the fairgrounds, county-owned for many years, has ex-
> panded and the number of buildings increased as the fair grew larger.
> The Ames County Highway Department will take over the former fair-
> grounds and buildings and use the land and buildings for the storage of
> equipment.
>
> The *Argus* is inviting people with memories of the fair to submit
> their stories to the paper, maximum of 500 words. The *Argus* plans to
> publish a selection of the stories in an upcoming issue.

News of the fair's closing hit Ben Wesley hard. He had spent twenty years helping to build and improve the fair, from arguing for new, updated buildings to expanding the 4-H membership to assure high-quality exhibits for rural and city folks alike to enjoy. Ben and those in his office worked hard before, during, and after each fair, and some people criticized them for it. "Should be spending more of your time working with the people of Ames County," one critic had said.

Ben was convinced that the county fair was one of the best tools he had in his bag of teaching approaches. At the same time that they were having fun, 4-H members had their work compared to the work of other young people in the county, and they could see how to improve. A good judge who rated the various fair projects had an important teaching role, pointing out where a woodworking project could be improved, how a hem could be sewed straighter on a dress, why one cucumber exhibit was placed above another.

Beyond the young people learning, city folk learned too. They learned about farming and agriculture, they learned a little more about where their food comes from, and the challenges farmers faced these days.

A couple of weeks later, the *Argus* printed several stories of Ames County Fair memories:

When I enrolled in 4-H back in 1950, I couldn't wait for the fair to begin. I had a calf project, her name was Annie. I worked all summer trying to teach that balky animal how to lead. I wasn't very big then, and Annie had a mind of her own. She dragged me all around the yard more than once. Pa said, "Just hang on to that halter rope, no matter what," and that's what I did. You should have seen my bib overalls after one of those calf-leading attempts. Dirt from one end to the other. I wasn't so sure I even wanted to take Annie to the fair. The last thing I wanted was for the other kids to laugh at me when I couldn't put a stop to some of Annie's antics.

Pa said, "Be patient. Calves can be just like people. Stubborn and sometimes slow to learn. But often they learn more than you think, they just don't want you to know it."

County Fair Eliminated

Well, I guess that's what happened. From the time that Annie stepped off of Ross Caves's cattle truck and onto the fairgrounds in Willow River, she was a picture of good behavior. I couldn't believe it. Another kid in the cattle barn asked, "How'd you get your calf to lead so well?" I answered, "Took some time." I wasn't about to share all the times when I was ready to give up on Annie. At one time I told Pa that Annie was either too dumb or too stubborn to learn how to lead. He just laughed.

On judging day, when I got to lead my calf around in a circle in the show ring with a bunch of other calves, and a very serious cattle judge stood out in the middle of the ring, I was scared out of my wits. What if Annie decided to go charging off like she had been accustomed to doing, me dragging along behind? I would have been so embarrassed. But she didn't do that. She did everything I asked her to do. She walked with her head high. She stopped walking when I stopped walking. And do you know what? I won the showmanship award, which means my calf performed better in the ring than any of the others. It was one of my proudest days as a kid. Pa was proud, too. He stood at the edge of the judging ring, smiling from ear to ear. I knew he was happy for me and for Annie, too.

Emily Davies
Link Lake

I have one big memory of the first time I went to the Ames County Fair. If I remember right, it was 1946, right after the war. Pa helped organize the Chain O' Lakes 4-H club in our community. We named it after the one-room school that all the kids hereabouts attended. Most 4-H members had dairy projects—we lived on small dairy farms where we milked a dozen or so cows. I had a little bull calf for my project.

What I remember most about that first fair was something you just don't see happen very often, or maybe don't want to see happen. Those were the days when barnstorming pilots went from fair to fair and offered a ride in their airplane.

Well, I'd never seen a plane close up before. I saw it parked just beyond the cattle barn, in a field on the other side of the race track. It was red, a double-wing style with two open cockpits. After we'd cared for our calves, another kid and I walked over the plane, to look it over. See it up close.

The pilot, a guy I'd say was in his twenties, was leaning on the wing and smoking a cigarette. "You boys like a ride in my plane?" the fellow said. "See your farm from the air; check out Willow River like a bird does."

"What's it cost?" I asked.

"Fifty cents, that's all. And I'll give you a half-hour ride." When I heard the price of a ticket, my heart sank. I only had a couple of dollars to last me the entire four days of the fair. Pa would have had a fit if he knew I'd spent fifty cents on an airplane ride.

While we were standing there, another fellow marches up, hands the pilot fifty cents, and before you knew it, that big red plane came to life. It made a heckuva racket. Well, the pilot drove his plane down to the far end of the field—it was somebody's cow pasture—and that plane seemed to shake with excitement as it roared even louder and came tearing down the field right past where my friend and I stood.

I don't know what happened, but the wheels of the plane struck the wire fence at the end of the pasture. Fence posts and tangled wire flew, but the plane didn't. It dumped head first into the ground, smashing the propeller and denting the front end of the machine something fierce.

Several others saw the accident, and we all ran over to the crippled plane, which had a little plume of smoke coming from the dead engine. The pilot crawled out of the cockpit and gingerly stepped down from the wing. I noticed that his nose was bleeding. The passenger crawled out of the front cockpit as well. He looked shaken, white as a sheet.

"Do I get my fifty cents back?" he muttered to the bleeding pilot. The pilot didn't answer.

Well, that's one thing I remember about the fair. I got lots more of these stories.

Trig Sorenson
Pine River

While Ben sat reading the county fair stories in the *Argus*, thinking about all the tales he had about the Ames County Fair, he heard a commotion in the outer office. He overhead Brittani saying, "You can't go in there without an appointment. Give me your name and I'll put you down. I have something tomorrow afternoon at three."

"I don't care what you've got at three; I want to see Ben Wesley right now. That's why I drove all the way over here."

"Sorry," Brittani said. She had a way of saying "sorry" that made most folks want to grab her by her skinny neck and shake her.

Hearing the give and take in the outer office and recognizing Joe Evans's voice, Ben walked to the outer office.

"Ben, just the man I'm looking for," Joe said, lowering his voice. "Can we talk for a few minutes?"

"Sure, come in the office," said Ben.

"You'll be late for your next appointment, Ben," Brittani said, not too politely.

"Tell them to cool their heels," Ben replied.

Ben and Joe entered Ben's office. Ben closed the door.

"That secretary of yours is something else," Joe said.

"A little too caught up with keeping me on time," Ben responded, forcing a smile. "What can I do for you?"

"It's about the fair closing down," Joe said. "Why'd that happen? You in on it, Ben?"

"Nope. Since they closed my previous office, I've had nothing whatever to do with the fair. Not a thing, except for sitting at a little booth during fair week last summer."

"I tell you, Ben. Those of us small farmers have had a tough go of it for a long time now, and then this. First they close your office. Then they eliminate 4-H. This Osborne outfit thinks they can do what your old office did. Well, they can't. Not for us little guys anyway. We can't afford you, Ben. We just can't. The big guys can. Who needs your help most—it's guys like me. Families that are struggling to make a go of it."

Ben listened to what he already knew. How many times in the last few months had he heard from his old friends, people who he had been working with for ten, sometimes twenty years? People who wanted him to work with them, but didn't have the money to pay for his workshops, or have him stop out at their farms. He didn't keep count, but it had been dozens.

"This is the last straw. Closing down the Ames County Fair," said Joe.

"Osborne University had nothing to do with closing down the fair."

"Oh, I know that, Ben. And I know you didn't either. But I had to talk to somebody. Somebody who'd take time to listen."

"There's nobody sorrier about losing the fair than I am," said Ben.

"I guess I know that too," replied Joe. "I apologize for using up some of your time."

"Joe, any time you want to talk, you call me or you stop in. I'll find time to talk. And you won't be charged for it, either."

"You sure?" said Joe, smiling.

"I'm sure," said Ben. The two old friends shook hands and Joe left the office.

"I've written down the time," Brittani said. "Your next appointment called and will be a little late."

"No charge for my time with Mr. Evans," Ben said.

"It's already in the computer."

"Well, take it out," Ben said firmly.

"Can't, the record is already in Oshkosh."

"You figure out a way of getting rid of those charges, young lady, or you'll be looking for another job."

Brittani didn't say anything. She immediately picked up her phone.

Beth Wins Osborne Award

After the initial hullabaloo about the Cranberry Red–treated cranberries, Ben's office returned to some degree of normalcy, although Ben had yet to decide what normal operations might be. It seemed there was always some crisis to contend with. If it wasn't something that Brittani had said to someone that ticked them off, it was the constant reminder from Osborne's business office that their earnings weren't what was expected of them.

Ben counted one minor success. He did not hear from Joe Evans that he had been charged for their brief office conversation. On the downside, Brittani barely spoke to him after he threatened to fire her. Nonetheless, she kept a constant vigil on Ben's billable hours and continued to send out invoices and evoke the wrath of his clients.

Slowly, it seemed to Ben at least, the people in Ames County were beginning to understand that if they wanted help from Ben Wesley, it would cost them money. Of course, some never accepted that reality. For them, Ben would always be their ag agent and his services free. Brittani had an uncanny ability to schedule these people on Ben's calendar, and after Ben had met with them and they received their bill, they hit the roof. Just last week a big, burly beef farmer from Link Lake had an hour-long appointment to talk about how to improve the quality of his cattle feed. He and Ben had chatted for no more than a half hour. Ben had even sold him a bulletin on beef cattle management for five dollars, which he didn't mind paying. But when he got the bill that charged him "One hour consulting time—$100," he blew his cork. He came stomping into the office waving the bill in his hand.

"Ben, what the hell is this all about? You charged me a hundred bucks for a half-hour conversation and ten minutes of that time we talked about the weather."

Ben tried to explain that everyone was charged for at least one hour, no matter how long they spent in Ben's office or he spent at their farm.

"Ben, it just ain't right," the man argued. "You got to do something about this or none of us is gonna darken this damn outreach office door again." He stormed out of the office, still waving the charge statement in his hand.

"What was that about?" Brittani asked, after the man had slammed the outside door.

"Another billing problem," Ben replied. " We've got to do something about this."

"Nothing we can do," Brittani said with her all-knowing tone of voice. "Billing procedure is written right here in the rule book. Black and white. Nothing to change."

Ben decided that one of these days he needed to visit the business office in Oshkosh and try to explain that for folks out here in the country not everything is so cut and dried. Country people aren't accustomed to all this timekeeping. For many of them, it's why they live in the country and why they try to make a living farming. They don't do their work by the hour; they do it according to what needs to be done. Sometimes that means spending a long day on a project, even several days. Other times, a project may take only a few minutes.

When Ben arrived home that early December evening, he had a headache, something he never had when he worked under the old county agricultural agent system. He kept reminding himself that he must learn how to adapt to his new job. He was trying, but he never realized how difficult it would be. Beth greeted him with a big smile and a kiss.

"Guess what I found out today, Ben," she said. Ben couldn't remember when he had seen her happier.

"I've won Osborne's Outstanding Returning Student Award."

"The what?"

"Osborne University's Outstanding Returning Student Award. They've invited me to attend graduation ceremonies in Oshkosh to receive the award. It's a big deal."

"Well, good for you, Beth. I know you've been working hard."

"It's such a good program, Ben. I do everything right here on the computer. And I've been able to fit my studies around my job, too. When I have a question, I send an e-mail. When I want a repeat of a lecture, I can get that. I can study at night, early in the morning, anytime I want. It's just the best way to learn."

"I'm glad for you, Beth. Computers and I just don't get along that well."

"You're never too old to learn," Beth said, smiling.

"I'm not so sure about that. Computers give me fits."

"Come on now, Ben. Computers, for heaven's sake, are here to stay."

"Doesn't mean I have to be comfortable with them."

"Well, you should be. Just look how easy it is to learn in front of a computer screen."

"Easy for you to say," Ben said with a grin. He was headed for the fridge and a cold bottle of Spotted Cow.

Ben knew better than to say what he was thinking. He knew the power of computers and he knew how important they were for businesses, for educational institutions, for just about everyone. But he knew from experience, especially when teaching, how important it was from time to time to talk with people face to face, to watch their expressions, to see what they did with their hands, to capture the tone of their voice—all these responses told Ben something about how they were reacting to his suggestions, how they were dealing with his questions, how they were wrestling with what they already knew in contrast to another way of approaching a problem.

He wondered how much of this kind of interaction Beth was missing in her computer-based educational program. Obviously she was learning, and having a good time doing it. He began to wonder if his ideas about face-to-face learning were no longer important, that the allure and convenience of computer-learning had pushed his ideas into history.

He took a long drink from his beer and opened his newspaper. Recently he heard that newspapers, too, would disappear and that he'd be reading his news on some kind of screen. What was the world coming to anyway?

Part 6

50

Fred and Oscar

Since their confrontation with the big, mean fish back in the spring, Fred Russo and Oscar Anderson had avoided fishing the Tamarack River. That summer they fished a number of lakes in Ames County—Round Lake, Long Lake, Silver Lake, Marl Lake, Pearl Lake, and several others. But with the coming of winter, they decided to return to the Tamarack, as they had done for many winters. In one of the backwater areas of Tamarack, where the current was mostly nonexistent, the water froze early, providing support for a village of fish shanties that appeared each year.

One of those shanties belonged to Oscar and Fred. They had built it out of scrap lumber they found around their farms, and named the little building "Escape." It wasn't much to look at and it surely would not win any competition when put up against its neighbors on the Tamarack backwater ice. Several shanties boasted propane heaters, two or three had TV sets, and one even had a bar. One, painted a bright purple, had enough room for four fishermen inside—Oscar and Fred dubbed it the party house. And that's what it appeared to be, for they saw mostly beer cans piled up outside the door and few fish.

"Escape" served its purpose. It provided just enough room for Fred and Oscar. They sat side by side on a bench nailed across one end of the shanty, with two trapdoors in the floor that stood over fish holes drilled in the ice. In one corner stood a little sheet-metal stove that some blacksmith had made fifty or more years ago, with a thin stovepipe stuck through the roof

215

of the structure. Fred and Oscar had put in large windows on three sides of the shanty so they could see what their neighbors were doing, and if the day was pleasant, they might drill a hole in the ice outside the shanty and put out a tip-up, a self-standing device that had one end in the icy water and the other end thrusting upward, with a little flag that flew up if something took the bait.

"Sure a nice day," Oscar remarked as he held his fishing rod and stared into the hole in the ice.

"Yup, it is that," said Fred. "You bring along any of that venison sausage for your lunch?"

"Got a whole stick right here in my lunch pail," replied Oscar. "Brought along enough for both of us. Lunch time, I'll heat us up some on our stove. You got any of that good bread from the Link Lake Bakery?"

"Got her right here," said Fred. "We're gonna eat high on the hog today."

"Fish sure ain't doin' much. Ain't had so much as a nibble," Oscar said as he lifted his fishing rod enough to see if the minnow was still in place. "How's the fire doin'?"

With his gloved hand, Fred opened the door of the little sheet-metal stove and stuffed in a couple of sticks of oak wood that he'd brought along from home. A puff of oak smoke filled the little shack.

The two old fishermen sat quietly for a time, each wrapped up in his thoughts as he peered into the depths of the Tamarack River. They enjoyed each other, whether they were talking or not. Just having the other there was enough.

"You remember that big northern you caught last spring?" Oscar asked.

"Can't forget that bugger. Not only was he big, but he was mean."

"Yup, mean as hell he was," Ben said.

"You gettin' hungry?" Oscar asked, glancing toward his lunch pail.

"Yeah, I am," said Fred. "You wanna heat up some of that venison sausage?"

Fred reached for the cast-iron skillet that had a permanent place on a nail driven into the side of the fish shanty. He placed the skillet on the little woodstove while Oscar unpacked the stick of sausage and, using his

216

big hunting knife, cut off a half dozen thick slices and placed them in the old, well-seasoned frying pan.

The meat was soon sizzling, filling the fish shanty with delightful smells of seasoned sausage. Fred sliced some bread, smeared a layer of butter on the thick pieces, and with the tip of his knife speared a couple of pieces of sausage and made a sandwich for himself and for Oscar.

From a big thermos, Oscar poured a steaming cup of coffee for each of them. The two friends sat enjoying their sandwiches, appreciating the nice day and not much concerned that the fish weren't biting. They had each placed their fishing rods on the floor of the ice shanty, neither paying much attention to them, as they had not had a bite all morning.

"Hey, Oscar," called out Fred. His mouth was full of sandwich. "You better grab your fish pole or it's goin' down the hole."

Oscar reached for his soon-to-disappear fishing rod, spilling his coffee and dropping the remains of his venison sandwich on the floor. He caught the end of the handle just before it disappeared.

"Geez, I got one on," said Oscar. "Feels like a lunker from the way he's pulling."

"Let him have some line, let him have some line," suggested Fred.

Line stripped out of the reel and then it stopped.

"Set the hook and bring him in," Fred advised.

Oscar gave a tug on the line and then began reeling as quickly as he could.

"He's comin' our way," Oscar said excitedly. "He's comin' our way."

Oscar reeled as fast as he could crank the reel, taking up the slack in the line. "Wonder if he spit the hook."

"Just keep reelin'," said Fred. "You'll find out soon enough."

Oscar continued cranking rapidly. Sweat appeared on his forehead.

"He's still on," Oscar said. "I've got him comin' through the hole."

An enormous northern pike shot up through the fish hole into the tiny fishing shanty, as if it had been propelled by some mysterious underwater force. The giant fish began flopping all around the tiny space.

"Hit him in the head with something!" Oscar shouted.

"With what?"

"Use the skillet. Hit him with the skillet."

Fred began swinging the big cast-iron skillet at the fish, but couldn't connect. The second time he tried, he missed and accidentally struck the reel on his fishing pole, smashing it to pieces.

"Damn!" exclaimed Fred. "Smashed my new reel all to hell."

The big fish continued flopping, its tail striking the small woodstove and tipping it over, spilling hot coals on the floor of the little building. Immediately the fish shanty was on fire, flames shooting up the side of the wooden structure.

"To hell with the fish," said Fred. "Let's get outta here." The two scrambled toward the tiny door, their eyes smarting from the smoke of their burning fish shanty.

Fred and Oscar stood outside watching the shanty burn as other fishermen gathered to stare. Some fishermen were chuckling. It wasn't every day that someone set his fish shanty on fire, as most of the group believed had happened.

The group included Billy Baxter from the *Argus*, who was doing a story on ice fishing.

"What happened here?" Billy inquired.

"Big northern did it," said a stunned Oscar. "Big northern tipped over our stove."

"Where's the fish?" asked Billy.

"Cooked, I suppose," said Fred.

"No sign of a fish, alive or cooked," said Billy. "You sure that's what happened?"

"That's what happened," said Oscar.

The next edition of the *Ames County Argus* carried a brief mention of the event:

Ice Fishing Shanty on Tamarack River Burns

Longtime fishermen Fred Russo, 84, and Oscar Anderson, 86, lost their fish shanty to fire last Tuesday. Fishing on the Tamarack River, they claim to have hooked a giant northern pike that they pulled through the ice.

Fred and Oscar

They said that when they were unable to subdue the big fish, it tipped over a stove, which led to the shanty burning. No evidence of a fish was discovered.

51

Phillips and
the Outreach Office

*B*en enjoyed Christmas week. It was his first vacation since taking his new job back in July, and he appreciated not having to deal with a constant flow of problems and questions associated with his new office. Both kids were home from college, and both had done well during the fall semester; Ben was proud of them and he told them so.

Josh had one more year in his program at Mid-State Technical College. Beth had slowly accepted that there was nothing wrong with studying to become an auto mechanic, which was Josh's first love. He had tinkered with everything from an alarm clock he took apart when he was five years old to their old power lawnmower, which he overhauled last summer.

Liz, despite some excessive partying her first two years, still got good grades and now was settling down and focusing on her studies and career. It looked promising that she'd be accepted into medical school.

Beth had hung her Outstanding Returning Student Award plaque on the hallway wall for all who came into the Wesley home to see.

"Way to go, Mom," she had heard from both of her kids when they saw the award.

"Didn't know you were such a computer whiz," said Liz, who knew from her mother's weekly phone conversations what was involved when you enrolled in a degree program at Osborne University.

"Now we've got to work on Dad," said Josh. Both of Ben's kids knew of their dad's reluctance to learn much about computers, beyond reading his e-mail.

"Looks like Mom is ahead of you, Dad," Liz joked.

"Seems so," said Ben, not in the least bothered by his kid's ribbing about his inadequate computer skills.

Ben was scheduled to return to work January 5—to begin a new year, one, he hoped, better than the one just past. The biggest disappointment for Ben, beyond losing his job, was the closing down of the long-standing Ames County Fair. He simply couldn't believe that the county fair had been eliminated. On the upside, he had a job, a decent-paying one. And his rocky relationship with Beth had improved in recent months with his new job, and with her enrollment in Osborne's nurse-practitioner program. During the last couple of months he didn't hear her complain once about his work, or about living way back here "in the sticks," as she had commonly called Ames County. In fact, she proudly shared information with her friends and coworkers at Ames Memorial Hospital about the important position her husband held with "that prestigious Osborne University."

As Ben's country friends often told him, "Things could be worse." Of course they could be better, too. For the past several weeks, Ben had hated going to work. Hated facing the ever-present Brittani, the picture of computer savvy and office arrogance. One of his goals for the new year was to figure out what to do with her.

Ben continued questioning whether Osborne's limited research findings from Cranberry Red warranted as much publicity and promotion as he was asked to give this new "miracle discovery," as Osborne officials described it.

The first Monday morning of the new year, Brittani greeted him with "Just got a call from Dr. Phillips in Oshkosh." No "Happy New Year." No "How did your vacation go?" No small talk, only business. That was Brittani.

"What'd she want?" Ben had come to dread any communication with Oshkosh; it usually meant some kind of reprimand.

"She's coming over this afternoon. Wants to meet with both of us."

"About what?"

"She didn't say, but she sounded serious."

"She usually is," Ben said, not looking forward to the meeting.

Promptly at one, Sara Phillips strode into the office. She wore her usual formal business suit and carried a slim, brown leather briefcase.

"Good afternoon, Brittani," she said. Her voice was all business. "Let's meet in Ben's office."

"You want me in the meeting, too?" Brittani asked. She wondered if she had earlier heard correctly that Phillips wanted to meet with both of them.

"Indeed I do," replied Phillips. "And please place the 'closed' sign in the door window, and turn off the outer office light."

Brittani did as instructed and joined Phillips in Ben's office. Ben had taken his place at the side of the little conference table. Dr. Phillips greeted Ben and then sat at the end of the table. "Sit over here," Phillips said to Brittani, "across from Ben."

Ben felt a burning sensation in his stomach, a symptom he had noticed lately when he faced a stressful situation.

"I don't want to mince any words," Phillips began. "I am extremely disappointed with both of you."

The room was filled with silence.

"I want this new year to be a better year, a lot better than the past six months," Phillips continued.

"So do I," blurted out Brittani.

"Let me do the talking, please," said Phillips. "First, you two have got to get along. All I hear is bickering. Petty disagreement. Problems with billing. Overcharging. Not following the rules. One thing and another." Phillips made a sweeping motion with her arm.

"I follow the rules," said Brittani. She began to fidget in her chair.

"Brittani," Phillips scolded. "Let me finish."

"And this business of who is boss. For heaven's sake, you two act like a couple of kids. Neither one of you is the boss. If you need to worry about a boss, look in this direction. I'm in charge of this office. Or to look at it another way, both of you are in charge. The two of you have to work as a team to make this office work. Does that make sense?"

"It does," said Ben quietly.

"But . . . but I thought I was office manager," argued Brittani.

"You are," said Phillips. "But that doesn't mean you are in charge of the place. You're not Ben's boss. And Ben, Brittani tells me you threatened to fire her. You can't do that. You can't fire her. Only I can do that."

"Oh," Ben replied. In his previous position as county agricultural agent he was responsible for the hiring and, yes, firing of the administrative staff, if it became necessary.

"Are you both clear about what I just said?"

"I am," said Ben, somewhat relieved to have the air cleared about these matters.

"But . . . but," sputtered Brittani.

"But what?" said Phillips, staring icily at her office manager. "Get used to it, Brittani. This is the way it's going to be. Coworkers. Not one in charge of the other."

Brittani looked down at the table in front of her.

"A couple of other procedural things. Ben, I want you to review every billing invoice before it's sent to Oshkosh. Make adjustments if you think necessary, but include the reasons. Of course you will do this on your computer."

"But, I'm not really very good with computers," Ben said, more meekly than he had intended.

"I know that," said Phillips, smiling. This was the first time she had smiled during the entire meeting. "I've taken the liberty of signing you up for an online course on computer operations, Ben. You can work on it at night, on weekends, whenever you can find some time. There's no excuse for not having a working knowledge of computers."

Again there was silence in the room.

"Okay, what questions do you have?" said Phillips, looking at Ben and Brittani in turn.

"I think I've got it," replied Ben.

"Can I talk with you in private?" said Brittani.

"No, you cannot. Whatever question you have for me, Ben should hear. If you're going to work as a team, you've got to share things with each other. You got that, Brittani?"

"I . . . I guess I do."

"All right. Let's get back to work. This is going to be a busy year, and an exciting one as well, with Cranberry Red coming out."

Dr. Phillips stood up and left. No handshakes, no further words.

Both Ben and Brittani sat looking at each other, each somewhat stunned by what they had just heard.

"Happy New Year," Ben said. Brittani didn't answer.

52

Chris Martin

*B*en noticed several changes in Brittani since the meeting with Phillips on the first working day of the new year. Once or twice a week she arrived late, sometimes more than fifteen minutes. She seemed less zealous about keeping Ben's schedule filled with appointments, and for whatever reason, she had begun being more civil toward him, with questions such as "How you doing today, Ben?" and "How's the computer course going?" The last comment she made with a big grin on her face. Then just the other day she said, "Tell you what, Ben, you get stuck with something in that computer course, let me know. Maybe I can help you out."

"Thank you, Brittani," Ben responded. "I appreciate the offer."

As it was, Ben found himself almost enjoying the computer course. Now, for the first time he was learning to work his way through Internet searches, how to "Google," as Brittani called such work. Although he didn't say so to Beth, who continued gushing about her Internet degree program, Ben's impression of Osborne's courses had increased by several notches. The course he was taking was well organized, thorough, and offered ample opportunity to ask questions via e-mail and have the answer within a short time. The course he took was especially designed for Osborne employees, so a considerable amount of time was spent on such things as reporting project times, billable hours—the kinds of things his office was required to do.

During the last couple of weeks, he asked Brittani if she would have time to discuss computer reporting with him, and the two of them had spent more than an hour doing so on two different occasions.

"Brittani, the billing schedule for farmers must have some flexibility," Ben explained.

"But, Ben, you know the rules. They're all laid out for us."

"Tell you what; let's see if we can change some of these rules."

"Change the rules? Nobody can change Osborne's rules," Brittani said somewhat dejectedly.

"What do you say we give it a try? Start small. Ask that the minimum charge time be a half hour rather than an hour. For some folks a half hour is all the time they need with us."

After their discussions, the two of them agreed to petition Osborne's business office in Oshkosh for a rule change—that a half hour rather than an hour be the minimum billable time. They also asked that the first visit, whether it be in the office, over the phone, via e-mail, or to the client's home, be free.

"Doesn't hurt to ask," Ben said. Both he and Brittani put their names on the request.

Three days later, they simultaneously received brief e-mail messages from Oshkosh:

Recent request for billing rule modification. Approved.
Joe Schneider, Business Manager

"Well, what do you think of this?" Ben said when he walked out to Brittani's desk, where she had just finished reading the same message.

"Guess it doesn't hurt to ask," she replied, smiling broadly.

That simple rule change, along with Ben's opportunity to make adjustments in hours billed based on circumstances, eased some of the conflict with clients, although a good many of them still considered his services too expensive and after their first visit, he didn't see or hear from them again.

On this particular mid-February day, business at the Osborne University Outreach Office had nearly ground to a stop. A snowstorm had blown in from the southwest, one of those moisture-laden storms that roared out of Iowa, spread up into Wisconsin, and then collided with a blast of cold air that drifted down from Canada. The storm dumped several inches of heavy, wet snow that clogged highways, hung on the bare branches of the trees, and painted a classic picture of winter all over Ames County. The snowmobilers loved it. The one ski hill in the county depended on such storms. And the children of Ames County gleefully listened to their radios and watched their TV sets for news of school closings. They were not disappointed. Snowmen appeared on front lawns in Willow River. The sledding hill on the edge of the Willow River Golf Course was clogged with sleds, tubes, toboggans, and plastic saucers of various colors. It was a day of celebration. A day to commemorate winter. One of the reasons people lived in Wisconsin.

For the adults, it was a day for slowing down, perhaps not going to work, but if you did, when you got there you did what you hadn't had time to do before the storm rolled in and reminded everyone that Mother Nature was really in charge of what went on in central Wisconsin, especially in winter.

Both Ben and Brittani lived close enough to their office that they could walk. Brittani, who had gotten new cross-country skis for Christmas, skied to the office. Ben pulled on his four-buckle boots and walked through the snow, enjoying every difficult step of the way.

Brittani had arrived before Ben and greeted him with "Ben, is that you? It looks like a snowman coming through the door."

Ben took off his down parka and shook off the snow. "What a great day it is," he said. "I'm not going anywhere. Good day to catch up on office work."

"You had two farm visits scheduled for this afternoon. I've already cancelled both of them," Brittani said.

"Thank you," said Ben. He decided to complete a couple of late reports, sort through the inventory of bulletins the office had for sale, and, perhaps, find a little time to finish off the computer course. The beauty of an Internet course was he could work on it anywhere a computer was handy.

Ben was busy reading the online Osborne employee manual for information about how to do a particular required report when he heard a voice in the outer office. He'd been so engrossed he hadn't heard the outer door open.

"Geez, is this a snowy one or what?" he heard someone say. "Is this Ben Wesley's office?"

It was a man's voice, a younger man from the way it sounded.

"Yes, it is," Brittani replied. When Brittani wanted to, she could exude charm. This was one of those times.

"Well, my name's Chris and I'd like to talk to him. Someone told me there would be a charge. How much might that be?"

"No charge for the first visit," Brittani responded, now really pouring on the charm.

"Name is Chris Martin," the young man said when he met Ben in his office. "I'm Hoak Martin's son; we live just beyond Link Lake."

"Sure, I know you. You were in 4-H, weren't you?"

"I sure was. A fun time."

"How's your dad doing? Haven't seen him in a couple years."

"He's had some health problems. He's in his seventies, you know. He and my mother moved into town last fall."

"And what about you? I can't remember when I last saw you. You were just a kid leading a little Holstein calf around the show ring at the county fair."

Chris laughed. He was tall, with short-cropped black hair and brown eyes. He sat ramrod straight in the chair. "I got back from Iraq last November, my second tour of duty and my last. I've had about all that I can take."

"Iraq, huh," said Ben.

"I enrolled in ROTC in college, got my commission, and then thought I'd make a career of the military. I was in the Transportation Corps—thought that would be interesting, and safer. It was, until those bastards started setting up roadside bombs. They killed as many truck drivers as they did infantry."

"So I heard," said Ben.

"But enough war talk. I'm out of the army now and I plan to take over Dad's farm, except I want to grow vegetables, set up a roadside stand, sell at the farmers' market, that sort of thing. And I want to grow organically. I've seen too much of chemicals, heard too much about chemical warfare."

"Well, good for you, Chris. We've got a sizable group of growers like you, some of them organic, some of them using limited pesticides, all wanting to sell locally."

"Can you help me get started? I haven't got much money—saved a little when I was in the service. I do have the farm. Dad said it would be mine when he and my mother passed on."

"First thing I would recommend is that you join the Ames County Fruit and Vegetable Growers Cooperative. Here's Curt Evans's phone number; he's the new president. They've got about twenty-five members and are getting bigger every year."

"I'll do it," Chris said. "And what about you? Dad said you know more about vegetable and fruit growing around here than almost anybody."

Ben laughed. "I doubt that," he said. "But I'll help when I can. As Brittani may have told you, I have to charge you for my services these days."

"She didn't, but I heard that from someone else. How much?"

"One hundred dollars an hour," replied Ben, who wished he didn't have to charge young fellows like Chris Martin a nickel. To Ben's way of thinking, guys like Chris Martin were the future of agriculture, especially in an area like Ames County, where fruits and vegetables grew well and markets were not far away.

"Well, that's the way it is, I guess. You want something, you have to pay for it," said Chris.

"I can sell you a bulletin for ten dollars that includes a lot of what I would tell you." Ben got up and walked to the bulletin rack, where he pulled out a copy of "Fruit and Vegetable Growing in Ames County" and handed it to be Chris. "I wrote this a couple of years ago so most of the information is current."

"I'll take it," Chris said, pulling a ten-dollar bill from his pocket.

"Pay Brittani on your way out."

"I will. By the way, is that secretary of yours married?"

"Brittani, our office manager? Nope, Brittani is very much single," Ben said, smiling.

53

Secret Meeting

*W*hat was that fellow's name?" Brittani asked after the tall, dark, and ramrod straight visitor left the office.

"It's Chris, Chris Martin. He grew up over by Link Lake; his dad is Hoak Martin. He just got out of the army, back from Iraq, and wants to take up farming."

"Oh," said Brittani. It was not like her to inquire about clients; usually she treated them as so many potential billable hours, possible bulletin buyers, and maybe participants in a workshop.

"He didn't mention a follow-up appointment. He say anything to you, Ben?"

"Only that he didn't think he could afford me," Ben said.

"Lot of that going around, isn't there?" said Brittani.

Ben glimpsed Brittani reaching for the Link Lake phone book while he thumbed through the mail that had just arrived.

"Martin is the last name," Ben said with a smile.

Ben had never seen Brittani blush before.

*A*t home that night, Ben received a phone call.

"It's Slogum," the voice said.

"Shotgun, how the heck are you? Making it through the winter okay?"

"I am," said Shotgun. "Kinda like winter. Gives me some time to meditate, read a few books, strap on my snowshoes and appreciate the snow."

"Sure wish I had time for that sort of stuff."

"Say, Ben, the reason I'm callin'—and before I go on, this is totally off the record, one friend to another. Nothin' to do with Osborne University or the outreach office."

"Okay," Ben said, now wondering what all the mystery was about.

"Well, here's the way it is," began Shotgun. "You know a bunch of us smaller guys in the business ain't too taken with what Osborne's chargin' for your services."

"Sure wish I didn't have to do it," Ben said quietly.

"Ain't your fault, Ben. We all know that. We also know you gotta have a job, gotta make a livin'. All of us gotta make a livin'."

There was a brief silence on the line. Ben could hear Shotgun breathing.

"Do you suppose, Ben?" Shotgun hesitated, then continued. "Do you suppose you could come out to my farm, next week, say Wednesday night?"

"I expect I could do that, Shotgun. Provided we don't have a snowstorm."

"Ben, I'd sure appreciate it. Be doin' a bunch of us a favor."

"Who you talking about, Shotgun?"

"I'm talking about the co-op. I've invited the board of directors to come out, too."

"Anything I should prepare for?" Ben asked.

"Nope. Don't prepare. Just come. And don't tell nobody. You okay with that? Big thing to ask. We don't wanna get you in trouble. Don't want Osborne to find out."

"Deal," said Ben. He found himself looking forward to this meeting more than just about anything he had done in the past several months. And, he had to admit to himself, he rather looked forward to slipping something past Osborne University.

"Got to drive out to Slogum's place tonight," Ben said to Beth at the dinner table. "I should be back before eleven."

"What in the world you driving way out to Slogum's for in February?" Beth asked. She always wanted to know Ben's whereabouts. It was part of her nature, or perhaps a reflection of her insecurity. But on the plus side, if something ever happened to him, Beth would know where he was.

"Don't know what he wants, he didn't say exactly—sounded important though." Ben didn't mention anything about the growers co-op; if he had, Beth would have asked more questions. And he didn't mention that he should keep the meeting secret either, that would surely have triggered questions.

The late February night was cold, the temperature hanging right around ten degrees, and the moon was bright. It was one of those winter nights that had a mystical feel to it, with moonlight filtering through the bare tree limbs and casting blue shadows on the snowplow-created snowbanks that lined the roads. Over the years, Ben had driven the road to Shotgun Slogum's place more times than he could remember, and he always enjoyed the trip, no matter what season of the year. He especially enjoyed the ride in winter. There was essentially no traffic; the world was gray and white, broken by the occasional green of the pine windbreaks that surrounded most farmsteads.

Arriving at Shotgun's farm, Ben parked his car near three others and walked the short distance to his friend's kitchen door and rapped. He stamped his feet on the porch to remove the snow while he waited for a reply.

"Come in, Ben. Come in; a bit nippy out there tonight," Shotgun said as he opened the door. The two old friends shook hands after Ben removed his gloves and stuffed them in the pockets of his parka. "I'm glad you could come."

Ben looked around the room. Several people sat at the kitchen table, drinking coffee and eating store-bought cookies.

"Ben," Shotgun began. "I think you know all these folks. They're the new board of directors for the Ames County Fruit and Vegetable Growers Cooperative. This is Curt Evans, our new president."

"Hi, Curt," said Ben. Ben had earlier heard that he had been elected the group's president. Curt was Joe Evans's younger brother.

"And this is Wanda Klusinski, the group's new secretary-treasurer."

"You're John Klusinski's daughter, aren't you?"

"You've got a good memory, Ben," the young woman responded.

"I remember you when you were about this tall," said Ben as he gestured, smiling.

"Finally," Shotgun said, "this fellow over here, this shy one who doesn't do much more than drink coffee and eat cookies, is Clyde Mueller. You know him, of course."

"Clyde, how are you?" Ben said, smiling. He remembered helping Curt set up his pick-yourself strawberry-raspberry project several years ago. In fact Curt, along with Shotgun, had been instrumental in establishing the highly successful Ames County Farmers' Market.

"You like some coffee, Ben?" Shotgun asked.

"Sure would," Ben said. He wondered what this group of quite successful fruit and vegetable growers wanted with him on this cold winter night, and as someone might say at a place that's about as far from civilization as you could get.

Shotgun, who had helped Ben organize the cooperative and had served as its first president, began. "We've been talking," he said. "The board and several more co-op members. We've been sayin' how much we miss the workshops you used to put on for us every year."

"I miss doing those, too," said Ben.

"No fault of yours, Ben, but you've been working mostly with the big guys, the ones who can afford you," piped up the usually quiet Clyde Mueller.

"I guess that's right," said Ben. He looked down into his coffee.

"We've got a proposal for you, Ben. Something for you to think about," said Curt. "I know this is tricky business, and it could get you in trouble if word got out. But . . ." Curt hesitated for a moment. "But the cooperative really needs your help. There's a bunch of new ideas coming along. Take Cranberry Red, for instance. We've read about it in the paper and heard about it on the radio. But we just don't know if we should be thinking about using it or not. And we've got new members joining. Just this past week, we signed up Chris Martin—guy's just back from fighting in Iraq."

"I talked with Chris last week and I sent him in your direction," Ben said. "But what's your proposal?"

"Same old Ben Wesley," Curt said, smiling. "Cuts right to the chase. Well, here's our offer. We'd like you to do some workshops for us on your own time. Off the Osborne books. And we've figured out a way to pay you, too."

Ben noticed that everyone was looking at him, wondering what his reaction to the proposal would be.

"We've decided to charge a little extra for membership dues, and we'll use that money to pay you. We don't expect you to work for nothing. But we can't afford Osborne's rates. We just can't."

Silence in the room.

"Anybody want some more coffee?" offered Shotgun. Several hands went up.

"I feel terrible that things have come to this," Ben finally said.

"Ben, it's not your fault. We all know that," said Wanda.

"So whattya think, Ben?" asked Shotgun. "You game for this?"

"I'll have to think about it," replied Ben. Shotgun wasn't surprised by the response; in fact, he took it as quite a positive sign. He knew Ben Wesley well. If Ben was opposed to something, he said so right up front. If he was considering doing something, his usual response was the one he just made.

"I'll get back to you," Ben said. "Thanks for the coffee, Shotgun. And thanks for organizing this little get-together."

54

Teaching Strategies

*T*he next evening Ben called Shotgun. Ben told him that he would be more than happy to set up some sessions for the co-op members and would conduct them on Saturdays, or on Sunday afternoons if that would work out. Ben once more apologized that he was not able to set up the meetings as he had in the past, when he still worked as a county agricultural agent.

"Ben, don't worry about it," said Shotgun. "We all know the predicament you're in, and we don't want you to lose your job."

"I appreciate that all this is hush-hush."

"Yup, and we intend to keep it that way. There will be no announcements in the paper, nothing over the radio. We'll not even mention this in our newsletter. It's all word of mouth, one co-op member talking to the next."

"Hate to say this, Shotgun, but if you call and Beth answers the phone, don't let her know what this is all about," said Ben.

"I got it," Shotgun said. "I know how women can be about these things."

"Thanks." Ben appreciated that Shotgun didn't inquire further about what was going on between him and his wife. Ben surmised that Shotgun had figured out that Osborne could do no wrong in Beth Wesley's world. Because of the outreach office's fee schedule, most of Ben's clients these days were the larger, more prosperous farmers, and of course the larger cranberry growers. Ben had never been able to help Beth understand since he began working for Osborne that some of the smaller farm operators didn't have the financial resources to pay for his services. Beth was surely not aware how many hours he had spent with these farmers when he was county agricultural agent.

Beth's mind worked differently than Ben's. More different every year it seemed. She had this survival-of-the-fittest attitude. Perhaps she got that from working all these years at the hospital, competing with other nurses, feuding with some of the more arrogant physicians, and arguing with the administration about trivial things.

She was a fighter, no question about that. Her thinking went something like this: If you can't compete, if you can't make it on your own, then you should try something else. She of course used herself as an example. She worked hard and lately she had studied diligently in Osborne University's nurse-practitioner program to give herself a competitive advantage.

Ben remembered the time a year or two ago when he had spent many hours working with a market gardener who was down on his luck and needed Ben's help so he could figure out a way of saving his small business. The fellow didn't have enough money to put in an irrigation system, and dry weather had cut his vegetable crop yield in half. Ben helped the fellow obtain a loan from the bank, and took him to several irrigation equipment companies to help him decide on the best system for his small acreage. The following year, the farmer was back on track and never forgot what Ben had done for him.

When Ben shared all this with Beth, she had simply said, "Sounds like you should have let the fellow go under. Not everyone can make it, you know." Ben hadn't replied to her rather sharp comments, but he hadn't forgotten them either.

Over the years, a series of these one-at-a-time successes earned Ben the positive reputation he had in Ames County. Of course there had been some failures. And a time or two Ben's good nature and accommodating personality had resulted in his being taken advantage of. Nonetheless, his approach was to work with just about anybody who walked through the agricultural agent office door.

Lately, his frustration was trying to meet the expectations of Osborne University, including developing an increasingly larger paying client base—it wasn't happening—and trying to maintain a reputation that had taken him twenty years to build. Even the large cranberry growers that Osborne University incorrectly assumed would fall all over themselves in wanting to learn more about Cranberry Red, where to buy the product, and how to use it, were hanging back. Ben never said so to these growers— he thought it best he shouldn't—but he wanted to praise them for wanting more information before they moved into something new. He wanted to tell them to keep asking questions. Remain skeptical. He wanted to say, "Just because something is new doesn't mean you should buy it." This was what he had been telling people for twenty years, but now he thought it best to keep his mouth shut. He could imagine what Dr. Sara Phillips would say if she heard he was raising questions with growers rather than doing the promotion he was expected to do.

Not even the successful sale of Healthy Always Cranberries resulting from harvesting Jeff Johnson's experimental plot had made much differ-ence in the minds of the large growers. They wanted more evidence. They wanted to know about yields, any changes needed in pest management, any harvesting modifications, and above all, whether they could make addi-tional profit from spraying their crop with Cranberry Red. Ben had heard these kinds of questions many times over the years. They were important.

Sometimes Ben wondered if the folks at Osborne University really understood that just because a product sounded unbelievably useful and resulted in benefits that went far beyond what everyone had ever hoped for, those who were supposed to leap at buying the product might be skep-tical. He had taught these farmers to be skeptical. Ben realized that what he had been doing for the past twenty years was getting in the way of what he was supposed to do now. He had been teaching people how to think on their own, how to gather facts and then make a decision based on their individual circumstances, their goals, and their aspirations.

Now he was supposed to convince cranberry growers to buy a pig in a poke? He just couldn't do it; it flew in the face of everything he believed in. Yet, he was convinced that Cranberry Red increased the health benefits of cranberries. He would need to do some careful thinking about how to incorporate this information into an educational program for cranberry growers that included as many answers to their other questions as he could find.

If only he had time to do this. Osborne had him on notice to increase his billable hours, to sponsor more workshops, to make more money for the university. Even Brittani had recently said, "Ben, our office schedule is crazy. Where do you think we're headed?"

"I don't know," Ben said. "I just don't know."

Gunnar's Research

Ben Wesley wasn't the only Osborne employee doing things without the university's knowledge. As a scientist, Gunnar Godson couldn't forget about what had happened last summer when he had captured several giant night crawlers that he believed had been exposed to Cranberry Red accidentally spilled on the research station's lawn. He surmised their size was somehow related to the Cranberry Red spill, and he had been experimenting to get to the bottom of what he theorized to be true. Before freeze-up last fall, Gunnar collected eighteen rather normal-looking night crawlers, built an indoor receptacle that he filled with soil from the outside, and divided them into three groups, putting six in each group. He recorded the measurements of all eighteen night crawlers as he placed them in their respective containers. Gunnar noted that the worms were all essentially the same size.

He devoted one corner of his lab at the research station to his experiment, admonishing his assistants to say nothing to anyone about what he was doing. They all agreed to keep quiet. He labeled the first group of night crawlers a control group; he did nothing with them except add a little water from time to time to provide them with conditions that nearly matched those in nature. For the second group, as the soil dried, he added water to which he had added five drops of Cranberry Red per gallon of water. For the third group, when the soil became dry, he moistened it with undiluted Cranberry Red, to replicate what had happened outside last summer when the chemical had been spilled.

Every two weeks, starting in December, Gunnar measured the night crawlers in each group. As any good scientist would do, he carefully recorded everything that he did, everything that he observed, and of course the measurements of the night crawlers.

From the beginning he hoped that his hypothesis would be wrong, that the night crawlers treated with Cranberry Red would show no effects. After all, he was the one who had developed Cranberry Red in this very laboratory, and it was his employer who was depending on this product to provide a handsome profit.

When he measured the size of the night crawlers in the control group at the end of February, he noted only a few tenths of an inch of growth. When he measured the night crawlers in the group that received the diluted solution, he found they had doubled in size, some of them had increased to eighteen inches long. Not only had the crawlers in the second group grown to grotesque lengths and diameters (the size of a man's index finger), but they were also hyperactive, turning and churning in the soil, a writhing mass of tangled reddish snakelike bodies. In the third group, where he had subjected the crawlers to undiluted Chemical Red, by February all had died. Some of them had reached nearly two feet in length before they expired in a twisted mass.

His worst fears had been realized. Cranberry Red had a profound affect on night crawlers, beyond anything that he had guessed. Whether exposed to the diluted solution or the concentrated dose, the night crawlers grew many times larger than normal and those that lived exhibited other characteristics far different from normal night crawlers.

Now Gunnar faced a dilemma. What should he do with this information? If he told Osborne officials about it, he would surely be fired, as the president of the university had demanded in no uncertain terms not to do any experiments on side effects of Cranberry Red. What was the ethical thing to do? Gunnar talked about his problem with his wife that evening, after dinner.

"You need this job, Gunnar," she said quietly. "We need the money to live. Think about our little girls."

56

Brittani and Chris

*T*he seasons can change abruptly in central Wisconsin. One day it's winter, the next day spring comes out of the closet and announces itself with a flourish. On this March morning, Ben smelled spring in the air. He caught the fresh scent of green grass, which had emerged on the side of his home where the snow had melted several days previous. He picked up the subtle smell of warmer, moist air that had been sweeping over snow-covered farm fields that surrounded Willow River, turning the dirty remnant snow piles to mush and allowing bare ground to emerge.

Just yesterday Ben had seen a pair of sandhill cranes that had returned from their winter quarters to still mostly snow-covered fields. He chuckled as he watched them standing on one leg and then the other, obviously not comfortable standing in the cold snow. This morning Ben heard a cardinal calling. He looked for the red bird high up in a tree as he left his house and walked to the car parked in the driveway. He felt good. Conditions at the office had improved greatly. He had begun to enjoy working with Brittani and he believed she had come to enjoy working with him, as well. Brittani continued to take care of Ben's scheduling, of course, but now she asked him about anything that seemed a bit unusual, for instance requesting some background on a new person he was to visit, or whether he thought it made sense to drive all the way to Tomah to meet with a cranberry grower.

He had finished his online computer course and for the first time felt comfortable when he sat at his computer, at least considerably more comfortable than just six months ago. And he believed he had mastered the Osborne rules, at least those that pertained to the outreach office.

Ben had met monthly with the Cranberry One-Fifty celebration planning committee. Now, in March, everything for the big event began to come together. Each month the various groups planning activities had reported on progress: The Cranberry Queen committee said twelve candidates applied; the winner would be announced at the August celebration. The parade committee reported more than fifty entries so far. A polka band had been signed for the dance on Saturday night, and more than twenty-five artists and craftspeople from all over the area had consented to show their work. Billy Baxter, editor of the *Ames County Argus*, had been running regular announcements about the festival in his paper.

Ben wished things had been going as well at home. After the recognition Beth had received from Osborne in the fall, and the praise she had gotten from her children and friends, she once more began questioning Ben's ambition and his desire to improve himself. She didn't consider his completing a fairly complicated course on computer use to count toward anything more than an attempt to catch up, to reach a place where most other professional people had arrived some time ago.

The previous week, after dinner one evening, she asked, "Have you heard anything about Osborne offering you a promotion?"

"A promotion?" Ben answered, surprised.

"Yes, a promotion. You've been working hard, traveling many miles, meeting with lots of people. You should be due for a more responsible position."

"Beth, I haven't been on this job for a year. I doubt the folks in Oshkosh have given a thought to promoting me." To himself, Ben thought he was fortunate to have a job, especially after the dressing down he and Brittani had gotten back in January. Ben had not told Beth about the meeting with Dr. Phillips. If he had, he knew, it would have upset her.

"Well, it seems you should be entitled. You got this new office up and running. You obviously have shown Brittani how to do her job. You should get credit for that."

Ben listened but didn't say anything. He couldn't believe what he was hearing.

"Have you asked Dr. Phillips about what Osborne has in mind for you—some position in Oshkosh, perhaps?"

"I don't think it would be right to ask."

"There you go again, Ben. Worrying about what you think is right. You'll never get anywhere unless you do some asking. You've earned a promotion and a raise in salary. You've got to be a little aggressive. Push a little. Go after what you deserve."

Ben didn't say anything in reply. But he thought how he and his wife were certainly thinking differently these days.

Arriving at his office on this warm March day, Ben greeted Brittani with "Good morning, what a great day it is."

"It is that," Brittani replied. She was wearing a bright yellow dress— maybe she was pushing the season a little—that contrasted well with her black hair and dark eyes. Ordinarily she wore slacks, sometimes even jeans and a sweater, to work.

"Chris Martin called for an appointment," Brittani said. "I've got him scheduled for ten. Says he only needs a half hour."

"Okay," Ben said. "Nice young man. Need more like him going into farming. He's a graduate of the College of Agricultural and Life Sciences in Madison, you know. He's taking over his dad's place."

"I didn't know that," said Brittani as she busied herself at her computer, trying not to show her obvious interest in Chris Martin's background.

When Chris arrived at the office a few minutes before ten, Ben was on the phone with another client.

"It will be a couple of minutes," Brittani said when Chris stopped at her desk. "Could I get you a cup of coffee?"

"That would be nice," he said. "It's Brittani, right?" He had a deep, clear voice.

"Brittani Stone," she said. "As in rock, but with an 's' in front." It was an old joke from her high school days. Brittani poured the coffee into an official Osborne University cup. Their hands brushed when Brittani handed him the cup of steaming coffee. "Have a chair—Ben should be off the phone shortly. Ben told me you went to school in Madison."

"I did, graduated from the ag college in 2002. How about you?"

"I graduated from UW–Whitewater in 2004, business major," responded Brittani.

"You like working here?" Chris asked as he took another sip of coffee.

"It's okay. Could be better. Could be worse."

"I've heard lots of good things about Ben Wesley—I knew him when I was a little kid in 4-H."

"Ben's a good guy. Works hard. Honest as the day is long and a nice guy to work with. And he knows what he's talking about." Brittani tried hard not to sound like another promotion for the outreach office.

"So I've heard." Chris took another drink of coffee. "Good coffee. You make this?"

"I did. Not part of my job description, but since the first of the year I've been doing it. Makes the office a little friendlier."

"That it does," said Chris. Brittani noticed he had the biggest, brightest smile she had ever seen.

"Chris, come on in," Ben said as he opened his office door. "Bring your coffee with you. Brittani makes a great cup of coffee."

"She sure does," said Chris as he looked once more toward Brittani and smiled.

Ben and Chris talked for nearly twenty minutes. After reading the booklet on fruit and vegetable growing he had purchased from the office on the previous meeting, Chris had several questions. He wondered what new strawberry varieties might have been developed since the booklet was written. And whether Ben had any advice about what vegetable varieties he should plant this first year. He also asked Ben to help him develop a business plan that he could take to the banker in Willow River in preparation for obtaining a loan. Ben asked several questions and shared a few stories he'd heard from other members of the Ames County Fruit and Vegetable Growers Cooperative.

"Don't be afraid to ask the co-op members about anything. These people know the business, from the ground up, so to speak." Ben smiled at his attempt at humor.

Chris stood up to leave. "Do I pay you?"

"No, Brittani takes care of the business end of the office. She can send you an invoice if you'd like and you can pay later."

"I like to pay my bills right away," Chris said. "I learned that from my dad."

Chris walked over to Brittani's desk, with Ben behind him. Chris was reaching for his billfold in his back pocket.

"It's a half hour," Ben said. "Talk to you later, Chris. Good luck."

Brittani looked at the clock on the wall. "Not even a half hour," she said. "Let's make it 'no charge.'"

"Thank you," Chris said. "But I'm prepared to pay. I don't expect any favors."

Brittani, looking radiant in her yellow dress, smiled.

"Tell you what," Chris said. "How would you like dinner, say Friday night? A kind of thank you."

"I'd like that," Brittani said. "Here's my phone number. Call me and I'll tell you how to find my apartment."

Two Faces of Osborne

No question about it, May was one of Ben Wesley's favorite months of the year, along with October. By May winter gave up the battle once and for all and sulked off for a few months to rest and regroup for another siege come November. As the old timers said about Wisconsin, "We have nine months of winter and three months of poor sledding."

Trees formed leaves in May; tulips opened and displayed an array of mostly yellows and reds. Songbirds returned, filling the tree tops with love-making song. Bluebirds and tree swallows competed for the nesting boxes that had become more popular in Ames County in recent years, thanks to some of Ben's work in promoting bluebird preservation. In the marshy areas of the county, sandhill cranes filled the air with their primitive, throaty calls that echoed through the valleys. Wild ducks that frequented the small ponds and lakes in the county showed off their hatches, as little ducks paddled behind their mothers in single file. By the end of the month the lilacs—light purple, dark purple, and white—burst into full aromatic bloom. Ben liked their slightly sweet smell, for it reminded him of his youth, and the row of lilacs that grew just to the west of the farmhouse where he grew up. By the end of the month, the lupines opened, hillsides and roadsides of deep purple lupines, with flowers resembling those of peas, as indeed the two plants were relatives.

Ames County farmers burst into action during this month that seemed never to arrive, preparing seedbeds and planting their crops. The potato farmers had gotten their seed in the ground in April, as did those who grew peas. May was for sweet corn, field corn, and green beans. And by the end of the month, with fingers crossed because spring frosts were a common threat, tomato plants were gently placed in small and large gardens.

Graziers, a fancy name for an old-fashioned idea, turned their dairy cows out to pastures that had begun to green up nicely. These were the farmers with smaller herds who resisted hauling feed to their confined cows and then having to haul out the manure. Graziers allowed the cows to find their own feed, as cattle had done for hundreds of years, and distribute their own waste. No hauling in, no hauling out for these farmers— during the non-winter months of course.

Ben was in his office, with the windows open. The first time this spring. A warm breeze brought in the smell of fresh-cut grass from the lawnmower he heard operating. Ben was reading the headlines in the *Ames County Argus* when he spotted the following article:

Osborne University Building Recreational Park

Award-winning Ira Osborne University, headquartered in Oshkosh, announced this week its plans to construct a recreational park on land it owns next to its research station on the Tamarack River in western Ames County. Construction has already begun on this ten-acre park that will include nature trails, a bird walk, a softball diamond, an array of playground equipment for younger children, and an improved swimming beach.

Upon completion of the park, Osborne's president, Dr. Delbert George, said, "We plan to donate this park, land, and equipment to Ames County. It will be our way of saying thank you to all those who have so graciously applauded our efforts in providing an alternative college education for students around the world, as well as supported our research efforts leading toward the discovery of new products such as Healthy Always Cranberries treated with our now famous Cranberry Red."

A dedication ceremony for Ira Osborne Commemorative Park will take place later in the summer, a date to be determined

Ben put down the newspaper and turned to read his new batch of e-mail messages; it seemed there was always something from someone at Osborne in Oshkosh who had something to say. Today's e-mail was from Dr. Quinton Foley, vice president for research:

Mr. Wesley,

It has been called to my attention that sales of Cranberry Red are much lower than projections. Do you have any insight as to why this is the case? Could you send me a list of the cranberry growers you have contacted? Do you need to develop a new sales strategy for Cranberry Red with these growers?

As you know, the primary reason we hired you was to promote Cranberry Red. We have a considerable investment in this product. We are expecting you to hold up your end with direct sales contacts and whatever other sales strategy you believe will succeed. I expect to hear by June 15 what you have accomplished along these lines.

Ben sat back in his chair, thought for a minute, then printed the message. He took it out to where Brittani was sitting at her desk, working on completing the April report of activities and accomplishments that was due by the end of the week.

"Wow," Brittani said when she finished reading the message. "You now got the big shots on your case."

"Appears so," said Ben. "What am I supposed to do? I've contacted just about every cranberry grower in central Wisconsin; almost every person is waiting to see more information about Cranberry Red."

"I know that," replied Brittani. "Tell you what I'd do if I got that missive."

"What would you do?" Ben said. He was smiling as he waited for her answer.

"Well, I'd tell Dr. Foley to stick his message where the sun doesn't shine."

Ben laughed out loud at the rather surprising response from his office manager.

"I probably shouldn't do that," Ben said as he stopped laughing.

"Yeah, probably not. But it seems like a good idea. Good God, what do those people expect of us?" she asked.

"More than we're doing," Ben responded. He returned to his office. He could feel another tension headache developing in the back of his neck. A beautiful spring day had become just another day at the office, with demands beyond what he could meet.

Another little voice in Ben's head seemed to demand some attention, more so it seems as the days passed. What if Cranberry Red wasn't as great as Osborne made it out to be? Could that be why the pressure for promoting Cranberry Red had increased so much since last fall? Why the new park? And now? Could there be some relation of Cranberry Red to the park? Was Osborne trying to build up a wall of community support in case they ran into some problems? On the one hand, Ben began wondering if he had gotten himself into the middle of something that went significantly beyond what he was aware of. But on the other hand, Beth had long reminded him that he was just too blamed skeptical of everything. "Where is your faith in the goodness of people?" Beth had said. From long experience, Ben knew what happened when people's values and money collided. Money usually won.

Part 7

58

Fred and Oscar

At Fred Russo's suggestion, he and Oscar Anderson opened the annual fishing season on the Willow River Millpond, a small body of water created when pioneers in the middle 1850s dammed the Willow River to create waterpower for the grain mill and the adjacent sawmill. Both mills were long closed. The grain mill still stood; it was a three-story, red, wooden structure that had become a gift shop of some kind. It was the ideal place for tourists to see the water tumble over the mill dam. The small city of Willow River surrounded the mill pond; its main street hugged one side. Ebenezer Townsend Park, created on land set aside from a donation from once-prominent citizen Ebenezer Townsend, took up much of the opposite shore. It was here that Fred and Oscar had staked an early morning claim for a fishing spot.

The two old fishermen stood on shore, tossing their lines out into the clear, cold water of the pond—they were the only fishermen there. It was a blustery cold May morning, with the wind coming out of the northwest. Winter was having a tough time giving up.

"What kinda fish we supposed to catch here?" said Oscar after he had tossed his line out about a half dozen times without any action.

"Trout. There's brook trout in here," said Fred. "Native brookies."

"Rookies, what in hell is a rookie trout?"

"Brookie! I said, 'brookie!'" Fred yelled over the sound of a semi that had downshifted as it motored slowly along Main Street.

"Oh," said Oscar. He waited a few moments. "You ever catch a brookie trout?"

"Used to. When I was a kid. Caught 'em in the Upper Pine River. Caught a lot of 'em. Good eatin'. About the best eatin' trout there is."

"You ever catch a brookie trout in this millpond?"

"Nope, I haven't. Heard they're in here, though," said Fred.

"Who told you there's trout in here? You see another fisherman? Not a damn one. There're all someplace else . . . where the fish are bitin'," added Oscar.

"François over at the bait shop told me," said Fred.

"François. He don't know nothin' about where the fish are bitin'. All he wants is to sell bait. . . . Damn, it's cold out here. That wind just cuts right through ya."

"Gotta have a little patience, Oscar. Gotta be patient," said Fred.

"Ain't had so much as a nibble. I don't think there's even a turtle in this pond," grumped Oscar.

"You wanna catch a turtle?"

"No, I don't wanna catch no damn turtle. I wanna catch fish like we used to catch over on the Tamarack River," said Oscar.

"You wanna catch another one of them mean northern pike, like the one that chewed off your walkin' stick last year?" asked Fred.

"That was the meanest fish I ever saw. Burned down our fishing shanty, too. Bet it was the same damn fish. Out to get us. That fish was out to get us, Fred," said Oscar.

"You tell anybody about that fish chasin' us and chewing off your stick?"

"Only Shotgun Slogum. Don't think he believed me, either. Even if he did, he wouldn't tell nobody. Slogum knows how to keep a secret," Oscar remarked.

The two old friends, with their collars up and their hats pulled down, watched their bobbers ride the little chop on the pond created by the cold northwest wind. Fifteen minutes passed without a word between them.

Oscar finally broke the silence. "Fred, this here pond is the worst place I've ever fished. It's colderin' hell out here besides. Let's go over to the Lone Pine for a cup of coffee and warm up."

"Good idea," agreed Fred, reeling in his line.

59

Queen Selection

The Cranberry Queen selection committee consisted of Brittani Stone; Jeff Johnson; Mable Derleth, another cranberry grower, in her sixties, quiet, unassuming, with gray hair tied up in a bun; Willow River librarian Megan Fritz, fifty-two, who had intense, deep blue eyes and was known for her brightly colored sweaters (she chaired the queen committee); and lastly Solomon Paige, a regional poet from Neshkoro who had reluctantly agreed to serve. Solomon was in his early fifties and had long white hair that he wore in a ponytail. A string of colorful beads hung around his neck. He wore Franklin-type glasses that hung on the end of his rather long and bulbous nose.

The application process required that each candidate submit a one-hundred-word essay on how cranberries contributed to Wisconsin's economy, the state's cultural heritage, and its agricultural diversity. Each candidate was also asked to submit a short, original poem with some reference to cranberries, thus the reason for inviting a professional poet to serve on the committee.

The committee met twice just to work out the application process, a task that should have been straightforward but turned into a near donnybrook. The problem was with the committee—too widely diversified. Solomon Paige and Brittani Stone tangled during the first ten minutes of the first meeting. Brittani had a one-two-three, let's-get-this-done approach to things. Solomon went on about the emotional aspects of queen selection and how the process must be open to allow each applicant sufficient "breathing space for creativity." Brittani challenged Solomon to explain what he meant by "breathing space for creativity," and he then went on for five minutes trying to put into words the meaning of something that went well beyond words.

While this exchange went on, the rest of the committee sat with a why-did-I-agree-to-do-this look on their faces. After finally working out the application form, the committee did not meet again until March to begin reviewing the materials twelve young women submitted. Everyone on the committee first read all the essays and independently gave them a ranking of one to five. Then they read the poems and likewise voted one to five. In the midst of reading the poems, Solomon, in a loud voice, announced, "I would like the attention of the entire selection committee, please."

Brittani had grown increasingly weary of Solomon and his pronouncements. He made several at each meeting of the committee. *What a pompous ass he is*, thought Brittani, but she kept her opinions to herself.

"Yes, Mr. Paige," Megan Fritz responded. He wanted to be called Mr. Paige. "What is it?" Megan had chaired many committees during her long career as Willow River librarian, but this queen selection committee was proving to be the most challenging by far, and it consisted of only five members.

"I have a motion to make," Solomon said, in a voice too loud for the room.

"Well, as you know, we are a small enough group that motions hardly seem necessary. But what is your motion?" asked Megan.

"I move we disqualify all twelve queen candidates and start over."

"Start over!" Brittani exclaimed. She struck her open hand on the table to make her point. A loose pencil began rolling toward the edge of the table and dropped onto the carpeted floor. "Start over after all the time we've spent meeting! Why, in heaven's name?"

"Because their poetry is no good. Absolutely awful. An embarrassment to everyone."

"Gee, I kinda liked the poems," Jeff Johnson said, smiling.

"Do I hear a second to the motion?" said Megan, ignoring Jeff's comment. "Hearing none, the motion dies," affirmed Megan after no one else spoke.

"I must resign from this committee," Solomon said as he stood up, his long white ponytail swinging back and forth, the beads around his neck jumping up and down.

"Oh, sit down, Solomon," Mable Derleth said. She almost never said anything, but it was obvious from her tone of voice that she was disgusted with Solomon's antics. "We are not going to disqualify all the queen candidates because of their poetry. And you're not going to resign either."

Brittani smiled. Solomon slumped into his chair. Mable had deflated the man completely and he said little during the rest of the meeting.

The committee took a brief recess while Megan tallied the scores. When committee members resumed their seats, she announced the three candidates with the top numbers. A top score would be fifty: twenty-five for essay and twenty-five for poem.

"The three top candidates for Cranberry Queen," Megan began in a somewhat formal manner, "are Debra Backus, forty points, Carol Cunningham, thirty-eight points, and Laura Dalenski, thirty-five points. These three will move on to the final selection process. I will notify all the girls of the results and thank them for participating. I'll phone the top three girls and tell them about our final selection meeting in May." Megan shuffled all the application papers in a pile in front of her and once more looked up. "And thanks to each of you for all your hard work. We have but one more responsibility and that of course is to pick the queen from these top candidates."

*T*he evening of May 14 was cold and blustery, as May often is in central Wisconsin. The final selection of Cranberry Queen was open to the public and held in the community room of the Willow River Library. The five committee members sat in the front row, each holding a pad of paper. The three queen candidates sat facing the audience and slightly to the right of the committee. The room was filled with parents, friends, and others interested in the queen contest, which had been reported on thoroughly in the *Ames County Argus*.

Chairperson Megan Fritz, wearing a bright red and white sweater, stood up in front of the microphone. "Welcome, everyone," she began. "We are so pleased that you can see firsthand the selection of our Cranberry One-Fifty Queen." Megan went on to explain the selection process and how the top three candidates had been selected from the twelve young women who had entered.

Megan continued, "This final stage of the selection process will include a round of questions for each candidate, and an original poem read by each. Following that, we will break and while the audience enjoys some refreshments, the committee will tally the results and make the final decision. Our first candidate this evening is Debra Backus from Link Lake. She is the daughter of John and Judith Backus. Debra is a senior at Link Lake High School and is planning to attend the University of Wisconsin–Stevens Point this fall. Debra Backus."

The audience clapped as Debra stood up and walked to the microphone. She wore a plain black dress, with a white scarf around her neck. She had brown hair that hung loosely on her shoulders.

"Debra," Megan began, "what are some of the health benefits from eating cranberry products?"

"First, I want to thank the committee and everyone connected with this contest. It has been a truly interesting and educational activity for me. To answer the question, the health benefits from eating cranberries are many. Cranberries are high in antioxidants. We know that Native Americans used cranberry poultices to draw poison from wounds, and they believed eating cranberries could calm nerves. The Indians used a mixture of cranberries and cornmeal as a cure for blood poisoning. Today, eating cranberries can help prevent urinary tract infections and reduce the risk of gum disease, ulcers, heart disease, and cancer."

"Very good," said Megan. "Your second question is multiple choice. Of Wisconsin's several commercial fruit crops, what percentage of the annual income from these fruits comes from cranberries: 20 percent, 50 percent, or 80 percent?"

Debra paused for a moment. "Fifty percent?"

"I'm sorry; the correct answer is 80 percent of the income from Wisconsin's fruit crops comes from cranberries," Megan replied.

"Now, Debra, would you share your poem with us?" The young woman, a bit flustered because she missed her second question, unfolded a sheet of paper and began reading:

Cranberry Moon

On a quiet night in October
When the moon hangs low in the sky
I take my love to the country
To the cranberry marshes
To the marshes that stretch out before us
As far as we can see in the moonlight.
To the marshes that stretch out before us
As far as we can see into the night.

And there on the banks of the river
On the banks of the river called Tamarack
On the river that winds through the bogs
Through the cranberry bogs
We pledge our love to each other
By the light of the cranberry moon.

She bowed slightly, refolded the paper, and took her seat to loud applause and even a few whistles, no doubt from some of the high school boys who stood in the back of the room.

"Carol Cunningham is our next contestant," Megan said as she once more stood at the microphone. "Carol is the daughter of Bruce and Karla Cunningham from Willow River. She is eighteen years old, a senior at Willow River High School, and plans to attend the University of Wisconsin–Oshkosh this fall. A round of applause for Carol Cunningham."

Carol, a tall, slim girl, wore a cranberry-red dress with a pale yellow scarf.

"Carol, here's your first question: What is the scientific name for cranberry?"

After a long pause, Carol, her face nearly as red as her dress, muttered, "I . . . I don't know."

"*Vaccinium macracarpon*," Megan pronounced matter-of-factly.

"Your second question multiple choice. What percentage of Wisconsin

259

cranberries are consumed as fresh fruit: 50 percent, 20 percent, or 5 percent?"

"That would be 5 percent," the young woman said, smiling. "The rest go for juice, dried cranberries, and such."

"That is correct. Now to your poem, Carol."

Carol took a deep breath and began reading:

Ode to the Cranberry

Oh, Cranberry!
Oh, Cranberry!
How we hold you in high esteem.
Your tarty taste.
Your reddish hue.
Your history and romance.
Oh, Cranberry!
Oh, Cranberry!
We tip our hats to you.

She walked to her seat and sat down as the room echoed with applause.

Megan returned to the podium. "Our third and final candidate is Laura Dalenski from Waupaca. Her parents are John and Sophie Dalenski, and she is a senior at Waupaca High School. In the fall, she plans to enroll in Osborne University."

Laura, a tall, blonde girl, wore a powder blue dress with a red belt. She walked confidently to the microphone.

"Laura, you will also have two questions," said Megan. "First, how many acres of woodland, uplands, and wetlands does it take to support one acre of cranberries?"

"Between five and ten," replied Laura.

"That is correct. Your second question is multiple choice. How many years before a newly planted cranberry bog will bear fruit: two years, four to five years, or eight years?"

"Two years, like strawberries?"

"No, it depends somewhat on the weather and the variety planted, but a newly planted cranberry bog seldom begins bearing fruit until four or five years after it is planted," said Megan. "And now your poem, please."

With her hands at her sides, a somewhat rattled Laura began, "I call my poem 'Cranberry Seasons.'"

Cranberry Seasons

Cranberries in flower
Springtime in Wisconsin
Promise for the fall
Winter holiday delight.

She walked to her chair and sat down. There was a brief silence because some people expected a longer poem, but then there was scattered clapping.

Once more Megan Fritz returned to the microphone. "Aren't these young women great? Stand up, please," she said to the trio of young women. They stood facing the audience, smiling to loud applause. "Now we'll take a brief intermission and in a short time we'll announce the results."

Coffee, cranberry juice, and assorted cookies were on display on tables along one end of the room and people helped themselves while the queen selection committee adjourned to an adjacent conference room. After a half hour, long after the coffee pot had been drained, the cranberry juice gone, and all the cookies consumed, the committee still had not returned. An occasional loud voice could be heard coming from the meeting room, but the door remained closed. The queen candidates sat quietly in their chairs. After forty minutes, everyone had left except the queen candidates and their parents. Megan Fritz appeared for a brief moment. "I'm so sorry," she said. "We are having a bit of a disagreement in our committee. You might as well go home and we'll phone you our decision."

Three disappointed young women and their parents filed out of the library door. Someone driving by the library at midnight noticed that the lights were still on in the conference room, and people were sitting around the table.

The next day the Cranberry Queen was announced. The honor went to Debra Backus, with Laura Dalenski first runner-up and Carol Cunningham second runner-up. Someone later learned that the committee could not break a tie between Debra and Laura, so they finally flipped a coin and

Debra won. The problem was with the poetry and how much credit should be given to a longer versus a shorter poem. When asked to say a word about the contest's poetry, poet Solomon Paige grumped, "No comment."

60

Ups and Downs

*T*he early days of summer sped by. Ben met on four successive Wednesday evenings with members of the Ames County Fruit and Vegetable Growers Cooperative. They met in members' homes and no mention of the meetings was leaked to the press or anyone else who didn't need to know. Members personally contacted each other—no newsletters or other public information—to inform each other of the meetings.

Ben didn't have to know the Osborne University employee manual verbatim to know he was violating it. He worried a little about this and what the consequences might be if Osborne officials found out. He also felt badly that he had not shared the existence of these meetings with his wife, who wanted to know in detail everything that he did. He was running out of reasonable excuses as to what he was doing on Wednesday nights—he hoped she hadn't jumped to some wild conclusion that he was off seeing another woman. Beth had been especially cool toward him the last few weeks, but she didn't push the question as to what was really happening when Ben left the house with his briefcase and a big smile on his face, only to return a couple hours later rather exhausted. The fact that he returned home each of the evenings at a reasonable hour seemed to count for something. Besides that, it seemed that Ben and Beth had little to talk about these days. Beth's life was going in one direction, Ben's in another.

Ben wanted to tell Brittani about the meetings and almost did a couple of times, but he still wasn't sure that she wouldn't blab it to Osborne officials and everything would hit the fan. He doubted she would tell, though; she seemed as perturbed with Osborne University these days as he was, but you just never know.

What Ben enjoyed about meeting with the co-op growers was their enthusiasm and interest in learning, and secondly the fact that he could once more put on his teacher's hat. So often these days he was conflicted. He was a teacher, had been a teacher, and would always be a teacher by nature. Yet, although Osborne University didn't call him a salesman, that's what they expected him to be. It had taken him most of a year to realize this, but recently it had become abundantly clear that his top priority as an Osborne University employee was to sell Cranberry Red. Of course he was expected to earn money for the university in other ways as well, through consultations, workshops, and sales of publications. But Cranberry Red was at the top of his list of important things to be concerned about. He had also been thinking a lot these days about Osborne University's ties to International Farm-Med. To what extent were the university's ideas and dictates really those of IFM? Part of him knew that he shouldn't go there with his thinking, but he couldn't avoid it.

In addition to enjoying the workshop series with the co-op members, Ben felt good about the accomplishments of the planning committee for the upcoming Cranberry One-Fifty celebration. Although there had been a few glitches and a few feathers ruffled—there always are in these big planning efforts—the three-day celebration plans had come together beyond his fondest hopes. It was obvious that Ames County was proud of its cranberry history and its cranberry growers, and they wanted everyone to know it.

Taking stock of his first year on the job, Ben felt good about the office and the relationship that he and Brittani had worked out. They had developed a level of trust and respect for each other and had clearly begun working together rather than competing with each other. Brittani came to work these days with a big smile on her face and a bounce in her step—she seemed genuinely happy. But Ben knew it wasn't the office and its relationship with Osborne that was making the difference. He had surmised that

Brittani might be spending time with Chris Martin, who had returned to Ames County to farm his father's land. His suspicions were confirmed one night when the co-op group met at Chris's house.

"Say, Chris," commented one of the co-op members, "your coffee needs some improvement. What you need is a wife to show you how to make coffee."

"Maybe," Chris said, smirking a bit.

"Understand that something might happen along those lines," another co-op member piped up.

"Could be," Chris said. He was blushing a little.

"That Brittani Stone is quite a looker," offered Curt Evans, president of the co-op. "Wouldn't you say so, Ben? You see her every day."

"I guess you could say that," Ben answered.

Ben hadn't realized the relationship between his office manager and this tall, dark veteran had progressed so far. He was pleased to learn about it, but said nothing to Brittani when he saw her the next day.

A couple of days later when Ben arrived home from the office, he found an envelope addressed to him and marked "personal." Seldom did he receive letters anymore; it seemed everyone used e-mail to get in touch with him. The return address was Osborne University. He slit open the envelope with the pocketknife he always carried. It was a letter from Dr. Sara Phillips, with several accompanying pages. The letter read:

Dear Ben,

As is our policy at Osborne University, we conduct a yearly evaluation of all employees. Enclosed is the detailed analysis of your previous year's performance.

If you have any questions, please contact me.

Sincerely,
Sara Phillips, PhD
Director of Field Operations
Ira Osborne University

Ben thumbed through several pages of categories and numbers, then sat down and began carefully reading the evaluation of his first year of work. Each item was rated from one to nine—a one meant "completely unsatisfactory performance." Nine indicated "Well beyond expectations."

Understands Ira Osborne University's culture—2
Meets outreach office goals—2
Maintains congenial office working environment—3
Able to manage time and workload well—3
Works effectively under stress—3
Submits regular reports in a timely manner—2
Uses good judgment—2
Is productive with quality work—3
Communication skills—3
Enthusiasm—2
Attitude—3
Dependability—6
Selling skills, phone—2
Selling skills, in person—2
Marketing skills—2
Product knowledge—3
Belief in product and services—2
Builds loyal and repeat customers—3
Evaluation summary—2.67

Ben put down the papers, walked to the fridge, took out a Capital Special Pilsner, and snapped open the bottle. He took a long drink. The cold beer felt good on his tongue. He could feel a massive headache developing, one that would start in the back of his head, move around to both sides, and then settle just above his eyes.

He picked up the evaluation papers, slumped down in his recliner, and once more read through the list of numbers. He was furious. Never before in his now twenty-one-year career had he ever gotten such a low evaluation. It was humiliating, embarrassing. As he read the categories and the numbers more closely, he became even angrier. Not one category referred to his role as an educator. Not one. No mention was made of teaching strategies, of learner outcomes, of people's problems solved, of content knowledge and technical proficiency. No mention of what Ben believed to be the most important part of his job, trying to make a difference in the lives of people. The categories here referred to a salesperson—*Selling skills, phone*; *Selling skills, in person*; *Marketing skills.*

Slowly, Ben's anger subsided and he felt calm, as if some outside power had come into the room and said, "Relax, Ben." A great fog began to lift from his life. When Osborne University hired him and gave him the title of research application specialist, he had thought it was a fancy, twenty-first-century term for teacher. Now he knew it was not. "Research application specialist" was a cover for salesperson. Promoter. Marketer. Now he knew why he had so many headaches, why he was skeptical of Osborne and its lofty goals. This past year he had rediscovered who he really was, that he was a teacher, had always been a teacher, and wanted to be a teacher now.

He slumped further into his chair. How much longer could he work for Osborne University and maintain any semblance of personal integrity? Based on his evaluation it was probably not his decision to make—Osborne was likely right now trying to figure out a face-saving way of firing him and replacing him with someone who could excel in doing what they wanted.

And what would he tell Beth? What could he tell her? Could she handle the truth of the matter, or would she see him as a failure? As someone who was handed a great opportunity and then muffed it because of his ideals, because of his values and beliefs. Because of his personal integrity. He took another long drag on his bottle of Special Pilsner.

Ben decided not to tell Beth about his performance report because she would be extremely angry. He also decided not to share the information with Brittani because she had likely gotten her own evaluation and had not said one word about it.

He spent a long Saturday afternoon fishing with Lars Olson. He shared every detail of the written evaluation with Lars, every last number.

"What an ungrateful place, that Osborne University," Ben said. "I work my ass off and what do I get? A list of low numbers on a cold sheet of paper."

Lars let him talk without interruption. The fish weren't biting to break Ben's story line as he went on sharing what Lars had heard him say at other times.

"I try to do what they ask. I think I've traveled more miles this past year than I did in three years when I was an ag agent. I've learned most of their damned rules. Even took a computer course."

The two friends sat quietly for a time, watching their red and white bobbers that lay motionless on the smooth waters of Silver Lake.

"So, what are you gonna do, Ben?" Lars asked. Ben wiped his eyes with his hand, for he realized some tears had been forming.

"Lars, I just don't know. I've heard nothing more from Osborne, not a peep from anybody there. I don't know if they're figuring out a way to fire me, are hoping I'll change my ways and come around to doing what they want me to do, or if they expect me to quit and just disappear into the woodwork."

"Oh, I think I'd just keep doing my job," Lars said. "You've got a big celebration coming up in a couple of weeks. Cranberry One-Fifty should take your mind away from your troubles."

"What about Beth? She hardly talks to me these days. She thinks Osborne should be promoting me to a high-level position," Ben said with a laugh. "Boy, will she be surprised if they fire me."

"Ben, I can't tell you what to say to your wife. You'll have to figure that out by yourself."

"I guess so, Lars. I guess so." Ben retrieved the line on his fishing rod and cast it out once more. The red and white bobber lay motionless on the glassy surface of the lake, a vivid contrast to the turmoil Ben felt inside himself.

61

Cranberry One-Fifty

*B*en worked furiously the final days before the Cranberry One-Fifty celebration in August. He expected Dr. Phillips would remind him of his "excessive public service work," and tell him it was cutting into his billable hours. But he didn't care. He expected any day to receive his pink slip, a notice that his services were no longer needed, but he surmised that Osborne University wouldn't fire him just ahead of the big celebration; they didn't want to face the negative publicity. Ben assumed there might be some if he was let go after only one year on the job.

The celebration opened on Friday evening, with a banquet recognizing the centennial cranberry growers in central Wisconsin. Following the banquet, the community was invited to see the much-anticipated performance of the Cranberry One-Fifty pageant, a locally produced historical play. The planning committee identified twenty centennial growers and invited them and their families to a catered meal set up in the Willow River High School gym. The committee set up long tables of eight on the gym floor, with red and white table coverings. High school students decked out in black slacks and skirts and white shirts and blouses served the food catered by the Lone Pine restaurant. Platters of roast beef, baked chicken, green beans and corn, and of course bowls of cranberry sauce appeared on the tables, soon to be followed by large slabs of cranberry pie, all served by smiling young people.

The Willow River High School band, under the direction of Ms. Lois Walters, was in position on the gym floor in front of the stage that had been brought in for the celebration. The band played background music as people filed into the big room and found places at a table.

Ames County businesses plus other area businesses sponsored the event, which included awarding handsome plaques to each centennial family. Shotgun Slogum served as master of ceremonies. His family had been one of the very first to grow cranberries in the area, and likely the first to develop a bog on the Tamarack River. Ben hardly recognized Shotgun when he was dressed up. His beard was nicely trimmed and he wore a navy blue sport coat with pressed tan pants, not the faded flannel shirt and blue jeans Ben was accustomed to seeing.

"Welcome to this special Cranberry One-Fifty celebration banquet," Shotgun began. "I want to first introduce our Cranberry Queen and her court. Here is Debra Backus from Link Lake, our Cranberry Queen." Debra, resplendent in a red gown with a yellow rose corsage, stood up and waved from the stage while the crowd clapped loudly.

"And her court, Laura Dalenski from Waupaca and Carol Cunningham from Willow River. Would you both stand?" Laura wore a lime green gown and Carol's was a light blue. They also had yellow rose corsages. Both stood and smiled while the crowd clapped.

"As a special treat, I've asked Queen Debra to read her poem. Each queen candidate wrote a poem, which was a part of the selection process."

Once more Debra Backus stood and walked to the microphone. She looked out over the crowd and began reading in a strong, clear voice.

Cranberry Moon

> On a quiet night in October
> When the moon hangs low in the sky
> I take my love to the country
> To the cranberry marshes
> To the marshes that stretch out before us
> As far as we can see in the moonlight.

She read the entire poem, made a little bow, and returned to her seat to polite applause. Ben overheard someone at his table say to his wife, "That's not poetry. It doesn't rhyme. If it doesn't rhyme, it ain't a poem."

"Shh," his wife admonished.

Next Shotgun introduced Lars Olson and then Ben Wesley, who recounted memories of working as county agricultural agents with the cranberry growers over the years. In between the more formal parts of the program, Shotgun told stories and shared one-liners.

"Did you hear the story about the fellow who was caught in a snowstorm on his way to Wisconsin Rapids a few years ago?" Shotgun began as a few chuckles could be heard from the back of the room.

"Well, his car slid into the ditch and he began walking through the blowing snow. He saw a light up ahead and proceeded to tramp through the storm, on his way toward what he hoped would be shelter for the night." Shotgun paused for a moment and took a drink of water.

"When he got to the house, he rapped on the door. The farmer opened it and welcomed the stranger inside.

"'Would you have a spare bed for the night?' the stranded traveler asked as he brushed snow from his coat. 'I'm prepared to pay you of course.'

"'Sir, you are not the only one caught in this storm,' the farmer responded. 'Every one of my beds is taken. But if you don't mind, you can share a bed with the red-haired school teacher.'" Once more Shotgun paused as members of the audience listened intently.

"'My good man,' the stranded motorist said, 'I am a religious person. What you are suggesting I cannot do.'

"'Why is that?' the farmer asked, smiling.

"'Because I am a Christian man.'

"'So is the red-haired school teacher,' the farmer replied."

The entire audience burst into loud laughter, enjoying Shotgun's stories, although growers like Jeff Johnson considered him lost in the past when it came to gardening and cranberry growing.

After the centennial cranberry grower families were properly recognized, photographed, and applauded, and had returned to their seats after being lined up in a long row in front of the podium to receive their handsome plaques, Shotgun announced, "We'll now take a fifteen-minute break so those coming to see our special stage show can be seated."

There was a brief shuffling of chairs and table clearing in the gym, then the entrance of at least a hundred more people, who were ushered to chairs by the high school students. Once again, Shotgun took the microphone.

"Now we turn to a part of the program we have all looked forward to for a very long time. We are privileged to see the first performance of the Cranberry One-Fifty pageant, an enactment of the history of cranberry growing in Wisconsin." Everyone clapped as the lights in the gymnasium dimmed and the curtains on the stage slowly parted to reveal several Willow River High School students dressed as Native Americans and clustered in small groups on several parts of the stage. Flute music from the band could be heard in the background. The center of the stage was designed as a wild marsh. A spotlight illuminated a small group of Native Americans on their hands and knees picking wild cranberries into baskets.

Billy Baxter, author and narrator of the pageant, stood behind the curtains and offstage at a microphone. He began, "Cranberries have grown in Ames County and much of central and northern Wisconsin for hundreds of years. Native Americans knew about this tart red fruit long before the first white settlers arrived. Wisconsin's Algonquin Indians called this fruit *Alogua.* Here we see them picking the ripe red berries that grew wild in Wisconsin marshes." Billy's deep baritone voice easily reached every corner of the gym.

The spotlight shifted to three Indian women seated near a little campfire. Billy continued. "The Indians ate cranberries fresh, they baked them into bread, and they dried them and mixed them with wild game, creating what they called pemmican. Sometimes they mixed cranberries with maple sugar or honey, to make them even tastier with some of the tangy flavor reduced."

Once more the spotlight shifted, this time to a replica of a rustic trading post where a white man dressed in buckskins leaned over the counter while an Indian showed him a basket filled with ripe red cranberries. "The first known sale of cranberries in Wisconsin took place in 1829," Billy continued. "Daniel Whitney ran a trading post in Green Bay and he bought three canoe-loads of cranberries from the Indians."

Now the stage light dimmed and there was considerable shuffling and shifting going on. The flute music in the background continued as Billy said, "Cranberries also grow in the East, especially in Massachusetts and New Jersey. The early Dutch and German settlers in those states first called this native fruit craneberry, because the cranberry stem and blossom resemble the neck, head, and beak of a crane. Over time the word was shortened to cranberry."

Billy went on a bit talking about Henry Hall, a Revolutionary War veteran who started the first commercial cranberry operation on Cape Cod in Massachusetts in 1816. By 1820 Hall was shipping cranberries to Boston and New York City.

Now the lights came up on the stage, revealing a lone figure, a man dressed in a white shirt, brown trousers, and wide-brimmed hat. He stood overlooking the cranberry marsh. The band music shifted to a quiet rendition of the 1850s ballad "The Song of the Farmer." Billy Baxter continued, "Edward Sacket from Sacket Harbor, New York, started the first commercial cranberry operation in Wisconsin when he moved north of Berlin in 1860. He bought seven hundred acres of bog land covered with wild cranberry vines. Sacket had grown cranberries in New York, so he knew about their culture. Upon arriving in Wisconsin he cleared away brush, dug ditches, built dams, and even constructed a warehouse."

The spotlight shifted to a group of young people on their hands and knees, picking cranberries in six-quart pails.

"In the year 1865 Sacket's cranberry operation yielded 938 barrels of the tart fruit, which in those days was picked by hand. A good cranberry picker could pick two bushels a day and could earn as much as a buck fifty for his efforts."

The spotlight moved stage right, where a group of young people was square dancing. The band played "Turkey in the Straw" and the square dancer caller gave the instructions "All join hands and circle to the left, now swing your partner; do-si-do and promenade the hall."

The narration continued, "In the evenings, after a long, hard day of picking cranberries, the young people held huge parties and danced into the night. The cranberry harvest had become a major social event. Other growers, noting Sacket's success, started cranberry operations near Berlin on land thought worthless. These new cranberry growers included the Cary brothers, J. D. Waters, Ruddock Mason and Company, and J. D. Williams. By the late 1870s this area boasted more than one thousand acres of cranberry bogs, which yielded about one hundred bushels of cranberries per acre."

The music changed to a rather somber piece as the spotlight picked up Mr. Sacket looking over his deserted cranberry bog and holding his big hat in his hands.

"The Berlin-area cranberry boom turned to bust in the early 1880s," Baxter continued. "Heavy rains flooded the marshes, resulting in only half a crop and spoiled, partially ripened berries. An early September frost in 1883 doomed the crop; in many cases it was not worth harvesting. By 1885 cranberry growing in the Berlin area had essentially ended."

Billy paused briefly and then announced, "Now we will have a brief intermission as we move to Act 2. Sit back and enjoy the Willow River band." The band immediately began playing tunes from *Oklahoma!*, beginning with "Oh, What a Beautiful Morning." They had just finished the tune and were arranging their music for the next when a terrific crash came from behind the curtains, and "Judas Priest, whatta we do now?" boomed over the PA system. Billy hadn't realized his microphone was still on. A titter of laughter rolled over the crowd as the band moved into "The Surrey with the Fringe on Top," and then the band performed a boisterous rendition of "Oklahoma!"

Band members grinned, as they had an inkling of what had happened on stage. The band finished the third tune and immediately returned to playing the first—they had only rehearsed three tunes, as that was supposed to be enough time for the set change on stage. When they finished the third tune the second time the curtains once more opened, revealing the same cranberry bog that had been in Act 1 and, off to the side, a partial railroad depot, its roof tipped at a strange angle and the Cranmoor sign hanging crooked. The spotlight shone brightly on the disheveled depot. Looking carefully, it was possible to see a pair of moccasined feet under the depot replica; obviously one of the Native Americans from Act 1 was holding it in place.

Billy's narration continued, with no hint of the catastrophe or near catastrophe that had occurred behind the curtains during the intermission. "By 1875 cranberry growing had become well established in the Cranmoor area of Wood County. This area, with its combination of marshes and upland, naturally acidic soil, and ready access to water, made it an especially agreeable place for cranberry growing. With the coming of the railroad to the area, cranberry growing flourished."

The spotlight moved to a group of young men, each wearing hip boots and lined up in a row across the flooded cranberry bog. "By 1900 hand-picking of cranberries was replaced with hand-raking. Growers discovered that by flooding their bogs at harvest time, the ripe berries floated to the top of the water, and workers with rakes could far more easily harvest them than picking by hand. Hand-raking continued until after World War II, when the practice was slowly replaced with the harvesting methods used today."

Those sitting closest to front of the gym, much to their surprise, saw a stream of water pouring over the edge of the stage like a small waterfall and pooling on the gym floor near where the band was seated. Several band members shifted their chairs in order to remain dry. When the depot fell, it had punched a hole in the plastic that held the water in the bog. No one on stage seemed to know that the flooded cranberry bog was returning to a dry marsh.

Now the curtains closed once more and quickly opened again, with all the actors standing on stage and singing a song written especially for the pageant. The actors standing stage center stood apart from each other a bit, to allow the stream of water to pour between them. They acted like they hadn't noticed what was happening as they all began signing lustily to the tune of "On, Wisconsin!"

> On cran-ber-ries, On cran-ber-ries!
> We are number one.
> Run the others off the field now
> A winner sure each year.

You! Rah! Rah!
On cran-ber-ries, On cran-ber-ries
Drink their juice, eat them fresh
Fight on for healthy living
'Cause we know that's best.

The curtain closed and applause filled the gymnasium. Just as the clapping died down a bit, a huge crash came from backstage. The Cranmoor Depot had obviously once more fallen to the floor. Three janitors with mops and pails hurriedly appeared from a side door, intent on corralling the gallons of water that continued to pour from the stage.

Ben was smiling as he made his way to the door. The first major part of the Cranberry One-Fifty celebration had concluded with a minimum of mishap—at least from Ben's perspective.

Celebration Continues

*W*illow River's volunteer fire department swept clean and washed down Main Street and decorated it from one end to the other. Volunteers hung a huge white banner across the street with the words "Cranberry One-Fifty" in large red letters. Main Street business owners displayed photos, paintings, and exhibits of historic cranberry harvest equipment, all in one way or another commemorating cranberry growing and its contributions to the community.

Early on Saturday morning, the volunteer firefighters removed the fire trucks from the Willow River Fire Station, and in the empty spaces, on tables lined up along both walls and across the center, artists, photographers, and craftspeople from the area showed off and offered their wares for sale. The Ames County Whittlers displayed, on two tables, their recent efforts, including miniature carved old-fashioned cranberry rakes that they offered for sale. Two of the whittlers sat at the table, knives in hand, willing to show anyone interested how they did the carving.

Paintings of cranberry bogs and a quilt with various cranberry scenes sewed into it hung on the fire station wall alongside photos depicting modern-day cranberry harvest procedures as well as wildlife found in and around cranberry bogs—deer, raccoons, sandhill cranes, bald eagles. A corner table displayed framed poems and stories about early cranberry growing, with a big sign that declared "Writing contest sponsored by the Ames County Scribblers." The community room of the library featured a two-day sale of every imaginable cranberry food product: pies, cookies, breads, sauces, muffins, scones, cheesecakes, cranberry tarts, and much more.

A huge crowd from near and far turned out for the Saturday events, enjoying the exhibits, visiting with each other, and stopping by the food and beverage tents. Oscar Anderson and Fred Russo, freshly shaven and each wearing new John Deere caps, stood watching the goings-on.

"Quite a shin dig," Oscar commented.

"Yup, it's big alright. Really nice day, too," answered Fred.

"Yeah, I'm glad we don't have to pay," Oscar said.

"You want something to drink?"

"You're right, too loud to think."

And so the two continued their conversation, if it could be called that. Too much background noise prevented the two old farmers from hearing much of anything the other said.

The Willow River Kiwanis Club had erected a huge beer and bratwurst tent, strategically placed along Main Street so no one had to walk more than a block to buy a bottle of beer and a juicy, cranberry bratwurst made especially for the event at the Willow River Meat Market, which was one of the few old-fashioned meat markets remaining in the area. A cloud of bratwurst smoke wafted down the street, appealing to those who cherished their brats, not so appealing to a visitor who wondered what was cooking and why it smoked so much. Of course those manning the grills also prepared hotdogs and hamburgers, as well as grilled chicken.

Ben stopped by to chat for a bit with Lars Olson, who was working at one of the grills.

"Good show, Ben," Lars said. He wore a long apron with the words "I Grill for You" emblazoned on the front. "You did a good job with this. Let me embarrass you for a minute and say I couldn't think of anybody else who could have brought this community together like you did."

Ben smiled, appreciating the comment from his predecessor. "The planning committee deserves all the credit," Ben said. He touched his friend on the shoulder.

"Whoops, gotta turn some chicken," Lars said as he turned back to the big grill.

Ben walked along Main Street, greeting friends new and old. He spotted Joe and Julie Evans and their children, Joey and Melissa. They chatted a bit about the weather and how Joe's crops were doing this year after the disastrous hailstorm that about wiped them out last year.

Ben also greeted Gloria and Paul Mayer and inquired about their new market garden operation. "So far so good," Paul responded. "Weather's been good to us. Looks like a great tomato crop; potatoes look good, too."

"Glad to hear it. And how about the kids, let's see, their names are Jake, Jennifer, and Jackson."

"Hey, you got a good memory, Ben. Kids are doing great; they're around here somewhere."

Ben felt good as he walked along; he was pleased with what he had done to create this wonderful celebration. Adjacent to the grill the Willow River Flower Club sold ice cream of several flavors, including cranberry. Both adults and children stood in long lines to receive generous scoops of the tasty treat. Club members also served lemonade made the old-fashioned way, with real lemons. On Friday, members had hauled picnic tables from Willow River Park and located them near the big food tent. Ben noticed that nearly all the tables were occupied whenever he checked. Everyone clearly was having a good time.

Johnny Santoski sat under a big red umbrella near the food tent, cradling his accordion on his lap as he played everything from old-time polkas to Beatles tunes. Ben stopped to watch and listen. Despite all the worries he had about the celebration, he began to relax a bit as he realized that things were going well. The celebration was coming off as planned.

"Hi, Ben." Ben turned to see Billy Baxter from the *Argus*. He had a notepad in hand and a camera hung around his neck.

"You did a great job with the pageant," Ben said to his fellow committee member.

"Had a lot of help. Couldn't have pulled it off without the drama club at the high school. What a great bunch of kids."

"Too bad about the water spill," Ben said, smiling.

"Goes with the territory," Billy replied. "Could have been worse, I suppose."

"Getting a good story for the paper?"

"Sure am. Lots of good material here."

That evening, the Willow River police chief closed Main Street to traffic, and a polka dance went on into the night, with hundreds of young and old dancing to the strains of the Uncle Freddy Band, five farmers who began playing in the early 1970s and continued providing music over the years. Uncle Freddy, now in his eighties, was a bit hard of hearing and a little forgetful. His son had taken over the band, but Uncle Freddy was always there, playing his accordion and smiling like he'd just bitten into a freshly grilled bratwurst.

Ben asked Beth to go to the dance with him, "to kick up our heels," as they had when they were first married.

"I don't think so, Ben," she said when he asked. "Polka dances seem just a little old-fashioned for me, a little too country, too ethnic."

"Have it your way, then," Ben said, disappointed with his wife's attitude.

Because he chaired the planning committee, Ben felt some obligation to go, and he did. He saw Brittani and Chris dancing, doing the polka, dancing the old-time waltzes, snuggling during the slow dances. Brittani wore a bright red dress with a flowing skirt. They made a good-looking couple. At the end of one of the dance sets, they spotted Ben standing on the sidelines and walked over.

"Having fun?" Ben asked.

"Sure am," Brittani said. Her face was flushed from the dancing.

"Didn't know how much I missed these old-fashioned celebrations," remarked Chris. "This is about as different from Baghdad as you could ever imagine."

Uncle Freddy began playing an old-time waltz.

"Wanna dance, Ben?" Brittani asked.

"Sure," he said.

It had been a while since Ben danced an old-time waltz; it had been a long time since he had danced at all. For the past five years or so, Beth seemed too busy to go dancing.

"Celebration is going well," Brittani said. She was trying to follow Ben's halting dance steps.

"Better than I thought," replied Ben. "So many people volunteered to help."

They finished the dance, and Brittani and Chris walked off, holding hands.

Ben thought how much fun it had been dancing with Brittani, and how clumsy he felt as they moved to the music. *Guess I'm out of practice*, he thought. *And maybe part of it is I just don't have much fun anymore, working all the time, it seems.*

The Sunday afternoon cranberry parade was billed as the premier event of the celebration, featuring a flyover. The committee planning the parade knew that scheduling a flyover would attract people who might not ordinarily come to a parade, even though this one had more than a hundred units.

The parade was scheduled for 1 p.m., and by 11:30 a.m. you could scarcely find a place to stand along Main Street. Promptly at noon, the Willow River police chief parked his car across one end of the street, its blue and red lights flashing. His deputy parked the second police cruiser—the city only owned two vehicles—to block the other end of the street. The crowd waited, enjoying the nice weather, eating bratwursts, grilled chicken, hamburgers, and cranberry ice cream, and drinking homemade lemonade.

At five minutes of one, someone shot off an aerial bomb, which caused everyone to jump. The parade began moving down the street to the loud applause of those watching. First came Willow River's mayor, sitting in the back of a convertible and smiling broadly. He knew the celebration had brought thousands of dollars to his community.

The Cranberry Queen's float came next. Debra Backus and her court rode on a beautifully decorated farm wagon pulled by a restored John Deere B tractor. The young women, all wearing gowns of various pastel shades, smiled, waved, and tossed candy to the kids who scrambled to retrieve it.

A convertible with the words "Osborne University" printed boldly on each side came next. Brittani Stone, wearing her bright yellow dress, smiled radiantly as the car passed by. Ben had begged off being in the parade; he said he had too many details to worry about and needed to be available if some problem developed. He wondered who was driving the vehicle; the driver had his cap pulled low over his eyes and he was wearing dark sunglasses. When the car was opposite where Ben stood, he recognized Chris Martin. Brittani had talked her boyfriend into driving the convertible.

The president of Osborne University, Dr. Delbert George, walked behind the Osborne parade entry. He handed out colorful brochures describing the new commemorative park the university was building on the banks of the Tamarack River.

The Link Lake Historical Society entry followed next, with a team of black horses pulling a buggy driven by a woman in a mid-nineteenth-century costume and a man holding a red book and dressed in black from head to toe. A sign on the back of the buggy read "Pastor Increase Joseph Link: Founder of Link Lake in 1852, and a friend of the land."

Fire trucks from the neighboring towns passed by: Redgranite, Plainfield, Hancock, Coloma. All red and shiny. Horns blaring. Sirens screaming. Children covering their ears. The centennial cranberry growers and their families, in several convertibles, drove by next. Five Ames County snowplows followed, their diesel engines belching dark, foul-smelling diesel smoke.

But what about the flyover? people lining the parade route began to wonder. Usually such a special event occurred at the beginning of a parade, and now the parade was soon over and there were no airplanes, no National Guard jets roaring past, as people reading the parade announcement had anticipated.

The Willow River High School band marched by looking smart in their purple and gold uniforms. A troop of Girl Scouts followed and the Boy Scouts came next. But now the audience was becoming impatient. When's the flyover?

Someone finally spotted a lone airplane, a smallish propeller-driven machine, coming their way from the west and dropping lower as it approached. The plane was pulling a banner and as it got closer people could make out the words "Cranberry Red" on the long streamer.

"That plane better watch out for the flyover," someone said. The bright yellow flying machine, clearly a crop-dusting plane, as people identified the dusting mechanism beneath its wings, circled Willow River once and then twice. It flew low over the crowd, the long advertising banner fluttering in the breeze.

Two cranberry growers looked up. "Good God," said one. "What the hell kind of a flyover is this? The plane is pushin' that Cranberry Red stuff? Advertisin' comin' from all directions. Now it's even comin' outta the sky."

"You gonna use some of that Cranberry Red on your beds?" asked the second grower.

"Don't know enough about it yet," replied the first. "Wish they'd lay off on their damn advertisin'. Enough is enough."

The yellow plane turned wide and this time came even lower over Main Street, making a deafening roar as it screamed only a few feet above the tallest buildings, and lower than the water tower just south of town. Babies began crying; horses jumped. One horse reared and took off down the street, heading out of town on a gallop, its rider yelling, "Whoa, whoa," as she hopelessly tried to stop the beast.

People later talked about what happened next and wondered if it was planned or if the tow cable broke. Anyway, the long Cranberry Red banner came lose from the plane and fluttered earthward as the incredulous crowd watched. Like a kite with a broken string, the banner curled upon itself and slowly fell toward the crowd of parade watchers, now all looking upward.

Upon reaching the end of the parade route, the yellow airplane quickly climbed into the clear blue sky, wiggled its wings a couple of times, and disappeared into the distance.

The Cranberry Red banner came to rest over the top of the Kiwanis food tent, one end of the canvas banner landing directly on the hot bratwurst grill. It immediately began to burn. Alert Kiwanis members began tossing beer on the burning banner, eventually extinguishing it so that all that remained was "Cranberry R."

Ben turned to Billy Baxter, who had snapped several photos of the event. "Well, that was a bit of a surprise," Billy commented. "This your idea of another way to promote Cranberry Red?" Billy was smiling broadly.

"Hell, no," said Ben. He was not smiling. The smell of spilled beer and burned canvas hung in the air.

63

Anonymous Letter

Ben arrived home that Sunday evening, exhausted but pleased that the Cranberry One-Fifty celebration had come off so well, even though some people were more than a little disappointed with the flyover and International Farm-Med's brazen attempt at advertising Cranberry Red.

"Bet you're glad all that's past," Beth said when Ben walked through their door, ready to collapse.

"It was kind of fun," Ben said. "You heard what happened at the parade?"

"Glad I stayed home. Sounds like the flyover was a bust. Who hired that pilot anyway?"

"Well, *I* didn't," said Ben. "I can't be in charge of everything, Beth. I hope you'd realize that for a change." His words had a sharp edge to them. He wished Beth would be a little more supportive of his work and appreciate all that he and the planning committee had done for the community and for the cranberry industry.

"By the way, a letter came for you yesterday. I forgot to tell you about it last night."

"Well, thanks for telling me now," Ben said. He wished he'd used a different tone of voice as soon as the words came out of his mouth.

"Doubt it's very important. Some kind of free offer that'll cost us money. Looks like that kind of letter." She pointed to where she had tucked the envelope behind a book on the shelf in the living room.

Ben retrieved the letter and noticed that it had no return address. The envelope was plain, white, and business size. Ben's name and address were handwritten. He slit it open and unfolded a single sheet of paper; the message was also handwritten. It read:

Dear Mr. Wesley,

I have evidence to prove that Osborne University's new product, Cranberry Red, is dangerous and should be pulled from the market immediately. Although it likely does what it's supposed to do, that is, increase the antioxidant level of cranberries, it has side effects that are hideous, unpredictable, and as yet not fully known.

I know you to be an honest, ethical man, and I also know that you are an employee of Osborne University. I ask you to do whatever you can to stop the sale of Cranberry Red and prevent any more use of this dangerous chemical.

The letter was not signed.

"What's the letter about?" Beth asked matter-of-factly. She was working in the kitchen.

"Ah, from some crank. I get these once in a while."

"Why is that? You shouldn't be getting crank letters at home."

"Well, I do. Every so often," Ben said as he folded the letter, placed it back in its envelope, and stuffed it into his pocket. He didn't want Beth to find the letter. She would surely raise a fuss because she and a host of others believed Osborne University could do no wrong, and that any product from Osborne, whether it was a new product or a new online course in nursing administration, would be of the highest quality and should not be questioned.

Ben was curious about the letter. Its tone suggested the writer knew more about Cranberry Red than he or she had shared, but for some reason the person wanted to remain anonymous. From the very first time Ben heard about Cranberry Red, he had had concerns about the discovery, mostly because it was so new and in Ben's mind hadn't been sufficiently tested. This letter was the first real evidence confirming his suspicions, if he could believe what the writer said.

The next day Ben decided to drive to the Osborne Research Station and visit with Gunnar Godson; he might be able to shed some light on the situation. He first stopped at his office and asked Brittani to change any appointments he had for the morning, which she willingly said she would do. At least the office was a civil place these days, so different from a year ago. He wished that he and Beth got along as well as he and Brittani did. As the office situation improved, conditions at home grew frostier. During the past couple of years, Ben had simply not been able to understand Beth's thinking. He tried to share with her what he was doing and why, but she usually had some curt response that cut him off when he did. Lately, he found it easier not to share much. To keep what he was doing and what he was thinking to himself.

When he arrived at the research station, he found Gunnar working in one of the vegetable plots where he had been experimenting with some new variety of broccoli, attempting to increase its antioxidant level as he had with cranberries.

"Ben, it's good to see you. I'm working alone here today," Gunnar said as he stood up, wiped his hands off on his pants, and extended a hand to shake Ben's. "How are things going? Cranberry One-Fifty was sure a success. People are still talking about the parade. Especially the flyover," Gunnar added, chuckling. Ben enjoyed Gunnar's Swedish accent.

Ben laughed. "I expect that's what folks will remember most. How are things going with you?"

"Okay, I guess."

"Just okay? No new discoveries coming out of your lab?"

Now Gunnar laughed. "You're just like everyone else at Osborne, expecting something new and exciting to come out of this place every day." He said it with a smile, as he was aware that Ben knew well that when doing agricultural research it took time it to develop something, whether it was an improvement on something old or something completely new.

"Say, Gunnar," Ben began, becoming serious. "I have something to show you." He reached in his pocket and pulled out the anonymous letter and handed it to Gunnar. "What do you think about this? Does this person make sense? Any idea who wrote it?"

A strange expression came over Gunnar's face as he silently read the words. He handed it back to Ben.

"Well, what do you think?"

"This person has a point," Gunnar said.

"So, you believe something might be wrong with Cranberry Red?" Ben asked. "If there is, it's a serious matter."

Gunnar stood silently for a while, looking off in the distance, across the experimental cranberry bog and toward the Tamarack River that lazily flowed through the back of the property.

"It is a serious matter," Gunnar remarked.

"I wonder who wrote this letter," Ben said after Gunnar handed it back to him.

"Doesn't matter who wrote it. What matters is whether this person has his facts straight," replied Gunnar.

"Do you think he does?" asked Ben as he folded the paper and put it back in his pocket.

"I'm not supposed to tell you this," said Gunnar. "But you deserve to know."

"Know what?"

"Side effects of Cranberry Red."

"What side effects?"

"Let me show you something." Gunnar led Ben into the lab, where he took out the frozen night crawlers.

"Geez, I've never seen bigger night crawlers," Ben said. "Where'd you get these?"

Gunnar explained how a worker had accidentally spilled some Cranberry Red and how he'd later found these giant night crawlers on the very spot.

"Good God!" Ben exclaimed. "This is terrible. You sure Cranberry Red did this?"

"Follow me," Gunnar said as he walked to where he was conducting the experiment with three groups of night crawlers. Gunnar first showed Ben the control group.

"So, these look like perfectly normal night crawlers, pretty healthy looking ones, too," commented Ben.

Then Gunnar pointed to the third container.

Ben peered inside and looked at Gunnar with a perplexed look on his face. "Nothing here. I don't see anything."

"I started with the same number of night crawlers in each container," Gunnar explained. "Treated this container with full-strength Cranberry Red."

"What happened to the night crawlers?"

"They all died. Every last one of them. Grew themselves to death."

"Geez!" Ben said.

"Now look in this container. For these I moistened the soil with water containing five drops of Cranberry Red per gallon of water." Gunnar lifted the cover of the container and Ben looked in. He immediately jumped back, for he saw a mass of writhing, twisting night crawlers, some of them two feet long and as big around as a man's finger. They immediately tried to escape from the container; Gunnar slammed down the cover before they could.

"Son of a bitch!" Ben exclaimed. "Cranberry Red did this?"

"Yes, it did," Gunnar said quietly.

"Have you told Osborne officials about this?"

"Had the big shots out here to see the first big crawlers. They said I should tell no one about it and should do no more testing, which you can see I still did," Gunnar said, smiling. Turning serious again, Gunnar continued, "They threatened to fire me if I told anyone about this."

"I can't believe Osborne University would cover this up. I just can't believe it," Ben said, shaking his head.

"Neither could I," Gunnar said. "I'm glad you came out here. I had to tell someone."

"For what it's worth, I think Osborne University is ready to fire me, too," Ben admitted.

"Why?" asked a surprised Gunnar.

"Because I haven't promoted Cranberry Red well enough."

Gunnar thrust out his hand and shook Ben's. He was smiling from ear to ear. "I guess we are in this together."

"You got any idea who wrote this letter?" Ben asked. "Who else knows about these night crawlers?"

"My staff here knows, of course. They've been quietly helping me with the experiment. And the bigwigs from Oshkosh—President George, Dr. Foley, and Dr. Phillips—know; they were out here and I showed them the big, frozen night crawlers. They haven't seen my experiment though."

"None of the Osborne administrators would say anything," said Ben, scratching his head. "They've got too much invested in Cranberry Red."

"It's a puzzle, that's for sure," said Gunnar. "What do we do next?"

"I don't know. But we must do something," Ben replied. "Cranberry Red is much more dangerous than I thought."

Gus and the Tamarack River

Gus Caldwell remembered well that a year ago he and intern Kirsten Leary conducted a fish count on the Tamarack River and turned up a gigantic northern pike, one larger than Gus had seen in his thirty years working for the DNR. They'd also measured some huge brown trout, much larger than they expected.

When the DNR office learned about Osborne's University's plans to build a new park on the river, the Madison office asked Gus to check out the area and make sure Osborne University had complied with all the rules about setbacks, beach development, and other stipulations designed to protect the river and its adjacent habitat. Gus was also anxious to do another fish census of the river, to see how many and what size fish he might turn up this year.

Once more Kirsten Leary, University of Wisconsin–Madison intern, teamed up with him. Gus had come to enjoy working with Kirsten. He had learned a considerable amount about the basic biology of fish and their habitats from this university biology student. Kirsten had also learned much about the practical side of fish counts, water sampling, and assessing freshwater fish environments.

Gus always enjoyed his work because it kept him outside most of the time, and away from a dreaded desk. It also allowed him to visit some of the finest lakes and rivers in Wisconsin and get paid for doing it. The Tamarack River in central Wisconsin had always been one of his favorites. It was a lazy, twisting river that ran through marshland, cranberry bogs, and at times through thick forestland that came down to the river's edge. Like Wisconsin's many other rivers and lakes, it had its own personality, its own history, and of course its own stories.

On this early September day, Gus and Kirsten launched their DNR boat at the new Ira Osborne Commemorative Park. This was a mile or so from where the duo had, a year ago, measured the largest northern pike that either of them had seen, so they were interested in what the fish census would look like here. Besides, they could check to make sure that Osborne University had followed all the rules concerning building a park on a river. A careful look around had assured Gus that the rules had been followed, and he noted his finding in the notebook that he always carried in his shirt pocket.

They motored down stream for a half mile or so and began slowly working their way back, shocking, netting, measuring, clipping fins, and returning the unharmed fish back to the water. Nothing especially surprising turned up; no huge fish emerged, just the regular run of smallmouth bass, brown trout, and the occasional small- to average-size northern. But there was something different about the fish, something that Gus couldn't quite put his finger on. They appeared to look like the thousands of other fish he had measured and counted over the years; they may have been a bit larger for their ages, but there was something else about them. Something mysterious.

"Kirsten, do you see anything unusual about these fish?" Gus asked after they had worked for a half hour or so.

"Well, no, not exactly," Kirsten replied. She hesitated and added, "There is something strange about them though, but I don't know what it is."

"I thought the same thing, but I can't put my finger on it. Maybe we should take a few of these back to the lab with us, see if the lab people can figure it out."

They tossed two fish of every species they had measured into the live box on the boat, to take back with them back to the Madison laboratory. Just in case their hunches had some validity to them. Kirsten also took water samples every hundred yards or so as they worked upriver and toward the landing at the new Osborne park. These too, she would deliver to the DNR laboratory.

Gus cut the boat motor a hundred yards or so from the boat landing at Osborne Park and took up the oars for the remainder of the trip. Even with a good motor on a boat, he still enjoyed pulling on boat oars. It reminded him of fishing with his dad when he was a kid and no one owned a boat motor. To get to where you needed to go on a river or lake, you rowed. He was enjoying the day as he pulled on the oars, looking at the trees along the river that were just beginning to show a little fall color—a maple here and there with a hint of red leaves, an aspen showing a little yellow. As he rowed, he occasionally turned his head to make sure he was going in the direction of the boat landing. One of those times he felt something strike the left oar, like he had hit something, a rock in the river, or perhaps a fallen tree branch just beneath the surface.

"What the—?" He turned to look at the oar. As he pulled it out of the water, he noticed that the wide part of the oar was missing, completely broken off. "Will you look at that," Gus said as Kirsten looked in amazement at what had happened. "All these years I never broke an oar like that. Never did."

Gus was close enough to shore that he was able to paddle with the remaining good oar to the boat landing. After they had loaded the boat onto the boat trailer and pulled it out of the water, Kirsten looked at the broken oar more closely.

"Gus, this oar didn't break," she remarked.

"Didn't break? What happened to it?"

"These are tooth marks," the young woman said. "Something bit off the end of your oar."

"Geez," Gus responded. "You're right. Those are tooth marks. Best we not say anything about this. Nobody would believe us."

"Something going on in this river," Kirsten said. "Something mighty strange."

They headed down Interstate 39 toward Madison, neither saying anything about what they had just experienced.

65

Ben and Shotgun Slogum

*W*hat's your problem, Ben?" Beth asked the next day at the breakfast table. "You're moping around like you lost your best friend."

"I don't know," Ben said. "I'm not feeling right." Beth was the last person with whom he wanted to share what he was learning about the side effects of Cranberry Red.

"What next, Ben? You've got the best job in the world, working for one of the finest universities in the country. You're making fairly good money. What's with you, anyway? You sick?"

"Beth, when you gonna get off my case?" Ben said, bristling. "You haven't had a civil thing to say to me in two weeks."

"Whoa, a little temper flair," Beth responded, holding up her hands.

Ben was quiet for a moment. Part of him wanted to blurt out that Beth's wonderful Osborne University wasn't all that it appeared to be. That its officials had some serious ethical problems. But this was not the time to do it. He knew she would refuse to believe him.

"You better get going. You don't want to be late for work. Got to keep on the good side of Osborne, you know," Beth said. Ben was thinking, *It's a little late to get on the good side of Osborne after the evaluation I got in July.* Getting on the good side of that outfit would be a tall hill to climb, and with what he knew now, he wasn't at all sure he wanted to climb it.

On Saturday, Osborne University planned to dedicate their new park on the Tamarack River. The *Ames County Argus* had carried several stories in recent weeks, recounting the progress in developing the park facilities, and of course giving high marks to Osborne University for its "more than generous contributions" to the community.

Ben had gotten a terse e-mail from Dr. Phillips asking him to be present at the ceremony, to say a few words of praise for the endeavor and to introduce President George. "I trust you'll be able to handle the task." Ben could read the sarcasm in the tone of her message. She also reminded Ben that he should bring along Brittani and they should set up a table where they could distribute literature about the outreach office and its services.

The ceremony was scheduled for 3 p.m. Ben asked Brittani if she would drive on ahead and set up the display table. "I want to stop and see Shotgun Slogum on my way to the park," Ben explained. "I haven't talked with him in a while and I doubt he'll come to the ceremony. He doesn't much care for ceremonies like this."

Ben, how the heck are you?" his friend said when he arrived at Shotgun's place. "Come on in; think I may still have some coffee. Probably strong enough to grow hair on your chest." Shotgun laughed when he said it. "You goin' to that deal over at the new park?"

"Yeah. I'm supposed to say a few words. Brag up Osborne University a little, as if they needed any more bragging up."

"You got somethin' on your mind, Ben?" Shotgun said, looking at his old friend.

"Something's been bothering me for a while," Ben admitted as he sipped his coffee. "You're right, this stuff is strong as hell."

"I warned you," Shotgun replied. "What you got in your craw?"

Ben took the anonymous letter from his pocket and handed it to Shotgun.

"Who wrote this?" Shotgun asked. A serious look came over his tanned and wrinkled face after he finished reading.

"I don't know. But whoever did it has his facts straight."

"How so?"

"Don't go telling anybody about what I'm about to share, because I don't want to get Gunnar Godson in trouble, but I was out to the research station the other day and Gunnar showed me the experiment he'd been conducting with night crawlers."

"Night crawlers? Why night crawlers?"

Ben explained what Gunnar had shared about the spilled Cranberry Red and described the big, frozen night crawlers Gunnar had showed him. "Gunnar conducted an experiment with more night crawlers and discovered that even when low levels of Cranberry Red are added to the soil, the crawlers grew like crazy. I saw them. Mean, grotesque-looking crawlers."

"Holy Lucifer's lunch," said Shotgun. "Is that International Farm-Med outfit pullin' the stuff off the market?"

"Nope, they and Osborne University are sitting on the information. Cranberry Red is dangerous; can you imagine what other side effects it might have—now, a year from now, ten years from now? It's just not safe. The chemical needs a lot more testing; I thought that from the beginning." Ben took a long drink of coffee and glanced out Shotgun's window toward the Tamarack River, which he could see in the distance, moving peacefully along.

"This is serious stuff, Ben. Worsen' I thought. You told your bosses at Osborne about this?"

"Not yet. I'm not supposed to know about the night crawlers. Osborne people told Gunnar Godson that if he even hinted anything about Cranberry Red side effects to me or anyone else they'd fire him. He's just sick about the whole thing. After all, he's the one who developed the chemical."

"Man, they're playin' hardball."

"Yup, expect they'd fire me in a minute if I said anything. This is supposed to be their big moneymaker."

Shotgun Slogum sat quietly for a moment, obviously deep in thought, before he responded.

"Like I've always said, you start messin' with Mother Nature and she'll rear up and bite ya. She's been around here a lot longer than we have. Demands more respect than we're sometimes willin' to give her," Slogum said, running his hand through his white hair.

Ben glanced at Shotgun's refrigerator, where he saw news clippings fastened with magnets.

"What are those?" Ben asked.

"Oh, those are stories about the river. Whenever I read anything about the Tamarack River, I cut it out of the newspaper and save it." He pulled down the clippings and showed them to Ben. "This first one is about a couple of boys who turned up with cuts on their legs—happened last summer when they were swimmin' near where that new park is goin' in. This here second one is about when Fred Russo and Oscar Anderson's ice-fishing shanty caught fire last winter and burned. Most people didn't believe the old guys when they told what happened."

"I remember reading those stories," Ben said. "Kind of unusual in both cases."

"Fred and Oscar are my neighbors, you know. I talked to 'em after the fire and they swore that they'd hooked an enormous northern pike and 'twas the fish that knocked over the stove and caused the fire."

"That's interesting," Ben said.

"Fred and Oscar told me another story, too, said I shouldn't tell anyone else, but this seems the time to share it."

"About what?" asked Ben, who was still thumbing through the news articles.

"They told me a wild story 'bout a year ago—I didn't believe it at the time—of landing a fish that attacked 'em. Imagine that, a fish mean enough to go after a man!"

"So, what happened?"

"Damn fish bit Oscar's walking stick right in two, before it flopped back in the river and disappeared. That's what they said."

"Man, that's quite a story."

"Fred told me it was the gospel truth and I should keep my mouth shut about it for fear folks would think that he and Oscar was makin' up a whopper. Must say, it did sound like a whopper at the time. Now, I'll bet those old guys were tellin' the truth," Shotgun added. "Strange things happen on this river. Strange things. Rivers are like that. Always a little mysterious. Never know what's next."

Ben was thinking. He put down the two newspaper articles and turned to Shotgun. "I remember reading an article in the DNR magazine last winter. They had a story about the Tamarack River fish survey. I skimmed through it, but I remember the DNR guy who wrote it, Gus somebody, saying he was surprised at the size of the fish in the river and that they'd measured a huge northern pike. Biggest one the DNR guy had ever seen."

"I heard about that," Shotgun responded. "Suppose all this ties together?" Shotgun was running his hand through his beard.

Ben glanced at his watch. "Oh, oh, forgot about the time. I'm supposed to be speaking in less than a half hour. Gotta go. Thanks for the coffee."

Ira Osborne
Commemorative Park

*F*red Russo and Oscar Anderson arrived early for the ceremony at the park. They knew that parking was always a problem at events like this, and they didn't want to park Fred's Chevy pickup "in the back forty," as they described parking a distance from an event.

"Remember we used to swim here when we were kids?" asked Fred as they walked toward the river. They quickly noticed that they were the first people to arrive for the event, aside from a couple of men who were setting up chairs in preparation for the celebration.

"Yup, sure do. Great place. Sometimes we'd even go skinny dippin', especially on hot nights in July when we was makin' hay," said Oscar.

"Remember those days well. It's a great old river, this Tamarack. Great old river. Got lots of stories to tell. Lots of stories to tell."

The two men stood staring across the slow-moving water. It was a quiet day with scarcely a hint of a breeze. The water's surface was smooth as a polished dance floor.

"There's just something about a river," mused Fred.

"What about a river?" asked Oscar.

"Something special. Do you realize that we've never seen this water before and will never see it again?"

"What the hell is that supposed to mean?" asked Oscar.

"It means the river is always changin'. Never the same. Just like life itself. Always changin'."

"Good God, Fred, you becomin' some kind of philosopher?"

"Nope, not me. Just layin' out a fact. Plain and simple fact."

The two friends stood quietly for a time, looking out over the river and not saying anything.

"You wanna chew on a little of this beef jerky I got in my pocket?" offered Oscar.

"Is it tough?"

"Is it what?"

"Tough, can I chew it without knocking my jaws out of joint?" asked Fred. He watched as his friend hauled a big bag of jerky out of his pocket.

"No, it ain't tough. Here, have a piece." Oscar handed a hunk of the dried meat to Fred, who popped it into his mouth.

Fred began chewing vigorously and then stopped. "This jerky is tough as hell. Where'd you get this stuff—on sale someplace? It's no damn good."

"My piece is good, not tough at all. Your teeth must be gettin' bad."

"There ain't nothin' wrong with my teeth," responded Fred. He took the partially chewed meat from his mouth and threw it into the river. The piece of jerky had scarcely touched the surface of the water when there was a huge splash and a gigantic northern pike flew out of the water, its enormous tail flopping. As fast as it had surfaced, it disappeared once more into the water.

"Good gawd," exclaimed Fred. "You see what I just saw?"

"It's that big bastard of a fish we almost caught twice," said Oscar.

"I sure as hell wouldn't go swimmin' at this beach," said Fred. "Sure as hell wouldn't. That son-of-a-bitch fish would chew your leg off. He's a mean, hungry bastard."

As Ben drove from Shotgun's to the site of the new Osborne park, he couldn't get Shotgun's words out of his head. "Mess with Mother Nature and she'll bite you back."

Then the pieces all came together. The answer he'd been looking for. Evidence of broader side affects of using Cranberry Red beyond affecting night crawlers. The connection between Cranberry Red and the mysterious happenings on the Tamarack River.

Ben found a place to park his car, surprised at how many people had turned out this sunny afternoon for a park dedication and a chance to swim at this new beach. He saw Brittani sitting at a little table with a big sign propped up in front of her: "Osborne University Outreach Office." They exchanged greetings and he hurried to the speaker's stand, as the program was to begin in about five minutes. He saw the two old farmers Oscar Anderson and Fred Russo standing off to the side, seemingly watching both the river and the speaker's stand.

He spotted the dignitaries sitting in front of the speaker's stand: President Delbert George; Vice President for Research Quinton Foley; Cindy Jennings, representing the Ames County board; and Dr. Sara Phillips, director of field operations. Ben slid into an empty seat beside Phillips.

"Ben, you're late," Phillips warned. Her voice was cold. "The program is about to start and you're supposed to introduce President George after Ms. Jennings says a few words of welcome."

"Sorry," Ben said. He was thinking about how he would handle what he knew he must do.

Promptly at three, Cindy Jennings, dressed in a dark pantsuit, took her place at the podium, on a small stage that had been constructed on the riverbank. A short distance in back of her, a red ribbon stretched from one side of the newly created swimming beach to the other. The ceremony included cutting the ribbon and allowing anyone who wished to be among the first people at Ira Osborne Commemorative Park to try out the new swimming beach.

"What a great day this is," Cindy began. "We are here to dedicate Ames County's newest recreational site, the Ira Osborne Commemorative Park. Let's have a big round of applause for Osborne University and its generous contributions to our community."

Everyone clapped loudly, a few people even stood to show their appreciation for this wonderful gift from what was becoming the Midwest's most well-known university. The event had attracted at least a hundred people from throughout the county. Many families attended, their children expecting to be the first to swim at the new park.

Cindy went on for a few minutes talking about the Ames County park system and how this would be the most modern park on the Tamarack

River, perhaps in the entire county, and how pleased everyone should be of that fact. Then she turned toward Ben and said, "I want to introduce you to Ben Wesley, whom most of you know from his work at Osborne University's outreach office in Willow River."

Ben walked slowly to the podium and then looked out over the crowd. He recognized many faces, people whom he had worked with, members of the Ames County Fruit and Vegetable Growers Cooperative, cranberry growers, home gardeners, former 4-H members, members of the Willow River Flower Club. All were there with their families, with children waiting for the ribbon cutting so they could be the first to swim at this new Tamarack River beach.

"Thank you, Ms. Jennings," Ben said quietly. He began to perspire; he could feel sweat running down his face and into his eyes. Out of the corner of his eye he glimpsed President George, who was smiling broadly as he waited for his turn at the podium, waiting to hear the applause of an appreciative audience.

"I wish I didn't have to share what I'm about to," Ben said haltingly.

"Louder," someone shouted from the back of the gathering. The audience sat on rows of folding chairs, some of them sinking into the soft sand along the river's edge.

"I wish I didn't have to tell you what I'm about to," Ben said in a clearer, more confident voice. He noticed a perplexed look on President George's face.

"This park is not what it seems. It is a dangerous place." Ben spoke clearly so all could hear. "The Tamarack River is contaminated with the byproducts of Cranberry Red. The river is not safe for swimmers. The fish in this part of the river are dangerous and may attack you. I have the evidence here in my hand. We don't know yet about other side effects." He held up the news clippings from Shotgun Slogum's refrigerator. As he did, he glimpsed President George rushing for the podium, his face red with anger and disbelief.

Ben continued, "Do not cut this ribbon. Do not swim in this river. Osborne University has deceived you. Their miracle discovery . . ." Ben didn't finish his sentence before President George reached the podium and wrested the microphone from him.

Meanwhile, Oscar Anderson and Fred Russo, upon hearing Ben's words, had lifted the red ribbon and stepped under it. They now stood side by side, their hands outstretched to prevent anyone from entering the river.

"Don't listen to this man," George shouted to an audience that was now standing, looking at each other in disbelief, staring at the river that appeared so quiet and inviting, trying to understand what they had just heard.

"This man speaks nonsense," George shouted as he pointed to Ben, who was walking off the stage. "He doesn't know what he is talking about."

But people knew Ben Wesley. They respected him and believed him when he spoke. They began leaving, taking their unhappy children with them.

President George continued his rant, but no one was listening. Soon the chairs were empty. The red ribbon fluttered in the breeze. The Tamarack River flowed peacefully by, its dangers hidden beneath its rippled surface.

"Looks like that big old northern's gonna go hungry today," Fred Russo said to his friend.

"Yup, looks that way," said Oscar Anderson. "Sure looks that way." Both men were smiling as they walked toward Fred's pickup.

"Ben Wesley, you are fired." An extremely angry President George shook his finger in Ben's face.

"So be it," Ben said as he turned and walked away, his head held high.

When Ben returned home from the aborted park dedication, Beth had obviously already gotten the news. Propped on the table was a note:

Ben,

This is the last straw. What were you thinking? Have you lost your mind? I have taken a few things, and I am on my way to Chicago, where I will live with my sister until I can get things sorted out. I will call the kids and let them know. You'll hear from my lawyer.

Beth

Ben slammed his fist down on the table. "Dammit!" he exclaimed. "Dammit to hell."

Ben wasn't surprised at his wife's departure, but he thought her timing could have been better. To lose your job and your wife in the same afternoon was more than a little difficult to take.

"Dammit," he said again. He walked to the refrigerator, took out a bottle of Spotted Cow, snapped it open, and slumped down in a chair. His mind was a muddle of thoughts. He knew that Beth was not happy with him, hadn't been for some time. But he was a bit surprised that she just up and left, leaving behind a four-line note.

He remembered the good times they had together, especially when the kids were little. But lately they had grown apart—she having her ideas of what she wanted from life, and he so busy trying to make a living that he hadn't been paying enough attention to her.

Ben slept little that night, wondering what he could have, should have, done differently. When he woke up in the morning, he said aloud, "Life goes on."

67

Fallout

*T*wo weeks after the aborted park dedication and Ben's subsequent firing from his job with Osborne University, a letter arrived, again in a plain envelope without a return address. Unfolding the carefully handwritten letter, Ben noticed that it was signed by Sara Phillips, his former boss. What did she have to say? After all, he didn't have to answer to her anymore. Ben sat at the kitchen table and began to read:

Dear Ben,

You don't know how difficult it is for me to write this letter, but my conscience forced me to do so. Although you may not have been aware of it—how could you from my recent actions?—I have a lot of respect for you, for your ethics, for standing up for what you believe in, and for your willingness to step forward, as you did at the recent park dedication ceremony. That took a lot of guts, knowing that Osborne University would surely fire you as a result.

I wanted you to know that I wrote the "anonymous" letter that you received a short time ago, the one warning about the dangers of Cranberry Red side effects. I feel badly that I set you up to do what I should have done myself. When I saw firsthand what Cranberry Red had done to some lowly night crawlers, I was appalled. But I felt I needed to remain silent to keep my job. I should have spoken out. I should have insisted that both Osborne University and the International Farm-Med Company stop promoting the product and pull it from the market. I did not. Now I am so sorry that I didn't stand up for what I believed to be the right thing to do.

I thought the least I could do was to write you and let you know about my previous letter. For what it's worth, I resigned my position the Monday after the park fiasco.

All the best to you. I know you will find a new position where you will not be faced with the ethical challenges that Osborne University thrust on you.

Fondly,
Sara Phillips

Ben went back and carefully read the letter a second time. He couldn't believe it. Sara Phillips, high and mighty Sara Phillips, had effectively pulled the plug on Cranberry Red. Her letter had triggered a series of events that would have taken much longer to play out had she not written it.

Phillips was the last person Ben had thought about when he ran through his mind all those who might have written the anonymous letter. He had suspected that someone working at the research station had done it, someone working with Gunnar Godson who knew all about the work. But the research staff had remained loyal to Gunnar and had said not a word.

The day after hearing from Phillips, Ben was puttering in his garden when he heard the phone ring. He rushed into the house and answered it.

"This is Cindy Jennings from the Ames County board."

"Hello, Ms. Jennings," Ben said. He still remembered well her role in helping to eliminate all the county agricultural agent offices in Wisconsin.

"How you doing, Ben?" she said. Her voice was friendly.

"Okay, I guess."

"I wanted to call you earlier and tell you how gutsy it was to stand up to Osborne University, especially in front of a crowd, and even more especially because you worked for them."

"Thank you," Ben said quietly.

"I also want to apologize," Cindy added.

"For what?"

"For supporting closing down all the agricultural agent offices in Wisconsin. That was one of the dumbest things I ever did. And I'm sorry."

"I'm sorry, too," said Ben, as he was once more reminded of the twenty great years when he had been an agricultural agent.

"But I've got some good news."

"Good news. I haven't gotten much of that lately," Ben admitted.

"The executive committee of the county board met today, and we voted to reinstate the agricultural agent office and hire you back. The county will cover your salary, the salary of a secretary, and office expenses. So many people were turned off by Osborne University's antics. The board got formal petitions from both the Fruit and Vegetable Growers Cooperative and the cranberry growers and many phone calls and letters to reestablish the county agricultural agent office with or without state funding."

"I don't know what to say."

"Just say you'll do it."

"I will," Ben said. "I gladly will. And I'll ask Brittani Stone if she'd like to work with me again."

"Oh, and I should tell you, we have already contacted the University of Wisconsin in Madison. We've contracted with them to provide research information for the office, almost like it was under the old system."

Ben couldn't believe it; he would have his old job back—most of it anyway. He had been thinking about looking for an agricultural agent job in another state, and had even prepared a resumé. But now he wouldn't have to do that.

He immediately called Brittani and told her the good news, and without hesitation she said she would be more than pleased to work with him again.

"You won't have to worry about keeping a record of my billable hours anymore, either," said Ben.

They both laughed.

Afterword

After the Osborne park incident, word quickly spread about the dangerous side effects of Cranberry Red, forcing Osborne University and its partner, International Farm-Med Company, to pull the product from the market. The Department of Natural Resources brought a multimillion-dollar lawsuit against Osborne University and its partner.

Facing the lawsuit, Osborne University closed both the research station on the Tamarack River and the outreach office in Willow River, leaving Gunnar Godson and his staff, plus Brittani Stone, without jobs. Brittani's marriage to Chris Martin was planned for next June. As much as she never believed it might happen, she was about to become a farmer's wife.

The College of Agricultural and Life Sciences at UW–Madison hired Gunnar Godson as a research associate, to continue his work on increasing the antioxidant levels of cranberries along with other Wisconsin fruit crops. He and his family moved to Madison.

The court case against Osborne University and International Farm-Med Company dragged on for several months. Osborne University's legal counsel and IFM's attorneys argued that the problems with the fish in the Tamarack River were due to causes other than Cranberry Red residue. Beth Wesley, along with several others, testified to the virtues of Cranberry Red–treated cranberries. As a nurse, she spoke eloquently about how these new cranberries would save thousands of lives. Of course it didn't help Osborne and IFM's case when she said, "So what—a few fish in the Tamarack

River were affected. Just think of the thousands of people who would be helped. What should come first, fish or people?"

Beth also said she was testifying on behalf of the thousands of students from around the world who were in the midst of completing degree programs, herself included, and that with the possibility of Osborne University closing they would be left with nothing but several thousands of dollars of lost tuition money.

Oscar Anderson and Fred Russo also testified.

"I tell ya," Oscar Anderson said, looking straight at the jury, "them fish we caught in the Tamarack River were killers. First big fish I caught there took after me. Chewed off my walkin' stick. Cut it right in two, and it was hickory. Hickory wood that fish sliced off. Hickory wood is hard."

The jury was smiling as Oscar told his story. "Then there was the time when me and Fred was ice fishin' in our little shack right there on the backwater of the river. Mindin' our own business and cooking up a little venison sausage on our woodstove. Well, I tell ya, we hooked onto this fish, a northern, it was. And it was a bigun." Oscar held out his arms to show just how big he thought the fish was. "That fish came a-flopping into our fish shack and came right after us. Managed to tip over the stove and burn down our shack before it slid back into the hole. That damn fish burnt down our fish shack. Yes, it did. Something got into that northern. Something sure stirred him up. Grew him big and made him mean."

Gus Caldwell, representing the DNR, testified, "We found abnormal growth rates of fish in the Tamarack River when we did our fish surveys. We also found measurable amounts of the Cranberry Red chemical in the fish we examined in our state laboratory. Additionally, we found trace amounts of Cranberry Red in the water samples we took from the Tamarack River as recently as a few weeks ago."

A representative from the U.S. Food and Drug Administration testified that his agency was challenging International Farm-Med Company's claim that they could legally sell Cranberry Red–treated cranberries to the public without FDA approval. International Farm-Med attorneys claimed that the FDA lacked jurisdiction because the treated cranberries were sold as a health food, a dietary supplement, and thus did not need approval for sale from a governmental agency.

*T*he jury deliberated less than half a day and found Osborne University and International Farm-Med Company guilty of all charges. The next day both Osborne University and IFM declared bankruptcy and closed down.

Once more working as Ames County agricultural agent, Ben Wesley, with the able assistance of Mrs. Brittani Martin, continued to provide educational programs for the people of Ames County, from the smallest market gardener to the largest, most prosperous cranberry grower. The agreement with the county board also included reestablishing the 4-H program and the county fair. The county agricultural agent's office was once more in the Ames County courthouse, in the same place where it had been since the first county agent arrived in 1915. On the office door the words "Ben Wesley, County Agricultural Agent, Brittani Martin, Office Manager" appeared in large black print. Ben smiled each morning when he pulled open the office door and was greeted with Brittani's bright welcome: "Good morning, Ben. Looks like another beautiful day in Ames County."

Author's Note

Readers of my other Ames County novels— *The Travels of Increase Joseph,*
In a Pickle, and *Blue Shadows Farm*—often ask the location of Ames
County in Wisconsin. The county is fictional of course, but when pressed
to answer its location, I say it's near Waushara, Marquette, Wood, Portage,
and Adams counties in central Wisconsin.

Fictional Ben Wesley, the main character in *Cranberry Red,* worked as a
county agricultural agent in Ames County. I worked for five years as a
county extension agent in two different Wisconsin counties after I graduated from the University of Wisconsin–Madison and completed a brief
tour of duty in the army. Wesley is a composite of several of my county extension colleagues. In the novel, the program for which Ben worked was
the University of Wisconsin Agricultural Agent Program (UWAAP). The
actual program, which exists today in every Wisconsin county, is Cooperative Extension, which is a part of the University of Wisconsin–Extension.
Cooperative Extension (the "cooperative" refers to a partnership of
counties, the U.S. Department of Agriculture, and the University of Wisconsin) came into being with the passage of the Smith-Lever Act of 1914 by
the federal government. United States Department of Agriculture funds
help support Cooperative Extension activities, as do state and county tax
dollars.

County-based Extension educators are University of Wisconsin faculty
and staff. They teach in the areas of agriculture and agribusiness, community and economic development, natural resources, family living, and 4-H

and youth development. These men and women conduct workshops, do radio and TV programs, write newspaper columns, answer phone queries, and are generally available to assist the citizens of the state. Cooperative Extension specialists work on University of Wisconsin System campuses, where they have direct access to current research and knowledge. These specialists provide a direct link between the campus researchers and the county staffs, and thus provide a service to the people of the state, as supported by the Wisconsin Idea. See my book *The People Came First: The History of Cooperative Extension* (Madison: University of Wisconsin–Extension, 2004) for information about Cooperative Extension's past. See http://www.uwex.edu/CES/ for up-to-date information about the organization.

The fall after I graduated from the University of Wisconsin–Madison, while I was awaiting orders from the U.S. Army, I raked cranberries by hand in a cranberry bog near Wisconsin Rapids. The bog was very similar to the one that Shotgun Slogum owned in my fictional Ames County. It was cold, often miserable, but always interesting work.

Cranberries are native to Wisconsin and several other U.S. states; by the middle 1800s cranberries were commercially grown in Wisconsin. The historical information I provide in the novel is as accurate as I could make it. Today, cranberries are Wisconsin's most important fruit crop. They are grown in central, north-central, and northwestern Wisconsin counties. Wisconsin leads the nation in cranberry production, and has done so since 1995, when Wisconsin beat out Massachusetts for top honors. For more about Wisconsin cranberries, go to www.wiscran.org, the website for the Wisconsin Cranberry Growers Association.